Dangers in Love

Dangers in Love

Book One of Dangers in Love Series

Ana Denise

Contact Information:
http://www.authoranadenise.com
TikTok: author.ana.denise
Instagram: authoranadenise
Facebook: Ana Denise

Front Cover design by: Deranged Doctor Design
ISBN: 9798988462941

First Edition: August 13th, 2024

SIGN UP FOR MY AUTHOR NEWSLETTER

Be the first to learn about Ana Denise's new releases and receive exclusive content!

www.authoranadenise.com

Chapter One

Destiny

"Come on, Destiny. The California Roll is calling my name," Candace called out as she walked towards the front door of our two-bedroom apartment.

We lived in the heart of Sacramento.

"I'm coming, Candace."

I walked through the open door and out of the house behind her.

The cold air pierced my skin, shooting

through my thick coat and long-sleeved shirt. The sun had set hours ago, dropping the temperature several degrees.

Candace, my best friend of eight years, and I went to dinner three times a week. Our schedules were completely opposite because of our differing occupations. So, whenever we both were free, we went to dinner. Tonight's dinner consisted of sushi, our favorite.

Candace locked our apartment before we walked down the stairs.

We piled into Candace's SUV. Once the warmth blasted into the cabin, I relaxed in the passenger seat.

Candace smirked, then looked over at me. The lights from the dashboard highlighted her face. Her skin reminded me of the color of honey. Her light brown eyes were vibrant.

"I thought you'd be used to the cold weather by now," Candace commented.

She looked at the back-up camera before she backed out of the parking space.

"I doubt I'll ever get used to it."

In second grade, I moved from Florida to California. No matter how long I lived in California when the cold snap arrived, it took me by surprise. So, climbing into Candace's car, shivering until my teeth chattered, I remembered my days in Florida when I didn't have to worry about winter coats and fur-lined boots.

Candace pulled out into traffic once it was safe to do so.

"I'm glad I bought you that coat for Christmas."

Christmas occurred three days ago. Since Candace's parents moved back to Argentina, their hometown, and my parents moved back to Florida, Candace and I decided to have our own intimate Christmas. Candace couldn't get time off from her job to travel to Argentina. I stayed in town so she wouldn't spend Christmas alone. We had a wonderful time exchanging gifts, laughing over memories we created over the years, and eating delicious food we prepared at home.

"It's my favorite gift."

I smiled as I looked out my window. Christmas lights were still on houses and trees, lighting up the night. The lights passed by in a flash as we drove. Candace, an observant person, was tired of me wearing my ratty old coat, as she called it. I'd had it for two years and bought it at a great discount in the local mall during an end-of-winter sale.

"It better be. I went through hell to get you that coat."

I raised an eyebrow. What did she reference?

"Candace. What did you do?"

"Eh." She shrugged. "Nothing too bad. I just wrestled that coat from a soccer mom."

"How do you know it was a soccer mom?"

She tapped her fingers on the steering wheel. We approached a red light.

"She had three little kids in soccer uniforms with her."

I gasped. "Candace. Why would you do that?"

She looked over at me and winked. "Are you kidding me? It was the only one there in your size. That coat had your name on it."

"You went through all this trouble to get me this coat?"

"Of course. You're my best friend."

Candace went above and beyond to get me the perfect gift. I couldn't ask for a better and more attentive best friend.

The light turned green, and we continued down the road.

"It's definitely my favorite gift, but you can't tell Mom."

She laughed. "We love our mothers, but they aren't fashion-forward. Your secret is safe with me."

My mom had also bought me a coat for Christmas. Sadly, it wasn't my style. I'd keep it tucked away in the back of the closet for the days when my favorite coat needed a wash.

Candace turned up the radio, and the lull of Latin music came through the speakers.

We rode the rest of our trip in silence, enjoying the music.

We arrived at the restaurant. The parking lot overflowed with cars. Perhaps a lot of people had sushi for dinner in mind for a Tuesday evening. Who would've known?

Once we parked, I wrapped my coat tighter around me before I stepped out of the SUV.

Candace and I trekked up to the door. We walked inside, freshness in the air. Japanese décor decorated the restaurant. Japanese music flowed through the speakers. The place hummed with wonderful vibrations.

The hostess led us through the restaurant. She walked us to a booth beside the kitchen.

We shrugged out of our coats, placed our purses on the seat beside us, and sat.

The hostess set the menus in front of us. We frequented the restaurant so often we didn't have to look at the menu. We never strayed from our usual.

"So, I need your expert opinion on something."

Candace clasped her hands together. She looked at me and smiled.

"Expert opinion?" I asked. "Well, it depends on what category my opinion is desired."

She grabbed her phone out of her purse. "Do you think I should pair this sweater with these blue jeans?" She showed me the outfit. "Or should I pair it with these white jeans?" She showed me the second outfit.

"The white jeans scream bold to me," I commented.

"Awesome." Candace ran her fingers through her thick, brown hair. "I thought the same, but your input is always necessary."

I loved how Candace could come to me about everything. Our bond, our friendship, was like no other. I had other friends I would talk to and hang out with occasionally, but those friendships could never exceed what Candace and I had. A lot of people made the association that soulmates were the people you'd spend the rest of your life with romantically. I believed soulmates would be anyone you couldn't go too long without talking to, or you'd feel lost. Candace was my soulmate. We connected on a level that no one could understand. Even though we were different in many ways, our differences made us one. Our differences brought us together.

Grabbing my purse, I rummaged through it in search of my phone.

"Guess what, Candace?"

Candace looked up. "What's up?"

I put my phone on the table. "I actually brought my phone tonight."

Half of the time we went out, I'd forget my phone on the dresser in my room or the dining room counter. Contrary to the rest of the general population, I wasn't dependent upon my phone.

Candace smirked. "Well, isn't that a surprise? Even if you had left it, it's not like you have anyone blowing your phone up 24/7."

I raised my eyebrow.

"I know you're joking. You send me at least a hundred messages every day."

Candace placed her hand on her chest. She smiled brightly. "Well, besides me."

We laughed at the comment. We were inseparable. Even when we were away from each other, we stayed in contact through text.

The waitress arrived shortly after. Candace ordered California rolls and tea, and I ordered a Shrimp Tempura and Sprite.

"Where do you plan to wear that outfit?" I asked once the waitress left our table.

Candace smiled. She looked around the room. Her cheeks became a touch of red. She shook her head.

"Nowhere special."

I hummed, leaning in closer, analyzing her carefully.

"Are you sure?" I asked.

"Yeah." She shrugged as she spun a curl around her finger. "It's just another outfit for work. I love to dress to impress."

Candace bartended for a living. She bartended at one of the most popular bars in town. She wore whatever she wanted, whenever she wanted. That's one aspect of my job that I hated. I had a strict dress code at work as an elementary school teacher. I had to stick to it, no matter what. Sweatpants and a hoody on a chilly day were a no-go.

"Do you work tomorrow?" I asked.

I was on winter break and didn't return to work until Monday. There were six more days of winter vacation left. I loved the time away from work. It was refreshing and relaxing. Since the cold limited me to the apartment, I lounged inside all day with my sketch pad and pencils, creating beautiful images. There was one downside to the break. I missed my students. I taught first grade, and the children were joyful to be around. I loved children with a passion. As a first-grade teacher, my duty was to make sure they had the best tools in life to receive the best education.

Candace had a weird schedule. She never had weekends or consecutive days off. She was their best bartender and could put a cocktail together in thirty seconds tops. She had every drink engraved in her memory bank. Working late nights into the early morning. When she crawled into bed to fall asleep at the end of her shift, I'd wake up to get ready to teach my students. When I came home from work some days, she was either getting ready for her shift or already gone for the night. We didn't see much of each other throughout the day, so we had to make it up on our days and evenings off.

"Yes, I do." Candace looked around the dining area before she looked at me. "I wish I didn't, though."

Our waitress brought our meals to us before I could respond.

We dug into our food, silence settling upon us. As always, the food exceeded my expectations with its delicious taste.

I sipped my Sprite and looked at Candace. She focused on her meal.

"Is someone bothering you at work again?" I asked.

The bar's customer demographic was primarily male. Candace was beautiful. Anybody with eyes could see that. Her beauty would catch anyone's eye. Sometimes, liquid courage would entice someone to do something they usually wouldn't do without that aid or encouragement. It had happened several times before. I wouldn't doubt that it would happen again.

Candace scrunched her nose up. She shook her head. "No." She paused. "Thankfully."

"Why don't you want to go to work, then?"

Candace grabbed her straw and sipped her tea.

"Don't get me wrong. I love talking to my regulars. I love the atmosphere. I just want to do more with my life than serve alcohol and meaningless conversations all day."

I understood her point. Candace had so much drive. She could conquer the world if she wanted to.

"I understand."

It wasn't common for Candace to complain about her bartending gig. I'd gone to the bar to hang out with her a few times, and she easily handled all her customers. She looked at home while she worked. She was comfortable, and I could see how she made everyone around her feel the same way.

"Have you found out more about the internship?"

Candace nodded. She placed her hands on the table.

"They only offer unpaid internships. I can't afford not to bring in money."

Candace hoped to pursue a paid graphic

design internship. Unfortunately, unpaid internships were only offered in our area.

I placed my hand on hers. "Don't let this little hiccup get you down." I gave her hand a squeeze. "This is just an obstacle on your path to success."

Candace returned a squeeze. "Somehow, you always manage to cheer me up."

I nonchalantly shrugged.

"What would you do without me?"

Candace smiled. "The same thing you'd do without me."

I raised my eyebrows. "What's that?"

Candace stuck her tongue out at me. "Be lost."

I laughed. "You're right about that."

We finished eating our dinner. After we paid, we put our coats back on.

"Dinner was amazing," Candace commented as we grabbed our purses.

I slipped my phone into my back pocket.

"Yes, it was. It's hard for sushi to disappoint me," I said as we walked through the dining room towards the exit.

Candace shot me a look. "Well, remember that time you tried the sushi from the gas station?" Her lips curled into a smile before she covered it with her hand.

I swatted at her arm. "You dared me, missy."

When we first became friends, we went to a gas station for candy one day after school. As we weighed our options, Candace dared me to eat the sushi they sold in the store. I later regretted it as my stomach wouldn't allow me to leave the bathroom for an entire day.

Opening the door for us, I missed the warmth I had grown accustomed to inside the restaurant. The cold air wrapped its strong grip around me and held on. I couldn't wait for Candace to start the car up and blast us with warmth.

"I did, but I didn't think you'd actually do it."

We laughed at the memory. We left the lit part of the parking lot. My eyes tried to adjust to the darkness as we walked to her SUV.

"I'm not one to back down from a dare," I commented.

I bumped my hip against hers.

"Yeah—" Candace began.

A loud, piercing pop sounded. It was so close my ears rang.

Where did the sound come from?

Why was it so close?

What made the popping noise?

Why did it sound like a gun?

Was it a gun?

"Ru—" I started.

A gut-wrenching scream escaped Candace's mouth.

I turned to grab Candace's hand. To my dismay, Candace's face displayed a great amount of anguish and pain. She fell to the ground face-first. My heart dropped.

Candace was shot.

Chapter Two

Destiny

I looked up. A high-pitched scream escaped my lips. A dark figure loomed several feet away in the darkness. They wore bulky clothes, making it impossible to tell the person's gender. They pointed the gun at me. I shut my eyes, having no desire to watch the bullet travel through the air to cause destruction. The clink of metal echoed. Opening my eyes, I looked down, completely shocked I wasn't doubled over in pain or saw blood. I hadn't been shot.

They looked at the gun.

Oh, my goodness. The gun had jammed. They tried to shoot me. Their intent was to shoot and harm me.

I had to go. Now. I looked towards the west of the parking lot. It was a wooded area. That would be perfect for my escape.

I darted across the parking lot. My boots slapped hard against the concrete. The cold air blasted me in the face as I ran into the woods. If they wanted to shoot me, they'd have to chase me. They had to hunt me down. I wouldn't be a sitting duck, making their objective easy for them. Thank goodness I chose to wear Uggs tonight instead of my favorite heeled boots. Those wouldn't have allowed me to run as fast.

What was I running towards? I didn't have long to think about it. They could've been on my heels, ready to pull the trigger for the second and last time. To stop me in my steps. I couldn't allow that to happen. I had to keep moving.

Wasn't there a police station within a mile radius of the sushi restaurant? I just hoped I ran in the right direction. I would be in trouble if I wasn't headed in the right direction. Big trouble.

Branches brushed against my pants and coat as I burrowed through the bushes and trees.

A branch snapped in the close distance. My heart was pounding loudly in my ears, and I abruptly turned north. My left Ugg slipped off my foot. The cold and dampness of the earth saturated my sock. No matter how cold it was, I couldn't go back for my boot. The attacker could be right on my heels. The fear and adrenaline that pulsed within me pushed me forward. That's the only thing that kept me going.

How long had I run? My lungs burned from the cold, crisp air. My energy was exhausted from the run, but the adrenaline pushed me forward. I couldn't stop.

If there was a police station close by, how long would it be until I arrived? What if I ran towards nothing? What if the attacker lurked in the woods, waiting for me to run straight into a trap they had set? Who was the attacker? Who was after me?

Streaks of light shined through the trees up ahead. It needed to be the police department. If it wasn't, I didn't know what I'd do. I needed to find safety.

Escaping the woods, I breathed a sigh of relief. Across the street was a small police station. Thankfully, there were three marked cars in the parking lot.

After checking both sides of the road for traffic, I ran across the road. The asphalt was hard and cold on my foot. I pulled the door open. The building was bright and warm. It smelled heavily of stale coffee. Placing my hands on my knees, I caught my breath.

I approached the counter where an officer sat. He focused on the computer in front of him. Dragging my fingers through my messy strands, I looked around frantically.

"I need help," I sniffled.

Slapping my hands against the counter, I looked around the police station. It was much smaller than I originally thought. The waiting area was the size of a shoe box. To the left were four closed doors. To the right was a hallway that led to the bathrooms.

Did I make a mistake going there? If the attacker was still after me, could this officer protect me? I highly doubted it. Would the attacker even come to the police station? I highly doubted it, but anything was possible. With the events that occurred, I wouldn't put anything past anyone. Anything and everything was possible.

The officer looked up. His hazel eyes widened in horror. He stood, and the name tag attached to his shirt came into view. It read T. Davidson.

"How may I help you?" he asked.

His eyes were a mix of sincerity and sorrow.

I pointed towards the door with a shaky finger.

"My best friend," I choked out as my voice cracked. Tears welled in my eyes, blurring my vision. My heart dropped. The sushi I had for dinner threatened to make an unwanted appearance on the streak-stained tile floor. "My best friend was shot."

The officer grabbed his phone off the desk. "What is the location?"

"The sushi restaurant, right around the

corner."

His fingers flew across the screen of his phone. He placed it to his ear. "We need an ambulance and police dispatched." He rattled off the address. "We have a woman down."

The officer stayed silent before he hung up the phone.

"Help is being dispatched to the scene."

Candace needed all the help she could get.

The officer motioned his hand to two chairs off in the corner. "If you could have a seat over there, I'd appreciate it. I need to go speak with the detective on duty."

"Thank you."

I walked over to the chairs and sat. Across the hall, there were several images of children and adults. They had gone missing as early as a week ago to several years ago. Visibly, I knew which cases were older and which ones were newer. For the older cases, the flyers were wilted. I stared so hard at one image it blurred.

What happened tonight? Everything was fine. Everything was normal. One horrible occurrence happened in a split second for everything to change. Everything changed for the worse.

A tear escaped my eye. Wiping it away, I tore my eyes away from the images. I didn't want to leave Candace there in the parking lot. My heart shattered into a million pieces. I had no other choice but to run and leave her. I hated that I couldn't offer her the help she desperately needed. I wanted to stay and help, but whoever shot Candace tried to shoot me.

Was someone after Candace? Was someone after me? Was someone after the both of us? Or was this a random act of violence, and we were just the victims of a pointless crime?

A door slammed shut, pulling me from my thoughts. My soul escaped my body. Was the attacker here to finish me off? I jumped and attempted to hide behind the chair. The chair didn't provide much coverage, but it was better than nothing. Closing my eyes, I waited for a commotion to erupt. I just knew a gun would go off, and the pain would resonate.

"Miss, are you okay? You are safe. I'm not going to hurt you."

I opened one eye at a time. A tall, fit man dressed in a gray suit stood in front of the chair. His long brown hair was pulled back in a low ponytail, his high cheekbones prominent. He trained his golden-brown eyes on me, holding out his hand.

"Who are you?"

I looked around. Was the police station getting smaller? Were the walls closing in on me? Was I going crazy? Was it just the two of them there? Or were there more officers behind the closed doors?

"I'm Zachary Miller. I'm one of the lead detectives in the police department."

I hesitated before I took his hand. He helped me stand with ease before he gave my hand a light squeeze. The warmth from his hand was inviting.

"I'm Destiny. Destiny Taylor." I took a step forward. "Can you help me?" I asked him.

His eyes softened. They traveled down my body before they met my eyes again. I looked down, and to my dismay, blood splattered my new coat. Candace's blood. I looked at my feet. One Ugg was scuffed with mud, and my foot was muddy and freezing cold.

Opening my mouth, no words came out. I couldn't say anything.

"Mrs. Taylor..." Zachary began. He spoke in a soft voice.

I shook my head. "It's just Ms." I looked over at the other officer. His face displayed every bit of his thoughts. They thought I was guilty. I wiped a tear that fell from my eyes.

"Ms. Taylor." He motioned his hand towards the closed office door. "Can you come sit in my office?"

"Why?"

They had no reason to think in the manner that they had. If I were guilty of shooting my best friend, I wouldn't have walked into the police station. Correction, I wouldn't have run into the police station. I would have gone in the opposite direction, making my escape across the country.

"I need to speak with you about what happened tonight."

I looked at my coat. The blood had dried into the coat Candace bought me for Christmas. My coat, my favorite Christmas present, was ruined. I looked at my bare foot, the coolness of the tile floor causing me to shiver.

How could they think I had something to do with Candace being shot? How could they think I caused all of this?

I pointed towards the door.

"No. You two need to get out there and help Candace. You need to find who shot her."

Zachary motioned to the officer. "Trevor has already dispatched help for Candace." He looked at me. "I need you to tell me what happened tonight." He paused. "So we can find out who hurt your best friend."

I looked back and forth between them. Their eyes bore into my soul. In their eyes, I was the prime suspect. If I were on the outside looking in, I'd think the same thing. Hell, I ran into a police station with blood on my coat and missing a shoe. If I were a suspect, this would be the dumbest move I could make.

"Okay."

Zachary opened the door to his office. The office was simple, consisting of a mahogany desk with a desktop computer, a notepad, and a cup of pens. One side of the desk had a black computer chair, and the other side had a metal, folding chair. The room smelled heavily of peppermint. I'd enjoy the festive scent if the situation that brought me here wasn't so horrendous. The reason at hand caused me to despise the scent.

"Have a seat, and I will be with you in a few

minutes."

Walking to the far end of the office, I sat on the hard metal chair. Zachary gave a sympathetic nod before he shut the door.

I stared at the wall. There was a picture of Zachary with a baby face and shorter hair. He stood beside another young man. It must've been taken years ago before his hair grew long. They held a giant fish in their hands as they smiled brightly into the camera.

A lump of sorrow lodged in my throat. Tears fell from my eyes. Wiping them away, I tore my eyes from the picture. Not even ten minutes ago, Candace and I were that happy. We had a great time over a delicious spread of sushi. Now, I cried my eyes out in a police station. I hoped and prayed she would be fine. If only she would survive this gunshot wound so we could continue with our lives. This would be a small hiccup in her path to achieving her goals, but she could conquer it. We could conquer anything that we put our minds too.

I stood, walked the short distance to the window, and peeked out the blinds. The window pointed towards the woods. In the distance, the other side of the woods was lit up. The police and ambulance must've already arrived.

I couldn't tear my eyes away. I willed the paramedics to do the life-saving measures I knew they went to school for. They needed to save Candace. I didn't know how badly she was hurt, but I hoped it was something minor. Candace needed to pull through.

Who could that have been? Who could've wanted to hurt Candace? Why would they want to hurt her? Who would've wanted to hurt me? Why would they want to hurt me?

I didn't have any enemies. The last person I remembered upsetting was the older woman at the gas station when I pulled up to her favorite gas pump right before she arrived.

If the gun hadn't jammed, I would've been shot and forced to the cold, hard ground against my will. Just like Candace.

None of this made sense. Candace had a loveable, outgoing aura. Everyone loved her. Even if someone met her for the first time, they fell in love with her personality after the first five minutes of talking to her.

I closed my eyes. Candace falling to the ground was engraved in my memory. My eyes shot open, and I gasped. Taking a step back, I bumped into the metal chair. The chair screeched across the tile floor.

The door swung open, and I spun around. Zachary walked in. He stopped in his tracks when he looked at me.

"Are you okay?" he asked.

No.

Should I lie to him and say yes? Possibly.

Would that make me look like a suspect? I didn't know.

I didn't know anything.

"I mean, I know you aren't okay." He looked

past me, towards the window. "You look like something spooked you."

He got that right.

"I'm okay."

He walked to his chair and sat. Then he motioned for me to sit.

I pointed towards the woods. "Did you get an update on Candace? Is she okay?"

He grabbed a red pen and opened the notepad.

"Our only update is that they are on the scene."

I stayed in place. Silent. I already knew that. I needed an update that I didn't already know.

"I'll let you know more when I get the updates."

"Thank you."

I pulled the chair out, and I sat.

"Do you want to tell me what happened tonight?"

"Yes."

Closing my eyes, I took a deep breath.

Could I do this?

I opened my eyes. Zachary's eyes burned into my face.

I knew I had no other choice.

"Candace and I went to get sushi for dinner."

Zachary jotted something down on the notepad. He wrote with his left hand.

He looked up at me. "Did she come to your place to pick you up? Did you go to her place to pick her up? Did you two meet at the restaurant?"

"No." I folded my hands on the desk. "We live together in an apartment. Candace drove us to dinner tonight."

He nodded, continuing with another question. "Did you notice anything strange earlier today? Did you notice anything out of the ordinary?"

I thought back to when we left our apartment. There wasn't anyone outside lending a curious or suspicious eye. Everything appeared like any other day.

I shook my head. "Nothing at all."

Zachary tapped his pen on the desk repeatedly before he looked at me. He stared into my eyes.

"Do you know of anyone who would want to hurt Candace?"

Looking around the office, I stared at a plastic plant in the corner of the room. The plant looked lonely. It looked exactly how I felt on the inside. I needed this feeling to go away. Forever.

Did Candace have any enemies? I couldn't think of one person that would want to cause her harm.

"No. I can't think of anyone."

"Does Candace have a boyfriend?"

Candace hadn't had a boyfriend for the past three years. Her last relationship didn't even last a year, and she ended it. Her desire to do what she wanted, whenever she wanted, outweighed her desire to be in a committed relationship. She didn't want to be tied down to anyone. I didn't blame her. I felt the same way. That's why we were content with each other's company.

"She doesn't have a boyfriend but is a bartender."

Zachary perked up at the mention of her occupation.

"Which bar does she work at?"

As I gave Zachary the bar's name, he scribbled on his notepad.

"Do you think any of her customers would've wanted to cause her harm?"

Did I think some of her customers could cause harm? Possibly. Would they want to hurt Candace? I highly doubted it. Everyone loved Candace. Or so I thought.

"Men gave her attention at the bar, but I don't think any of them would hurt her."

Zachary cleared his throat.

"Ms. Taylor, I have to ask you a question, which might be hard for you to answer."

Zachary paused. Time froze as I waited for the next sentence to come out of his mouth. The next question that came out of his mouth was expected, but it still shocked me.

"Did you have anything to do with Candace being shot?"

Chapter Three

Zachary

Destiny's red-rimmed, beautiful brown eyes grew wide as saucers. The shock etched into her face hurt me, but I had no choice. Being a detective, I had to ask hard questions, which was part of my job description. Everyone was a suspect, even if they appeared to be a victim. There were many cases I worked on over the years where the suspects portrayed themselves as the victim. It's insane how a crazed person could pretend to be heartbroken when they're the cause of all the destruction.

Once I heard the commotion outside my office, I stopped working on the paperwork I needed to file yesterday. It had been a long day of returning calls, drinking coffee that tasted like water, and waiting for a witness to come forward with information concerning the young woman who went missing a week and a half ago. Her mother and stepfather were heartbroken that she went to a train station and vanished into thin air. She didn't vanish, but the video camera that tracked her stopped working before we could know where she went next.

When I first laid my eyes on the distraught woman, I stopped in my tracks. Her beauty completely mesmerized me. She had skin the color of milk chocolate, and her luscious brown hair was pulled back into a messy bun. From her appearance, I could tell she was frightened. She stared intently at the images of the missing persons in the area. That was the last thing she needed to look at.

She nearly jumped out of her body when she heard the door close. Trevor was right. What she saw tonight traumatized her. I couldn't imagine watching my best friend get shot right in front of me.

The real question was, how did she manage to get away without being harmed? Unless she was the shooter. Or the shooter knew her and didn't want to cause her harm. Those two options could be one of the two logical explanations. Nothing else made sense.

"Are you serious?"

Her voice grew an octave higher. She stood.

I gulped, my throat dry as cotton. I didn't want to consider her a suspect, but I had no choice. She had blood on her coat. Blood splatter is one of the first indications someone might have shot a gun after the presence of gun powder. She had to be standing mighty close for blood to get on her.

She didn't have any gun powder on her. She didn't reek of gun powder. She came in here, missing a shoe. Either she lost the shoe to steer the attention away from herself or she lost it when she made her escape. Something told me it was the latter, but only time would tell.

"You think I had something to do with this? You think I had something to do with Candace being shot?"

Dropping my pen on my desk, I motioned for her to sit.

"Miss, it's only procedure."

She scuffed as she sat. She looked at the dried-up, fake plant in the corner. "You might as well arrest me now, then." Tears escaped her eyes.

My heart hurt for her. She wiped her eyes before she placed her face in her hands. She let out a sob. A beautiful woman shouldn't have to cry her eyes out at a police station, being questioned by a detective. She should be happily living her life, out have a great time doing whatever brought her pleasure.

I held my hands up. I needed her to calm down.

"Ms. Taylor. I'm not going to arrest you."

Her sob wavered. She looked at me through the gaps in her hands. Her makeup must've been waterproof because it was flawless, no smudge to see.

How could she not appear together but still be so beautiful?

Balling my hands into fists, my hands turned ash white. I willed myself to think with the correct head. This was a witness that I needed to question. Not a potential woman to add to my extensive list of one-night stands. Boy, I had a long list. The last thing I needed to do was add Ms. Taylor.

"Why not?" She wiped her eyes. "You think I'm guilty of something."

Deep down, did I think she was guilty of something? My gut told me no, but I had to do my job. My job required getting to the bottom of every case handed to me. If anyone could tell me everything I needed to know about Candace, it would be Destiny. She knew Candace better than everyone else.

Picking my pen up, I tapped it on my notepad. "It's my job to get every detail, no matter how small. All these details will help us with this investigation. We need to know what happened and why."

She puffed her cheeks out.

"I wish I could tell you more, but I can't. I don't know anything else."

"What I can't understand is how you have blood on your clothes, but you weren't the one to pull the trigger."

She closed her eyes. Silence settled upon us. I waited for her to answer. She tilted her head back so she looked up at the ceiling.

"Candace was shot right in front of me." She looked at me. Her eyes were bloodshot and flowed with fat tears. "I'm lucky to be sitting here, talking to you right now."

Honesty and sincerity poured from her. What she witnessed tonight broke her heart. If there was any other way to gather the information I needed, I would do it. Just so I could avoid upsetting her.

"I just need to ask one more thing. How did you get here? Did you drive Candace's car from the scene?"

She looked down and ran her fingers through her messy ponytail.

"I ran through the woods. Candace had her keys. When she was shot, I didn't think to do anything else but run."

I stared at her. That explained her appearance and why she had only one shoe on.

I scribbled some more notes onto my notepad before I closed it.

I opened my mouth to respond when a knock on the door interrupted me.

I glanced at the door. If Trevor interrupted, there had to be an important update. I hoped this update would give us some good news. Clearing my throat, I stood.

"Can you excuse me for a moment?"

Destiny nodded before her eyes dropped to her lap.

Opening the door, I walked out and closed it softly before I looked at Trevor.

His eyes told me everything I needed to know before he opened his mouth.

"I just received word that Candace passed away on the way to the hospital."

I ran my fingers through my hair, no doubt messing up my ponytail. Cursing under my breath, I looked towards my office. This case just went from an aggravated assault to a homicide. How would I break the news to Destiny? She already wasn't doing well with the information she knew. On this cold Tuesday night, I didn't think I'd have to break such devastating news to a loved one. Sadly, I had no choice.

"Thank you for the update, Trevor."

Trevor nodded sympathetically before he walked back to his desk.

I stared at my closed office. This was the hardest part of my job. Being a detective had its ups and downs. This was a down.

I opened the door. Destiny looked up at me as I walked inside. She perked up, her big, brown eyes glimmered with hope.

"Did you get an update? Please, tell me

Candace is going to be okay."

I opened my mouth to tell her the news but couldn't form a sentence. I couldn't even form a word. For the first time ever, I was rendered speechless. I had never experienced this before when dealing with victims. My quietness gave Destiny the answer she feared most.

She stood. The chair screeched across the tiled floor. She brought her hands up to her mouth and covered it.

"No," she screamed. She shook her head. "No. No. No."

She repeated it again and again. Her eyes fluttered closed, and tears streamed down her face like a waterfall.

Her legs wobbled.

I ran over to her. Right before she collapsed to the floor, I grabbed her in my arms. Her sweet, vanilla scent surrounded me.

"No," she screamed.

She clawed at my shirt. Her nails dug into my skin. She continued to scream out, but I didn't care. I'd rather endure scratch marks all over my body than deal with this situation.

If I wasn't convinced she had nothing to do with the case before, I was convinced now.

"I'm sorry," I mumbled into her ear.

I managed to find my voice and I'd use it to provide comfort for her. I rubbed my hand across her back, hoping the gesture would soothe her.

She whimpered. "Please, tell me you're playing a sick joke on me."

She pressed her head against my chest.

"I wish I could."

Boy, I wish I could take her pain away. Dealing with victims was always hard for me, even after years of being thrown into situations such as this. Situations always hit me hard, but this one affected me more than I would like to admit. I could feel her pain as her tears soaked through my shirt.

"Please, tell me this is a horrible nightmare I can wake up from."

A knock at the door grabbed my attention. Trevor opened the door. He had a solemn look on his face. Destiny's cries could probably be heard from a mile away.

I nodded at Trevor, letting him know I could handle Destiny. He responded with a nod before he closed the door.

I held Destiny close to my chest. Her whimpers continued to fill the room. I rubbed her back. I didn't know what else I could say or do.

"I have to go," she said.

She sniffled before she pushed away from me. She rubbed her eyes, but it was no use. The tears continued to cascade down her face.

I grabbed her hand. It was soft and delicate.

"Destiny, I can't let you go."

Destiny looked at our entwined hands. She looked up to meet my eyes.

"Why not? I can't stay here."

She was right. She couldn't stay here. The situation called for her to be far away from here.

The suspect could know the area. There was no doubt in my mind that they saw the direction in which she had escaped. She had to get to safety, and she needed to get there quickly.

"You're right, but you aren't any more safe out there." I pointed outside. "We still don't know if this was intentional or random."

Destiny exhaled.

"Everything in me is telling me it was random, but who am I?" She shrugged. "I'm just the best friend of the dead woman."

Raising my eyebrow, I rubbed the brown stubble on my chin. I let Destiny's hand go. Destiny must be traumatized because she talked like she was. There was no way she could be alone in this type of mindset.

I needed to speak with Trevor. Pronto.

"Will you excuse me for a moment?" I asked her.

"Take all the time you need."

She sat in the chair, placed her elbow on the desk, and propped her head against her arm. She stared at the wall. Tears continued to fall.

With one parting look, I backed out of my office and shut the door quietly. I approached Trevor's desk. He stared at his phone, playing a game.

I cleared my throat. Trevor locked his phone before he looked up at me.

"What can I do for you?" he asked.

I motioned towards my office.

"She can't be by herself."

33

Trevor stared at me with his emerald-green eyes.

"What are you asking?"

Leaning against the counter, I rubbed my fingers across my chin, deep in thought. What could be done for Destiny? We were in the dark about who could've committed the murder. Destiny didn't have any idea who could've wanted to harm Candace. That left me in the dark, with no leads to follow up on.

"I think Destiny needs to go into protective custody."

Trevor raised his eyebrows. He stared at me.

"Do you want me to find protective custody for her?"

"No." I made up my mind at that moment. "I'll do it."

Trevor's eyes widened. He placed his hands on his desk. His mouth dropped open.

"You can't do that."

"Why not?"

I stood straight. Trevor had no right to tell me what I could and couldn't do. His name didn't have detective attached to it, mine did.

"You're working her best friend's case." Trevor's eyes flickered over to my office. "You have a ton of manpower to put into this case. You can't do it while you babysit the victim."

Trevor had a point. A lot of work would have to go into this case. We were starting from scratch. We had little to nothing to go off of.

"Can you give the case to Frank?"

Frank was the other lead detective that I worked alongside.

Trevor gave me a pointed look. His eyes darted around.

"Zach, I just can't…"

"Yes, you can." I pointed towards my office. "That woman is shattered. I can't imagine it'll be beneficial for anyone for her to go into protective custody with anyone else but myself."

"Miller, are you sure about this?"

When Trevor called me by my last name, he meant serious business.

"Davidson, I've never been surer."

That statement was the truest thing I'd said all night.

Trevor nodded. "I'll call Frank." He unlocked his phone. "I'll let him know we have a murder investigation that must be handled pronto."

"Can you have Frank call the next of kin?" I asked.

"Sure thing."

Trevor was a great man. He worked hard and took his job seriously.

"Thank you."

I walked towards my office.

"What do I tell him?" he asked.

Stopping in my tracks, I turned and looked at him. I hadn't thought much about the excuse I'd come up with for disappearing for a while.

"Can you tell him it's a family emergency?"

Trevor smiled as he placed his phone to his ear.

"Family emergency, it is."

I walked a few feet before I hesitated.

"Can this stay between us?"

In a way, I considered Trevor my friend. I knew what we discussed would stay between us. For Destiny's protection, I was going out on a thin line. Technically, I could lose my job for my decision, but I couldn't bear to see her leave there alone. She needed protection. Only I could provide the type of protection she needed.

"This stays between us."

"Awesome, I'll leave my notes on his desk. It's not much, but it'll help us go in the right direction with the case."

Walking back into my office, I looked at Destiny. Tears drenched her face. Her mouth wobbled with sorrow. Her eyes pleaded for help. She would receive help from me.

"When can I go home?"

She tugged her eyes away from the wall, and she probably stared at the duration of the time I was out of the office. She looked at me, deep in a daze. Her eyes were red, and she looked through me as if I wasn't standing in front of her.

I approached my desk and I sat.

"Destiny, I don't think going home is in your best interest."

Chapter Four

Destiny

My expression changed from sadness to shock.

"Why not? I can't stay here."

I stood.

Were the walls getting smaller? Did I just hear a distant noise? There's no way I'd stay here much longer. It wasn't safe.

"I have to get out of here."

Zachary just informed me of the worst news anyone could ever receive. My best friend, the woman I told all my secrets too, died. My heart shattered into a million pieces and pierced me deeply when I saw his sorrowful eyes. He didn't even have to tell me what happened. I could see it in his body language.

She was killed right in front of me. If the gun hadn't jammed, I'd be dead too. I'd like to say I was lucky to be alive, but I didn't feel that way. I didn't feel lucky. Guilt consumed me. Maybe this is what survivor's guilt felt like. Why did I survive, and my best friend hadn't?

He stood, and he held his hands out.

"Destiny, you need to go into protective custody."

Protective custody? No way. I didn't have the time. I didn't have the money. I had bills to pay, and my teacher's salary wouldn't allow me to take extended time off.

"I can't. I must go back to work in a few days. Duty calls, and I must prepare for my children to return to the classroom."

I couldn't fathom what it would be like to go home, knowing Candace wouldn't have the opportunity to return. She would never return to the chic apartment we designed specifically to our tastes. How would I be able to live in our apartment without her there? That was our shared space.

Zachary stared at me. His eyes widened before he tapped on his chin several times.

"I understand what you're saying..."

"No." I interrupted him. My heart would

explode at any moment. "With all due respect, I don't think you do."

I hadn't lost my best friend to a senseless gun act. I didn't have the least bit of understanding.

"Destiny, it's not safe for you to go back home."

Zachary motioned for me to sit.

I opened my mouth to respond but decided against it. I sat. I needed to hear what Zachary had to say. He was the lead detective. He handled situations like this for a living and knew better than I did.

"The suspect could be someone you know. The suspect could be a stranger you've never encountered a day in your life." Zachary paused. He stared into my eyes. "We don't know anything right now, and I'd hate for you to go back home unprotected and you end up hurt." He paused. "Or worse."

He had a point. The suspect could be our next-door neighbor for all we knew. I couldn't trust anybody. The only people I trusted with my life in this world were my parents and Candace. With Candace gone, my parents were all I had in my corner.

I cleared my throat. The perfect thought came to mind. "I could contact my parents. They'll let me stay with them for a while."

I'd also need their emotional support to get me through this rough time.

He shook his head. He grabbed his phone out of his pocket and tapped the screen several times before he placed it on the desk face up. The screen of his phone was of the ocean. "It'll be too dangerous to stay with your family." He exhaled, his eyes darting across the room. "You don't want to place them in harm's way."

He was right. I was already in danger. I wasn't going to be selfish and place my parents in harm's way. I'd have to brave this situation on my own.

"Where will I go?"

I couldn't imagine leaving California in such a manner, but I'd do whatever I needed to stay safe.

"Well, I thought it best to protect you."

Raising my eyebrows, I sat back in my chair. Who would've known the lead detective would've been assigned to watch me. I wasn't an expert on job descriptions, but he didn't seem like the person who would take on that job. If you asked me, it seemed rather dangerous. Didn't he have to hunt down Candace's killer? Wasn't that his job? Not watching over helpless victims?

"What about Candace's killer? Who's going to look for them?"

That was my main concern. Yes, I needed protection, but we needed all the manpower to find the monster that took her life. They needed to be removed from society and placed behind prison walls for the rest of their life so they couldn't harm anyone else. What sick monster could take a life? They had to have an empty soul to do such a horrid thing.

"My counterpart will handle the investigation from this point forward."

Did I trust him to protect me? I'm not sure. Granted, I did run here for help. I didn't have anywhere else to go. I didn't have a vehicle to escape in, so I had no choice but to run on foot. Whoever wanted me dead was still out there, most likely waiting for the perfect time to strike. Would they strike as soon as we left this police station tonight?

Could I trust anyone?

I was undecided about that, but I knew I couldn't protect myself. I needed someone that was trained for this type of war. The fact was Zachary was that person. He was the only person I felt safe with.

I bit the corner of my lip. Did I have a choice?

"I'll protect you with my life." Zachary placed his hand over his heart. "I won't let anything happen to you."

I stared into his eyes. His luscious, dark brown eyelashes framed them. The sincerity in them was vivid. He meant every word that left his mouth.

"Do you promise?"

It was hard for me to find it in my heart to trust. I've had my trust betrayed one too many times in the past. I didn't plan for it to be betrayed again.

"I promise."

His words were laced with truth.

"Okay."

Going into protective custody with the lead detective might be the best thing I could do. He is more aware of the dangers in the world than I could ever imagine.

"I'll have to take you somewhere to stay." He picked up his phone and unlocked it.

"Are we going to a special headquarters?" I asked.

Was the location going to be under 24/7 surveillance video? Was there going to be a secure privacy fence surrounding the property? Would other people be watching over me, providing even more protection?

He shook his head. "No, I'm taking you to my cabin."

"What?"

A cabin? A cabin didn't seem the safest place to fend off a murderer with a devious vendetta against me.

"I have a cabin about two hours from here."

He clicked a few times more on his phone before he showed me the screen. He showed me a small, beautiful redwood cabin tucked away in a nice, wooded area.

I only worried about whether it could provide the necessary safety and protection.

"It looks nice," I commented.

He flashed a smile for the first time that night. His pearly white teeth were on full display.

"It is nice." He stood before he turned and grabbed the coat off the chair. He put on the coat as he said, "Let's get you out of here. We can't have any contact with anyone."

I stood slowly.

"Wait. Can I at least call my parents?"

I spoke to my parents at least three or four times a week. If they didn't hear from me, they'd worry.

He hesitated.

"I'm not sure that's a great idea."

I placed my hands on the desk, pleading with him. "I can't go without them knowing I'm okay. Let me at least call them and let them know I'll be gone for a while."

"Okay." Zachary nodded. He handed me the phone. "Don't mention Candace. Legally, next of kin would be the one to find out first."

With trembling hands, I dialed my mom's phone number. I had memorized it from the day she received the number. I wanted to make sure if I ever needed it and I didn't have my phone, I would have it. My memory came in handy.

After the third ring, my mom answered.

"Hello."

A hint of skepticism touched her tone. She wasn't familiar with the phone number.

"Hi, Mom. It's me."

My voice trembled on my last word.

"Destiny." Silence. "What's wrong? Why are you calling me from this number?"

I opened my mouth to speak, but nothing came out. I couldn't imagine what would happen if this was our last conversation.

Zachary placed his hand on my arm. I looked

at him. He gave me a reassuring look before he gave me a comforting squeeze.

"I have to go away for a while."

Mom cleared her throat. Rustling sounded on her end.

"Away? What do you mean away?"

I looked at Zachary. His words rang true in my head. I couldn't tell my parents what happened with Candace. They'd find out soon enough from her parents, though. Sadly, I wouldn't be able to contact them until...well, there wasn't any estimated date I'd be able to contact them. I just hoped and prayed they'd find the murderer sooner rather than later so I could reunite with my family.

"I have to go away for a while," I repeated.

"Why? What's going on?"

Mom's voice was frantic and laced with worry.

"I can't say too much, but I'm going into protective custody."

Mom gasped.

"Robert, something's going on. Destiny said she's going into protective custody."

I glanced over at Zachary. He patiently waited for this conversation to be over. I wanted to talk to my parents, but I didn't want to irritate the man who would go out of his way to keep me out of harm's way.

"What? Angela, put the phone on speaker."

Ruffling sounded on the phone before Dad spoke.

"Honeybun, what's going on?" Dad asked, calling me the childhood name I grew accustomed to from a young age.

"I can't go into details, but I have to go away for a while." I paused. Tears burned the back of my eyes. "For my safety and your safety."

"I don't like this," Dad called out sternly. "Tell us what's going on."

My eyes must've pleaded for help. Zachary held his hand out, and I handed him his phone.

"Hello. This is Detective Miller speaking." Silence lingered before he spoke. "I understand your worries, but going into protective custody is in her best interests. I promise I'll take good care of her."

After a brief pause, he said, "Here she is."

He handed me the phone back. I pressed it to my ear and closed my eyes. I didn't know when I could make another call to them. I needed to savor the moment. I needed to savor the moment for a lifetime. Who knew if I'd be able to talk to them again? Candace didn't have the opportunity to speak with her family again. What if I had the same fate? What if I couldn't say goodbye to my parents before my destruction?

"Destiny."

My mom's voice pulled me away from my thoughts.

"Yes."

"We love you, and we will talk to you soon," she said softly.

"Call us as soon as you can, honey bun."

"I will. I love you too."

Exhaling, the end tone rang in my ear. I stayed silent, willing myself not to cry anymore, but the tears continued to spill.

I handed him his phone back. "Thank you."

The sweet gesture warmed my insides. Zachary could've said no and allowed me to wallow in my misery, but he didn't. He had a heart. He had a soul.

Zachary shook his head. "You don't have to thank me." He grabbed a pair of keys out of the top drawer of his desk. "I can tell your parents really love you."

"Yes, they do. They'd go around the world a million times, just for me."

He walked towards the office door, and I followed him. "It must be nice to have that type of support from your parents."

Was he implying he didn't have that type of support? Or he didn't have that support from at least one parent? Either way, I'd find out sooner or later. Staying in a cabin with a man without access to the outside world, I'd have all the time in the world to learn everything I needed and wanted to know about him.

I approached the door we'd need to exit from. Then, I waited for Zachary to finish up his conversation with Trevor. They spoke briefly before Zachary said, "I'll be in touch."

Zachary walked to the door and held his hand out.

"Wait right here."

He removed his gun from its holster. He slowly nudged the glass door with his shoulder. A gush of cold air rushed into the building. He pointed the gun and walked outside.

My heart pounded so loud while I waited. It echoed in my ears.

Looking over my shoulder, I could see Trevor standing in front of his desk. He gave a sympathetic smile.

"Don't worry, he's the best of the best. He won't let anything happen to you."

I nodded in response. I tried my hardest to believe that. Anyone who would go out of their way to protect me meant business.

The door opened. Zachary motioned with his hand. "Come on, Destiny."

I waved at Trevor before I wrapped my arms around my body. We were headed to safety. I had to keep repeating that over and over in my head. That was the only thing that would keep me sane.

Chapter Five

Destiny

I walked outside into the dark cold. Looking around frantically, I surveyed my surroundings. Everything was still, no movement to be seen. The temperatures continued to dip, causing me to shiver. Only one streetlight stood in the parking lot, which didn't provide the best lighting. The murderer could be watching from the woods right then, lying in wait.

Zachary took my hand, pulling my attention

away from the potential danger lurking in the woods. He led me to a dark-colored pickup truck in the far corner of the parking lot. The truck lit up as we approached. He opened the passenger door, and I climbed in.

He closed the door behind me. I rubbed my hands together, generating warmth. He walked over to the driver's side, opened the door, and climbed inside.

The truck roared to life. I looked around the truck's cabin, the dashboard illuminating the front seat with light.

Cool air blasted out of the vents. Thankfully, the air became warm shortly after.

Looking out the passenger window, the light from the inside made it almost impossible to see outside. My eyes needed to adjust.

"Can we leave?"

I stabbed the lock button on the door. All the locks sounded   .

Zachary looked over at me, eyebrows raised.

"We can go as soon as we put our seat belts on."

Yeah. Right. Seatbelts. The detective was on it. He had to follow the rules of the roads. He wouldn't allow my manic ways to change that.

Grabbing the seat belt, I put it on.

Once he had his seatbelt on, he placed the truck in drive. We started to move, and I exhaled.

"Where is the cabin?"

Hopefully, the cabin wasn't too far. I wanted alone time so I could cry in peace. Who would've known I'd have to go through this? We just celebrated Christmas together. The festive energy still ran through everyone's veins. My festive energy disappeared, replaced with sorrow.

"It's in Arnold. It's about two hours away," he responded.

I relaxed in my seat. A two-hour drive. I had no choice but to endure this drive.

He pulled out of the parking lot and headed east.

The hum of the heater filled the cabin. The silence made me anxious. I didn't need silence. I needed something to distract me. To distract my mind from all the horrible thoughts that threatened to creep in.

"What am I supposed to do with my phone? Is it safe to bring with us?"

He looked over at me briefly before he said, "Just put it on airplane mode and turn it off for the time being."

I did as instructed before I focused on the road ahead of us.

Bright lights flashed from behind. The reflection in the passenger side mirror caused temporary blind spots in my eyes.

I turned around. A pair of headlights was so close it blinded me. Was it normal for a vehicle to drive this close? Or were my nerves playing tricks on me? What if that was the murderer? What if they were following us? What if they were waiting for us to get far enough away from the police station to kill me? To kill us.

"Detective Miller."

His eyes flickered over me. He smiled before he looked back at the road.

"You can call me Zach. There is no need for formalities . You'll be living with me."

I looked back. The vehicle drove too close for my liking. It had to be a truck or a van for the headlights to be visible.

"Zach."

I grabbed the armrest, mentally preparing myself for the worst.

"Yes?"

His voice was calm and even. The opposite of how I felt.

"Who's following us?"

He looked in the rearview mirror as he continued driving down the road.

"It's probably nobody."

Probably? Probably wasn't convincing me. Evidently, he wasn't convinced either.

My heart pounded a million miles per hour. My hands turned clammy. "Someone's following us."

He looked in the rearview mirror again. He contemplated his next move. After a few moments, he put his blinker on. We approached a right-hand turn and turned off the road.

The light-colored work van continued to drive. The brightness in the mirror disappeared, along with my confidence. Embarrassment embraced me.

Was I losing my mind? Yes. Did I want him to think that? No, but I knew he already thought it. I acted like a lunatic.

He was right. I was wrong, and he proved that to me.

He came to a stop on the shoulder of the road.

"I'm sorry."

The tears I tried my damnedest to hold inside exploded out of me, along with a disgusting sob.

My apology wasn't exactly fitting for the situation, but I had no idea what else to say.

He placed his hand on my arm, his touch comforting. "I'm sorry."

I glanced over at him. His eyes were trained on me, intensified with worry.

"Why are you apologizing?" I asked through my sniffles.

Zach had no reason to apologize to me. He had done nothing but try to help me.

"I should be more understanding. After everything you've been through tonight ..."

I looked at my lap. I didn't want to be the pity party, but I had issues to deal with. Issues that were out of my control. Issues that I needed to deal with on my own. Not with the help of a stranger I met less than an hour ago.

"Can we go to the cabin now?"

Sitting on the side of the road prolonged our trip to the cabin. It further assisted in the murderer keeping a close eye on us if they were trailing behind us. We needed to get back on the road.

"Yeah. Let's go."

He put the truck in drive and turned around so we were headed in our original direction.

I stared out the window. The trees passed by, a blur of green scenery.

What had my life come to? I was twenty-five. My life truly hadn't even started yet, but I sat on the edge of my seat, running for my life.

The truck filled with country music as the scenery turned into the city. I looked at him, and he turned the volume up, his eyes never leaving the road. The bass of a man's voice came through, serenading my ears about his love for his wife.

"Is country fine?"

He squeezed the steering wheel before he looked at me.

"Yes, it's fine."

I looked forward, breaking our eye contact. We were headed for the highway. We were headed for my temporary home.

What if Candace had never left Argentina to come to the United States? What if her family had decided to go to another state in the United States besides California? What if her family hadn't moved for that last time? What if Candace decided to go another route in life? What if she decided to go to college instead of jumping right into work? What if Candace had decided on a different career path? What if Candace had decided on someone else to be her soulmate? What if I were the reason for what happened tonight? Would she still be alive?

"Are you in deep thought over there?"

I blinked. We were on the highway headed south. At this time of night, the roads were nearly deserted. An upbeat country played.

"Yes."

An overwhelming wave of grief engulfed me.

"Do you want to talk about it?"

I laid my head against the passenger window panel.

"No, thank you."

I couldn't express my thoughts and feelings to him. Especially someone who didn't even know Candace. That didn't even know me, for that matter. I just met him. It wasn't right. It would never be right.

I could imagine how Candace would think he was hot, just for me. I could hear her now. "Girl, you better go for that hot detective. He's so handsome and your type." I giggled before the happy thought left my mind. I couldn't be happy, considering the circumstances.

"If you need to talk, I'm here."

Those words went in one ear and out the other. The only person I wanted to talk to was Candace. I would also talk to my parents, but whenever I was sad, I'd go to Candace. She always knew what to say to me to make me feel better.

An awkward silence settled upon us as we traveled along the highway headed to the cabin. Zach occasionally asked how I was doing, but I didn't have too much to say. I was a wreck and a mess. I didn't know what to do with myself. To avoid bringing him down my depressive spiral of life, I stayed silent.

I glanced at the time once he killed the ignition in front of a small cabin. It was only minutes from midnight. Only minutes from entering another day. Only minutes from moving on to another day without Candace there.

"We're here."

I looked around. The still darkness terrified me. Panic settled over me. My hands shook with anxiety. Did anyone know we were going there?

Zach opened the driver's door. A gust of cold air blew into the truck. He closed the door before he walked around and opened my door. He looked at my feet before placing his muscular arms around my back and under my legs. He lifted me easily as if I weighed as light as a feather. The scent of his cologne clung to his chest, temporarily distracting me from the purpose. He smelled delightful, and don't get me started on his muscles.

Wood burned thick in the air from a neighboring cabin. The smell reminded me of Christmas. Sadly, this occurrence ruined Christmas for me. It's no longer a fun, festive time for me. It's now a sad, lonely, dark time. A time in my life that I'd never forget.

"This will be your new home for a while."

He closed the passenger door with his shoulder. The cabin appeared small, but I couldn't make too much out of it from the outside in the dark.

"Goodie," I responded. He walked us up the four wooden stairs that led to the front door, and the occasional creak echoed under our weight.

He sat me down at the front door. Surprisingly, I could stand on my legs after being momentarily hypnotized by his scent and strength. The key jingled in the door before it opened. Zach walked inside, turned to the right, and switched the lights on.

I walked inside and I looked around. The lighting was low and intimate. The air was stagnant and cold. The cabin was small and decorated in modern décor. There was a loveseat, two end tables on either side, a small flat-screen TV, a lazy boy, little marine trinkets throughout the room, and pictures of fish hung on the wall. In the far right corner was the dining room.

"Welcome to my home away from home." He motioned his hand around the cabin. "Let me turn on the heat. It's chilly in here."

He walked into the dining room. Within seconds, the heater hummed.

"It's beautiful."

I walked further into the cabin.

I wish I had a home away from home. Heck, I couldn't even afford our apartment on my teacher's salary. How would I be able to afford our apartment now? I only survived with Candace's portion of the rent. Without her, I wouldn't be able to live there anymore.

I brought my hand up to my head. Piece by piece, my life fell apart. By the time the murderer was caught, I'd be left with nothing. I'd have no choice but to move back in with my parents and start my life over. Living with my parents wouldn't be so bad. I feared starting over the most.

"Yeah." He nodded. "I put a lot of work into it."

He must be crafty. This place was stunning.

"It's evident."

"My grandmother left it to me."

Did that mean his grandmother passed away? Or did she just leave him a cabin? I wouldn't pry. I knew I'd find out sooner or later.

I looked to the left, and there were two closed doors.

The smell of burned dust filled the air.

"You did great with it. How many bedrooms?"

"It's a one-bedroom."

I looked at him. One bedroom. Two people that didn't know each other from the fly on the wall, sharing a bedroom? This couldn't be good.

"This was the best gift my grandmother could've left me," he continued. "Sometimes, I just have to get away from work, and this is the best place to come."

I couldn't imagine being a detective. Dealing with people going through a tragedy daily had to be hard work. He deserved this cabin for helping people as much as he did.

Walking over to the end table, I sat my phone

down before I picked up a fish figurine. I examined its intricate details before I placed it down.

He loved his fish.

"Can I take a shower?" I asked.

We'd figure out the bed situation once I showered. I was done with small talk for the night. I needed to stand under a stream of hot water and spill my sorrows. Alone. By myself.

"Yes." He pointed to the door closest to the front door. "The linen is in the closet. Take as long as you need."

I smiled even though, deep down, I wanted to die.

"Thank you."

I opened the bathroom door, and to my surprise, it was spacious. A white bathtub against the far wall. A white toilet sat beside the tan vanity. Across from the toilet and the vanity was a closet. Opening the door, I looked at a stack of towels and washcloths.

Grabbing a washcloth and a towel, I placed them on the vanity before I went to the bathtub and turned the shower on.

I could look at myself in the mirror above the vanity for the first time that night. I wished I hadn't. I looked horrible. My hair was now in a messy bun. It was a tight, formal bun at the start of the evening. My eyes were red and puffy, but my makeup still looked flawless. I silently admitted I received my money's worth out of it. I didn't know why I chose to buy the waterproof products. I never thought it would come in handy, but looking at my reflection, it did. I glanced down at my coat, and my heart dropped to my stomach. Candace's blood.

I gulped. A lump of grief lodged in my throat. I had to take these clothes off. After locking the door, I stripped out of my clothes. Without another thought, I tossed my clothes and single boot into the trash. I didn't want to see that outfit again. It was tainted in the worst way possible.

I placed my hand under the hot water stream, the perfect temperature. Just the way I liked it. Stepping under the stream of water, I closed my eyes. The hot water danced down my body, washing away the horrible day I just conquered.

Grabbing the body wash, I lathered my washcloth up. The smell of cinnamon filled the bathroom. I scrubbed my body with every ounce of strength I could muster. Salty tears washed down my face and into the drain.

What would my life be like now that I was a shattered woman?

Once my skin burned from the hot water, I turned it off. I grabbed the towel, which smelled of flowers, and I dried off. If only I could close my eyes and imagine myself in a field surrounded by an array of flowers. All I could see was Candace on the ground of the sushi parking lot. I could never go to that sushi restaurant again.

"I have some clothes for you to wear," the voice came from the other side of the door.

I wrapped the towel tight around my body.

"I'll take them."

Unlocking the door, I grabbed the clothes. I closed the door and locked it again.

He handed me a red sweatshirt and a pair of black sweatpants. These clothes would do the trick in keeping me warm.

As I slipped on the clothes, I wondered who they belonged to. Maybe they were his girlfriend's clothes. How would she feel about him taking me into protective custody? At his cabin? We were all alone out there.

Considering the situation, I hoped she would be okay with this living arrangement. If Zach were my boyfriend, how would I feel about my boyfriend having a young woman in his cabin?

I opened the door. The cold from the living room met my body, and I shivered. The heater needed to warm up this place already.

Zach walked into the living room from the dining room. He cradled a mug in his hand.

"How was your shower?"

He sipped his drink.

"It was fine."

It felt great being clean. I hadn't desired a shower this much since... ever.

It seemed like it took forever to get out of my clothes and wash the night's events away. If only I could permanently remove them from my memory. I'd be content with that.

"Would you like some coffee?" He held the mug up. "I made a big pot. I wasn't sure if you were a coffee drinker."

I wrung my hands together, then glanced up at him.

"I love coffee, but if I had a cup tonight, I wouldn't sleep for the next eight hours."

He laughed. He walked over to the end table and sat the cup down.

"I can still fall asleep at the drop of a dime after having a cup," he replied.

I was dealing with a coffee fanatic. This would be very interesting.

I looked at the couch. A soft blanket and a fluffy white pillow lay on top of it. We had the same thoughts about the night's sleeping arrangement.

"Am I taking the couch?" I asked him.

"No. I already have the bed in the room made up for you."

He pointed towards the room.

I glanced over my shoulder at the closed door. "You don't have to..." I began.

"My guest won't sleep on the couch. The bed is all yours."

I knew I needed rest after the exhausting day that I had. I knew I probably wouldn't get an ounce of sleep, but I couldn't understand why he'd kill his back on the couch instead of allowing me to sleep on it. He stood well over six feet. His feet would dangle over the side of the couch. If I were to sleep on it, I'd actually fit. Would I argue with him over his decision? No. He did me a favor by protecting me.

"I hope your girlfriend doesn't mind that I'm

staying here," I blurted out.

As soon as the words rolled off my tongue, I immediately regretted them. Why would I say something stupid like that? There wasn't anyone to blame but myself.

"Why would you think I have a girlfriend?" he asked.

I motioned to the clothes I wore.

"Aren't these her clothes?"

He chuckled. He rubbed the stubble on his chin.

"You're wearing the clothes my mother left here when she came here a few months ago."

Oh. If I could open the ground up and fall inside a deep hole, I would do it.

"You two are the same size, so I thought, why not? I figured her clothes would fit you better than mine."

The conversation needed to end there. I needed to disappear into the bedroom for the night.

"Well, goodnight." I waved awkwardly before I turned towards the bedroom. I placed my hand on the doorknob.

"To answer your question, no."

I didn't turn the knob. To my surprise, I turned around and looked at him.

"I don't have a girlfriend."

He paused and stared at me.

"Actually, I don't date."

Hmm. For Zach to be so attractive, why would he not date? He didn't seem like a bad guy.

There had to be more to the story.

Heck. I didn't look so bad myself, and I have a wonderful personality. Why was I single?

I turned around and opened the door. "Goodnight," I called over my shoulder.

I'd find out sooner or later. There's no doubt in my mind about that.

Chapter Six

Zach

Destiny would be the death of me.

Why did I decide to take her into protective custody? Yes, she was distraught. She couldn't leave the police station by herself. She's been in a daze since before discovering the terrible news. I couldn't allow her to leave. I feared something would happen to her the second she left my sight. I knew deep within my heart there was something sinister about this case. It wasn't right for two women to go to dinner and have a wonderful time and only for one woman not to be alive at night's end.

I wished I could work it myself, but I cared more about her safety. Frank was the second-best in the department. I knew he'd get to the bottom of the mystery. I needed to control myself. Her beauty mesmerized me, though. I had to face the truth. In all my years as a detective, I never made a decision this terrible. I'd have to deal with it, though.

Once the words left my mouth, I was doomed. I had a mission to complete, and that mission was keeping her safe.

The entire drive to the cabin, she was on edge. I felt bad when I had to pull off the road when she thought we were being followed. I didn't know how she felt. Deep down, I never wanted to know how she felt.

I got into this field because I wanted to help people. My goal was to make her feel safe. I had to do that with no strings attached. I had to keep my mind clear of her beautiful brown eyes and her luscious, plump lips. I had to keep my mind strictly on business. Yes, it would be hard, but I had no other choice. I couldn't mix business with pleasure, no matter how much I wanted to.

Was she interested in me, though? Her statement made it seem that way. I knew she wasn't married. She corrected me when I addressed her as a married woman. Did she have a boyfriend? I doubted it. The only people she wanted to call when I told her she couldn't be in contact with anyone were her parents. If I were in a situation like this, I'd want to be in touch with my girlfriend after my mother knew I was okay.

It pained me to see her clothes stuffed in the trash can in the bathroom when I went to take a shower. She was hurt, to say the least. I didn't blame her, though. Her best friend's blood was on her coat. Whenever she looked at that outfit, she would never forget what happened when she wore it. She had no other choice but to trash it.

After showering, I threw the bag in the garbage can out front. If Destiny got up through the night to use the bathroom, I didn't want her to have to look at them again. That was the least I could do for her.

The last time I slept on a couch was in my college days after I had one too many drinks at the party of the week. A nostalgic feeling washed over me as I snuggled under the covers and closed my eyes. The couch wasn't the most comfortable thing to sleep on, though. It was designed for sitting, but I had no choice. I'd much rather sleep in the plush, king-size bed in my bedroom, but that bed was off-limits. At least, for now.

Before I went to sleep, I cracked the door open. Destiny slept in the middle of the bed. I stepped closer and admired her. She looked like an angel. A real-life goddess. She had her hair down, splayed across the pillow she slept on. A murmur of a snore escaped her lips as she snuggled under the thick comforter. She looked at peace. That's what I wanted for her. To have some peace. Even if it was only while she slept.

Emerged in a deep, peaceful sleep, an exasperated scream woke me up. Completely discombobulated, I jumped off the couch and stubbed my toe on the end table. I jumped up and down in pain, then hissed a spew of curse words. I rubbed the sleep out of my eyes.

Enough about my toe.

Where was I? Who was screaming? What was going on?

The cabin.

Destiny.

Why did she scream?

I ran to the bedroom. Thankfully, she hadn't locked the door. I threw the lights on, the brightness blinding. She lay in the middle of the bed. Her body writhed. Her hair was frizzy, her forehead was wet with sweat, and her eyes were closed. Tears streamed down her face as her mouth formed a circle.

"Destiny. Destiny. Destiny."

I ran over to the bed and sat beside her.

She continued to scream.

"No, no, no."

"Destiny."

I placed my hands on her arms, and she fought me. She kicked and clawed with all her might.

"Candace. Please, don't leave."

My heart dropped. Destiny was having a

nightmare.

Her nails scratched my arms, leaving painful scratches.

"Destiny." My voice was stern. "Open your eyes."

Her brown eyes shot open. They were wide as saucers.

"Are you okay?" I asked her.

I knew she wasn't okay, but I had to ask her something. Anything to make her talk to me and tell me what was happening.

She looked around the room, taking in the flat-screen TV on the massive brown dresser. The paintings of the fish on the walls caught her eye. She forgot her location.

She grabbed her face into her hands.

"No." She took a deep breath. "Every time I close my eyes, I see Candace."

What could I say to that? Could I even respond to that? I didn't know how to. Of all the years I dealt with victims, I couldn't formulate a thought to say to her. She rendered me speechless.

She looked down at my arms. They were red and hot from her fingernails.

"Did I do that?" she asked, her voice soft.

I grabbed her hands. They were soft, delicate, and perfectly fit my hands, like a perfect puzzle piece.

"It's okay."

I didn't care if I had scratches on my arm that stung. All I cared about was Destiny's safety.

"No, it's not." Tears fell from her eyes. "I'm sorry."

I squeezed her hands. "You don't have any reason to apologize."

Her eyes fluttered closed, another tear escaping her eyes. I wanted to reach out and wipe them away, but I didn't want to scare her with too much affection. Hell, I didn't need to give her any affection. She needed protection. That's all I could ever give her. I decided to do this to protect her. There was no other motive behind my decision.

"Just lay down."

She shook her head. She folded her arms across her chest. She didn't move.

"I'll lay in here with you."

She looked at me for a second too long. Did I overstep my boundaries? Did she think differently of me now? I shouldn't have suggested it. I was wrong, and she knew it. I knew it.

"Okay."

My mouth nearly dropped open when she lay down.

I turned the lights off before I walked back to the bed. I sat and placed my hand on her arm. I wanted to cuddle her but didn't want to move too quickly. I didn't want to freak her out.

She faced me and curled into a ball right before the room filled with soft sobs.

My heart ached for her. I couldn't imagine the pain she harbored. I couldn't imagine what my life would be like if I lost Jake, my best friend.

We had been friends since we were in diapers. Our moms were best friends from college. Inheritably, we became best friends. We each had our own lives now, though. By that, I meant he had a wife and two young children. About once a month, we'd get together when he wasn't working or spending quality time with his family. Even if I lost Jake in a natural manner, I still would be heartbroken. If I had one wish, I would wish her pain away. I'd bring Candace back so she could be happy.

Her eyes fluttered closed. I stared at her. Occasionally, she'd open her eyes and look at me. She'd give me a smile that didn't quite reach her eyes before she closed them again.

After a few moments, her soft snores filled the room.

I rubbed her arm soothingly and cupped her face. She looked so beautiful as she slept. She looked at peace, even if it was just for the time being.

My eyes were heavy. It had to be early in the morning. Could I sleep there? It sure as heck felt like it. After the long day I had, I could fall asleep sitting up.

My eyes fluttered close.

***

Something jolted me awake. I looked around. The darkness of the night loomed. I lay in the bedroom of my cabin. My arms were wrapped tightly around Destiny. Her back pressed against my chest, and the smell of coconut surrounded me. The coconut came from her hair. My bulge pressed hard against my jean shorts. Her hand lay on top of my arm.

What happened? How did I get like this? When did this happen? Why was I hard?

I maneuvered my arms around her, careful not to wake her up. Thankfully, she continued to sleep. I stood and stretched, then adjusted my hard-on, completely disgusted with myself. How could I allow myself to get like this? She was vulnerable, for goodness sake. I shouldn't get hard over comforting her.

What would've happened if she had woken up with my manhood pressed against her? Would she have left feeling violated? I wouldn't want to imagine how she'd feel.

After one more glance at her asleep, I opened the door and entered the living room. I picked up my phone and checked for any calls or messages I might've received. There were no missed calls or messages waiting for me. Disappointment settled over me. No news only meant there was nothing to tell. If Destiny asked for updates, I wanted something to tell her. I wanted to be able to tell her everything. Right then, I knew nothing. That wasn't good. Having news this early in the investigation wasn't normal, even if I handled the case. I just wanted everything to fall into place for Destiny. That was the least I could do. Provide her with the information on who killed her best friend.

My phone clock showed six in the morning. If

I weren't away from work, I'd already be up. I'd hit the gym for an hour before I went to work for the day. I worked long hours. I stayed in shape by working out for at least an hour a day and eating healthy meals.

Being a classified bachelor, I had to cook my own meals, but my mother raised me right. I knew how to put together a delicious protein with a massive side of vegetables and a small portion of carbs.

One thing was for sure: if Destiny wasn't eating like she should have before, she would have three meals a day while living with me.

I walked into the bathroom and stared at myself in the mirror. I had a bad case of bedhead. Pulling my hair tie off my hair, I pulled my hairbrush through my wavy hair. I handled my hygiene once I had my hair in a neat ponytail.

Due to my extensive years of mini flings, I kept extra hygiene products in my cabin. Anything and everything I could think of was in the vanity. When I had to shop for Destiny, all I had to do was pick up a few items for her to wear.

I walked into the bedroom. Destiny slept in the same position. She looked like a goddess. I wanted to walk over, grab her face, and kiss her lips, but I refrained. I opened the dresser and grabbed a pair of sweatpants and a sweatshirt. Around this time of year, the cold air was unbearable. I had no choice but to bundle up in sweatshirts and coats. Walking into the bathroom, I changed out of my pajamas. I didn't have any plans to go too far from the cabin, but I needed to prepare for anything that might happen.

I walked into the kitchen. The kitchen was adorned with stainless steel appliances. The table for two was dark brown and brand new. I put on a fresh pot of coffee. Destiny didn't have any last night, but I'm sure she'd have a cup when she woke up. Coffee helped wake me up and get ready for my day. I couldn't ask for a better companion in the morning.

Was she an oatmeal person? Or was she more of an omelet woman? I didn't know too much about her, but I knew by the end of it all, I'd know her like the back of my hand.

One thing I did know was that I wanted to find Candace's killer. I wanted to satisfy Destiny in a way that no one else could. Peace wouldn't fall on me until the suspect sat behind prison bars for the rest of his or her life.

The journey to finding the suspect might be a short one that would take a few days. The journey might be long, taking weeks to months to locate them. No matter how far they ran or succeeded in evading us, we'd bring Candace's family and Destiny justice. There wasn't a case I hadn't successfully solved, and this wouldn't be the first one. I'd make sure of that.

Chapter Seven

Destiny

Candace. She looked beautiful. With her flawless makeup, she smiled brightly, no imperfection that could be seen for miles.

A gut-wrenching scream escaped her mouth. Her smile disintegrated. We looked at the gunshot wound at the same time before she looked at me. Her eyes were full of pain before she dropped to the ground.

A scream escaped my mouth as a strong

force grabbed my arms and held them down by my side.

I kicked, screamed, and clawed with all my might. They already hurt Candace. They couldn't hurt me as well.

I had to find out who hurt Candace. I was the only witness... to my knowledge.

Right when the murderer's face nearly came into view, everything faded away.

"Destiny."

Who called me? Where did the voice come from? Where was I? Was I dead or alive?

"Open your eyes."

I obliged. I stared into a pair of eyes that were now familiar to me.

"Are you okay?" he asked.

Obviously, I wasn't. Zach shouldn't be beside me right now. He should be in the living room, peacefully sleeping on the couch. Not tending to me while I had nightmares.

Having him by my side was comforting as I settled back down. Occasionally, I'd open my eyes to make sure he was still there, but the smell of coffee jolted me out of my sleep.

Sitting up, I looked around. I lay in a massive, king-size bed. The blankets were luscious against my skin. The dresser across the room held a huge flat-screen TV.

Coving my mouth, I yawned. I didn't remember falling back to sleep, but I felt somewhat rested. Did Zach sleep with me last night? He was there when I fell asleep. His cologne hung in the air, warm and inviting.

Pushing the covers off, I stood. I fixed my clothes before I opened the bedroom door.

Walking into the living room, Zach wasn't in sight. Was he outside ? Did he leave for a few minutes? Was I there all alone?

A cabinet closed in the dining room. Zach was there. I wasn't alone.

I walked into the dining room. It was the perfect size for this cabin, small and intimate. Zach's back faced me. He grabbed the coffee pot and poured the cup full.

"Good morning," I called out.

He sat the pot on the burner and turned to look at me.

"Good morning."

He wore his hair in a low ponytail. He smiled brightly, his perfect white teeth on display. He was handsome, to say the least. Looking at him every day would be pleasant. I could get used to this.

"How did you sleep?" he asked.

I looked at him. What could I say? I didn't sleep the best in that humongous king-sized bed until you came to my rescue and woke me up from my nightmare? I slept decently once you told me that you'd lie with me. No, I wouldn't say that. I could never say that. That tidbit of information wouldn't leave my mouth. It would stay with me.

"I mean, after you went to sleep the second time?" he clarified.

"I slept okay," I responded.

Surprisingly, I rested. My mind raced all night, from how I couldn't talk to my best friend ever again to how he turned my question around and left me speechless. I must've been exhausted because I didn't remember falling asleep.

"Okay is better than terrible," he commented before sipping his coffee.

"You're right about that."

If I had pockets in these sweats, I'd stuff my hands in them. Nervousness washed over me. I had no reason to be nervous.

He scoffed as he sat his cup down.

"Where are my manners? Would you like a cup of coffee?"

Coffee on a cold morning? Who could say no to that?

"Yes, please."

Zach smiled, and then he grabbed another cup out of the cabinet. "Do you like hot or iced coffee?"

I gasped as I placed my hand over my heart.

"How could someone drink cold coffee?"

Truly, I needed to know. Coffee should be enjoyed while hot. It was brewed hot, it needed to stay hot.

"Hot coffee it is," he said before he winked and poured me a cup.

The steam swirled out of the coffee, letting me know the coffee was the perfect temperature for this chilly morning. "Do you like cream?"

I scrunched up my nose. I love creamer, but

this morning called for something different.

"I'll take milk and some sugar."

He pointed to the cabinet beside me.

"Sugar is in there."

He went into the fridge and grabbed milk.

"Here's the milk."

"Thank you."

I took the milk and poured some into my coffee, watching the dark liquid become a creamy tan color.

"It's no problem," he answered.

"No." I paused as I screwed the top on the milk. "Not just for the coffee. For everything."

He analyzed me as he grabbed the milk and placed it back in the fridge.

"You don't have to thank me."

I spooned sugar into my coffee.

"I have to. You went out of your way to protect me. To be with me, and you didn't have to do that. I could never have expected that from anyone, especially you."

Zach grabbed his cup of coffee, walked over to the dining table, and motioned for me to join him.

I grabbed my cup of coffee and the spoon and sat across from him.

"I don't ever want to hear you thank me again. I did this act from the bottom of my heart, and I'd do it all over again."

Did he do this for other surviving victims? Or was I the lucky one to have a lead detective care for me? Granted, I feel better with my life in his hands than anyone else. After last night, I knew I couldn't trust anyone, but I had no choice but to trust him. After last night, I knew I couldn't get through this on my own. It was impossible.

Nodding my answer, I stirred my coffee. Taking a sip, I moaned in satisfaction as the hot liquid warmed me.

"You make a mean cup of coffee," I commented, changing the course of the conversation.

He could tell me every day for the next six months not to thank him, and I would still do it. I could not go without showing my appreciation for the care he had shown me.

He held his cup of coffee up.

"I've had plenty of practice. Considering I have a cup two times a day."

I agreed. "Yes, you have."

He sat back and looked at me. His eyes stayed on my face.

"So, I must ask you something."

I shrugged. At this point, I was an open book. "Ask away."

"What do you have against people who love iced coffee?" he asked.

I cracked a smile. Ducking my head, I tried to hide my smile. How did he manage to make me smile when I wanted to disappear into thin air? Did he have superpowers I wasn't aware of?

He laughed as he rubbed the stubble on his chin.

"Don't hide that beautiful smile."

Was he flirting with me? I had to be imagining it. He was just being a nice guy, doing anything to put a smile on my face.

Looking at him, I contemplated my answer.

"Don't tell me you're an iced coffee lover."

"Die hard," he responded.

I threw my head back, laughter bubbling within me.

"How can you drink iced coffee?" I asked.

Grabbing my cup of coffee, I blew on it. I couldn't imagine going for a sip of coffee and coldness meeting my tongue.

He shrugged.

"Those hot summer days just call for an iced coffee."

I smirked before I took a sip.

"You have a great defense to back up your case."

He smiled.

"I always will."

He paused, looking at me for a moment.

"I was trying to figure out if you're an oatmeal or omelet lover."

I scrunched my nose up.

"I'm not hungry."

I could stomach coffee, but putting food in my stomach didn't seem the best idea.

He gave me a sympathetic look.

"I understand you aren't hungry, but you still have to eat something."

I exhaled before I sipped my coffee.

"Oatmeal would be fine."

He smiled before he stood and walked over to the fridge.

"Oatmeal, coming right up."

I stood. "I can help."

He looked over his shoulder at me.

"There's no need. You just sit there and relax."

Did I imagine yesterday, when I received the devastating news, that I'd be in a cabin with a hot detective the following day? No. Did I imagine that I'd be waited on hand and foot? No. Why was he being so thoughtful? All he had to do was protect me from harm. He didn't have to cook for me. He didn't have to entertain me.

I sat, crossed my legs, and sipped my coffee. Zach hummed a tune I wasn't familiar with, but I enjoyed the melody.

"Do you like your oatmeal sweet?"

"Yes," I responded.

As he delved into the cupboard and grabbed a bottle of honey, I observed his every move. I watched as he poured some honey and milk into the pot. He made the oatmeal with intent.

"Oatmeal for the lovely lady," he said as he sat a bowl of steaming, hot oatmeal in front of me. The sweet scent filled my nose, causing my mouth to water. My stomach growled.

He sat across from me at the table with his own bowl.

"Thank you."

He gave me a knowing look. He stuck his spoon into his oatmeal.

"What did I tell you about thanking me?"

"I can't help it when you've been so welcoming to me."

He smiled before he looked at his bowl of oatmeal. I focused on my bowl. Once I cooled the heaping spoonful, I ate it, and the perfect amount of sweetness touched my tongue.

"How does it taste?" he asked me.

I gave a thumbs up.

"Awesome," he responded.

He focused on his breakfast. I took the time to check him out. He was young and attractive. From the looks of how he carried himself, he had a great head on his shoulders. There had to be more behind the handsome smile and open heart I wasn't aware of. What could it be?

"What do you like to do for fun?" I asked him after I ate another spoonful of oatmeal.

He smiled before he answered.

"I don't have too much time for fun in my field of work."

"Yeah? That might be true, but what do you like to do when you have time to yourself?"

He sipped his coffee before he cleared his throat.

"I love the outdoors. Something about being in nature centers me, but my favorite hobby is fishing."

That explained the pictures in his office and the decor of his cabin. Right then and there, I knew I needed to be honest with him.

"Can I tell you something?"

He stopped mid-chew. He placed his spoon down.

"I'm all ears."

"I've never been fishing before," I admitted.

He raised an eyebrow before a smirk appeared.

"Are you kidding?"

I shook my head.

"No. I've never been fishing."

He leaned back and stared at me.

"Where were you raised?" he asked.

After I spooned more oatmeal into my mouth and swallowed it, I said, "I lived in Florida for the first few years of elementary school before I moved here."

He gasped.

"I need to take you fishing as soon as it warms up," he commented.

Wait. Did I hear him correctly? Did he say he needed to take me fishing? Was he being nice or was that a mess up with his words?

"That would be great," slipped from my mouth before I thought about what I said.

He smiled before he grabbed his empty bowl and walked it over to the sink.

I looked at my bowl, shocked I still had plenty left to eat.

"What do you like to do in your free time?"

He rinsed his bowl.

Besides hanging out with Candace, I didn't have too many other hobbies.

"I love to draw."

He looked over his shoulder after he hung the bowl to dry on the drying rack.

"That's awesome. You must be talented."

Maybe we shared a hobby, but he didn't tell me about it. It would be nice to draw together.

"Sometimes, I use it as an escape from reality. Do you draw?"

Spooning more oatmeal into my mouth, I chewed thoughtfully and with intent.

He laughed as he sat down.

"I wish I could. I couldn't draw a stick figure to save my life."

I laughed along with him. It was nice to have a conversation outside of why I was there in the cabin with him, but the conversation had to happen.

"Have you received any updates on Candace?"

I knew it hadn't even been a full day yet, but I needed answers. I needed them now. Zach could only provide those answers to me. The silence that settled in the room validated the answer I didn't want to hear. His smile disintegrated into thin air.

"No." It seemed like a century had passed before he answered. "There's no update yet, but they are extensively searching."

My stomach turned, the oatmeal in my stomach churning. I couldn't eat anymore, no matter how little I already ate.

"If you'll excuse me..." I began as I stood.

"You didn't finish your oatmeal."

Defeat washed over his face. I could tell he was upset he hadn't heard anything yet. Hell, he had a stranger in his cabin that he didn't know and probably couldn't trust. He probably wanted the answers just as quickly as I did so he could get his space back. So he could get his life back.

"I'm not hungry."

With those parting words, I walked out of the dining room. Walking to the lazy boy chair, I plopped down. If I could, I'd go outside and walk to clear my head, but that wasn't possible. What if the murderer lurked, waiting for me to reveal myself so he could finish me off too?

Candace. Her beautiful, radiant smile. Her joyful soul. Her energy couldn't be matched by any other. Who would want to take her away from this world?

I remembered the day we met. It was the first day of high school. No longer being the top dog in school frightened me. I had to do things in life that sometimes made me uncomfortable. We both had Ms. Edwards as our first-period teacher. Candace walked in right after the bell rang. She wore a black dress that stopped mid-thigh, thigh-high polka-dot socks, and high-heeled boots.

"Excuse me, miss, you aren't in dress code," Ms. Edwards called out.

She looked down at her outfit. She shrugged before she blew a big bubble with her wad of pink bubblegum.

"Gum is against school rules."

She nodded before she folded her arms

across her chest.

"Where would you like me to sit?" she asked, ignoring what she had said.

There were two seats open. One to my right and one in the far-left corner of the room.

"In the principal's office."

Candace smirked before she turned around and walked out the door.

She came back twenty minutes later, strutting into the classroom. We were going over the syllabus as she sat beside me. Pineapple wafted into my nose as she sat back.

Once the bell rang, I looked over at her as she placed her binder in her bag.

"You look amazing," I commented, zipping my bag up.

She winked at me as she placed her bag on her shoulder.

"Thank you."

"Where did you get that dress?" I asked as I stood. "It's flattering. I need one."

We walked out of the classroom together.

"The mall. We can hit the mall up after school if you'd like."

A visit to the mall? Could I ever say no?

"That would be great."

"Awesome. You're my first friend here at this...." She motioned around the area before she smiled at me. "School."

"It doesn't seem like you want to be here," I said as we passed a group of guys giving each other high fives.

She shrugged.

"My parents and I just moved for the third time in the last five years."

"Yikes."

I placed my hand over my mouth as we passed by the water fountain. No wonder she wasn't too happy. She bounced between schools. I could only imagine once she had a great, solid friendship at one school, she was yanked from that school and placed in another.

"I take it you wouldn't be happy either?"

I shook my head.

"Not in the slightest." I reached my hand out. "I'm Destiny."

She placed her cold hand in mine, her red nail polish catching my eye.

"Candace."

"Did you dress out of dress code for a reason?" I asked as I glanced at my schedule.

She smiled.

"I'm making a statement."

That's exactly what she did. She made a statement so bold, everyone respected her. She didn't settle for what everyone else did or thought was right. She had her own mind, and I loved her for that. We became attached at the hip from that point forward. It was rare to see one without the other being too far behind.

"I'm sorry," broke me out of my thoughts.

I looked at Zach, who sat on the couch.

A tear fell onto my cheek, and I wiped it away. What could I say? What could I do? My heart ached. My heart shattered into a million pieces all over again. I never had a pain that hurt like this before. This pain needed to go away. Would finding her murderer make the pain go away? No. Would it somewhat make me feel better? I didn't know. I didn't know anything anymore.

Even though Zach was there with me, I felt alone and isolated. I appreciated everything he did for me, but I needed my family. I couldn't reach out to them until the murderer was caught. The last thing I wanted to do was put my family at risk.

"I think I'm going to lie down."

I didn't even wait for him to respond before I got up and walked into the room. Closing the door, the grief took over. Falling to the ground, my chest ached with sorrow. Curling into a ball, I cried. I tried to be strong, but grief didn't care who you were. When it struck, it struck hard. I had to let it go, or it would eat me up entirely.

Chapter Eight

Zach

My heart hurt. I had no other choice but to feel this way. How could I feel different when I was around someone who had their heart ripped out of their chest and shredded into a million pieces right in front of them? I could feel her pain.

When she went into the bedroom yesterday and closed the door, I knew what would follow. Anyone with common sense would expect it. She sobbed for a good while. I could hear every sniffle, every exhale, and every inhale.

Walking over to the door about ten minutes after she walked into the bedroom, I knocked. Silence resonated. She didn't say anything.

Was she trying to avoid me? I hoped not. I knew I couldn't say anything or do anything to bring Candace back, but I could be a shoulder to cry on. I could be someone she could confide in. She didn't have anyone else she could contact right now. I'd be more than happy to be her confidant. Even if she had someone she could talk to, I hoped like hell she'd let her walls down and talk to me. I wanted to help her and bring her comfort. I wanted her to know everything would be okay, even if her life had fallen apart.

I knocked again. A sniffle followed by a weak, not-so-convincing, "I'm okay." She lied. Why did she lie? She didn't have any reason to lie to me. We both knew she wasn't okay, and I didn't want her to pretend to be. She deserved to grieve her best friend's death the right way. I didn't want her to cover up her feelings.

"I'm here if you need to talk."

I knew she knew that already, but I needed to reassure her every chance I got. I never wanted her to doubt that. She could talk to me at two in the morning if she needed to.

"Okay."

She came out about an hour later. We chilled in the living room while we watched reruns of 90s shows.

The conversation between us stayed light. I

didn't want to pry too much on our first official day together. I didn't want her to run to the room again in tears if I could help. I wanted her to know she could shut down when she needed to and talk to me about anything. I was there to listen.

I made a mental note to call Destiny's job and inform them that she was in protective custody and wouldn't return after winter break. She loved her job, and that was the least I could do to ensure she didn't lose it during the case.

I also needed to make a trip into town when I grabbed her another pair of clothes to wear for the night. My mother had only left a few pairs, and we were running out. She probably didn't mind wearing my mother's clothes, but I wanted her to have her own things here. This would be her home until we found the suspect.

A small piece of me wished I had never offered to be her protector, as I knew I could track the suspect down a lot faster than Frank. Frank was a great detective, don't get me wrong, but it took him a bit longer to put the pieces together than it took for me. A large piece of me was grateful I offered to protect her. I couldn't stand to watch her walk out of the police station, fearing she'd never be seen again. For fear I'd never see her again. Something about her that drew me in. Maybe her aura? I didn't know, but I was sucked in from the point she walked into my office and spoke with me.

It took me a while to fall asleep last night. I wanted to stay up as long as I could in case

Destiny needed me. I didn't want to fall into a deep sleep for fear I couldn't hear her. If I was in a deep sleep, she pulled me out of it hours later with an agonizing, ear-piercing scream.

I jumped off the couch. The bedroom. I ran into the bedroom and threw on the light. Destiny lay in the middle of the bed, shaking. Sweat touched her forehead. She screamed out, the pitch hurting my ears.

"No. No."

"Destiny. Destiny."

She continued to shake, tears streaming down her face.

"Sweetheart."

I placed my hands on hers.

She started to fight me, but this time around, I hushed her as I squeezed her hands.

Her eyes flew open. They were red-rimmed and wide with terror.

"What happened? Did I scream?"

I nodded.

"I'm sorry."

Her voice wobbled with sorrow.

How could I respond? She's apologizing to me for having nightmares. I should be the one apologizing. She's the one going through hell. She's the one suffering a loss that I didn't even want to try to understand. My heart hurt for her.

"Come here."

Maneuvering around the bed, I pressed my back against the headboard.

She hesitated. Was she scared of me? Was

she scared to get close to me? After a moment, she scooted over and leaned her head against my chest. Her hair smelled of berries, my favorite shampoo. She used my shampoo, and it smelled damn good on her. With her body laid against mine, I closed my eyes.

I knew nothing about providing comfort. I never cuddled my women after we had our mini fling. The difference right then was that Destiny, and I hadn't had a fling. Yet, I comforted her. Yet, I gave her all the affection that I could muster. Yet, I gave her affection I never knew existed within me. What was happening to me?

Not even five minutes later, her soft snores filled the room. I opened my eyes. Her body relaxed as she placed her hand against my chest.

What could I do? Where could I go? If I moved, I'd wake her up. She needed to rest. I needed to rest. Closing my eyes, I drifted off to sleep.

Something jolted me awake. I was pressed against Destiny. How did we get into this position? I didn't recall moving through the night.

My phone vibrated in my pocket. The vibrating stopped as Destiny moved over in the bed, getting comfortable.

Getting out of bed, I stretched. That sleep was refreshing, the best I'd gotten in a while.

Did it have anything to do with this being the second time I'd slept with a woman in my arms in several years? The first being the previous night? Was it because I slept with Destiny in my arms?

Tiptoeing out of the bedroom, I grabbed my phone.

Trevor. There would only be one reason he'd be calling, especially this early. He had to have some updates for us. Or more questions for Destiny. Either way, something of importance would be discussed.

"Hey, Trevor."

I walked into the kitchen.

Silence.

"Hey, Zach. Did I wake you up?"

Did I need to be honest? Or should I lie? It seemed like he already knew the answer.

"Yes."

"Woah." Trevor whistled. "You're usually up at the crack of dawn, not sleeping in like you're in college."

I looked at the time on my phone. It was only a few minutes past eight. Trevor might be exaggerating for anyone else, but he wasn't exaggerating for me. By eight, I was usually up for hours.

"Being on FMLA might do that to you," I responded as I grabbed the coffee pot.

Coffee would wake me up. I needed a cup now, considering what information I'd receive and would relay.

"Yeah," Trevor agreed.

I filled the coffee pot with water before I poured it into the coffee maker.

"How is Destiny?" he asked.

I placed a filter into the coffee maker before I

filled it with coffee grinds.

"She's okay."

That's the best explanation I could give. Did Trevor need to know Destiny woke up in the middle of the night, screaming at the top of her lungs? No. Did he need to know I comforted her and helped her fall back to sleep? No. All of that was irrelevant, and it needed to stay between us.

"I couldn't imagine being in her shoes."

I clicked brew, and the coffee pot turned on.

"Yeah, I couldn't either," I said.

If I lost Jake, I'd be broken. I wouldn't know what to do with myself. I wouldn't be myself. I'd be a shell, lacking every type of semblance to my life.

"So, I have updates."

Great. Enough with the small talk that I wanted to pass. He needed to provide information that would somewhat give Destiny some ease. Or ask questions that'll help lead the investigation in the right direction.

The coffee pot whirled before the hot liquid streamed into the pot. The kitchen smelled heavily of hazelnut.

"Give them to me, Davidson."

I prepared myself for anything and everything.

"We are waiting for updates on the autopsy."

Even though we knew that Candace died from a gunshot wound, an autopsy would tell us the whole picture.

"Hopefully, we'll get the report back fairly

quick," I responded.

"Yes." He cleared his throat. "We should, especially since the holidays have come to an end."

The holidays usually slowed things down, with everyone taking time off from work. We were only days from the new year.

"Is there anything else?" I asked.

Informing Destiny about the autopsy wasn't ideal. She needed more. I knew she expected more. She deserved more. I would do everything in my power to provide more.

"Yes. I have a question for Destiny. Is she available to talk right now?"

"She's asleep at the moment, but I can ask when she wakes up. What do you need me to ask her?"

"Destiny can answer for herself."

Her soft voice drew me in. I turned around. Destiny stood in the doorway of the kitchen. She leaned against the doorframe, her hair in a messy bun. Then she covered her mouth as she yawned. A soft moan escaped her lips, and my manhood perked up unexpectedly.

"Good morning, Destiny." I directed my attention back to Trevor. "She's up. I can hand the phone to her so you two can talk."

Destiny shook her head.

"The speaker is fine. I want you to hear everything."

I smiled. She wanted me to know everything that was going on. Did that say something about the relationship we were starting to build? What kind of relationship did we have? I knew it would be strictly business, but we were past that now. I slept in the same bed as her after she woke up with nightmares. More than once.

I placed the phone on speaker.

She stepped closer, leaning her hip against the counter inches from me. I wanted to reach out, grab her hips, and pull her against me, but I maintained my cool. I couldn't do that. I couldn't ever do that.

"Hi, Trevor."

"Hello, Destiny. We need to ask you a few questions about the scene."

Looking at me, Destiny lightly tugged her lip with her teeth. She was nervous. She had every right to be.

"Okay. You can ask me anything."

He cleared his throat. I waited patiently, not sure what questions would be asked. I knew they needed to be asked, but I hoped they didn't put Destiny in a depressed mood again.

"We located Candace's purse, wallet, and keys."

Where was he going with this?

He continued. "Was there anything else Candace had on her that you're aware of?"

She stayed quiet, deep in thought. She rehashed the night's events. I hated she'd have to do this. Hopefully, she'd only have to do it until we found the suspect.

"She had her phone."

"Are you sure?" Trevor asked.

Destiny's eyes flickered over to me before she responded.

"Yes. I'm sure. She used it at dinner."

The line became silent. Trevor wasn't a detective, but he quickly put the pieces together. If Candace had her phone at dinner and it wasn't found on the scene, it only meant one thing. The suspect took the phone.

Why would the suspect take her phone? There could be two reasons. One, there had to be something on the phone that somehow connected the suspect and Candace. The suspect had to have known Candace, or Candace had known the suspect. Maybe they had crossed paths a time or two before. Two, the suspect took the phone to make us think it was someone familiar with Candace to throw us off the right track. The suspect could be a total stranger, a random crime.

"Did they see them take anything before you ran?" he asked.

Destiny scoffed. She folded her arms across her chest, my eyes taking notice of her breast. I cursed under my breath. I wanted to kick myself for staring. We had no time for that.

"I didn't have time to see them take anything. I ran for my life. I wouldn't be here if I hadn't reacted so quickly."

Silence took over, the occasional drip of the coffee pot evident.

"So, they took her phone?" she asked after a

moment.

"That's the only point we could come up with."

She exhaled, looking down. Her pain resonated off her body. This was all too much. Destiny had too much information thrown at her all at once. She seemed overwhelmed.

"We also located your purse but no phone or wallet," Trevor continued.

"Destiny has her phone," I told Trevor.

That could mean one of two things. One, her wallet had her identification, and they knew exactly where she lived. That was why it wasn't safe for her to go back home. Two, the suspect took the wallet to make us think a robbery occurred instead of a planned attack to throw us off the right track. Either way, this suspect picked specific things to take from each purse for a reason. This suspect and their moves were calculated. They moved with intent. Who was after Destiny?

"They know where I live," Destiny said, barely above a whisper.

She stared at the wall in a daze.

"Trevor, I think that's enough for today."

Destiny didn't need to hear anything else. Hell, that was too much for me to hear in a day. I didn't want to hear that the suspect was coming after Destiny.

Why else would they take her wallet? From both purses at the scene, the suspect chose specific items to take. They took Candace's phone and Destiny's wallet. There was intent behind their every movement.

"Okay, I'll be in touch."

Trevor ended the call as the coffee maker stopped brewing.

"What does this all mean?"

Her voice was low and shaky.

She knew the danger she was in, but how could I answer her to the best of my ability?

"I'm glad I took you into protective custody."

Her eyes grew wider, and her mouth formed a small O. "Anything else?" She asked.

I didn't want to add more fear into her head, but I couldn't find it in my heart to lie to her. She didn't deserve that.

I grabbed two cups from the cupboard and sat them on the counter.

"They're coming after you."

Chapter Nine

Destiny

They were coming after me. I knew that in the back of my mind, but hearing those four words hit me hard. They took my breath away. My heart dropped into my stomach.

I was a pawn in someone's sick, twisted game. The question was, whose game was this? Who had Candace been communicating with? Was it someone from her past, like her ex? Was it someone new that she didn't tell me about? I didn't recall Candace telling me about anyone she communicated with. Maybe it was a coincidence that the murderer took Candace's phone and my wallet.

"Why? Why would they want to come after me?"

All of this made no sense. Whatever went down to cause this whole fiasco to happen, I had nothing to do with it. Why did I have to suffer because of it? Why did Candace have to lose her life because of it?

"You're a living witness."

He poured coffee into the cups before he walked around me. His hand brushed against my hip.

Did he do that on purpose? Or was it a mistake?

He went into the fridge and grabbed the milk.

"When they are found, you could put them away for life for the crime they committed."

I loved how he said when. He didn't doubt that they'd be located. He knew they'd be located. The only thing he didn't know was the exact time or moment it would happen.

He handed me the milk. I thanked him before I poured some into my cup.

"They're coming after me because I'm the only one that can say what happened that night?"

He stayed quiet for a second.

"That's right. In a criminal's eye, the best witness is a dead one."

What could I do? He wasn't sugarcoating

anything, and I was fine with that. I didn't want him to sugarcoat. I needed to know exactly how bad it was. I didn't want to be caught off guard.

"I don't want you to worry, though. I won't let them hurt you."

Silence hung in the air.

"I can even teach you how to defend yourself."

Zach's words were comforting. He wouldn't go out of his way to bring me to his cabin and personally watch me if he didn't believe he could protect me. He also wouldn't have done that if he didn't believe they would hurt me.

I spooned sugar into my coffee before I stirred it. Zach could only protect me now. My family was out of the question. They didn't need to be placed in harm's way. Zach was trained in providing protection.

"I'm trying my hardest to trust you," I admitted.

He sipped his coffee, staring at me. His eyes were full of sincerity.

Was that a twinkle in his eyes? Did I want him to have a twinkle in his eye? Yes? Maybe? I didn't know what I wanted.

He took a step closer.

"What's stopping you?"

I looked away. His stare was too intense. What stopped me?

"Life."

It was a one-word response, but the response held a load of meaning. That response took him by surprise. I smiled before I walked out of the kitchen and into the living room.

The couch was made up like a bed, but I knew he woke up in the bed with me this morning. His scent clung to the pillow I woke up cuddled to this morning, warming my heart. His generosity gave me butterflies, and his desire to keep me safe almost made me want to like him.

Almost.

I could sense his eyes staring into the back of my head. I sipped my coffee before I turned around and looked at him. He stared at me. I could tell he wanted to say something and chose his words carefully.

"You have to give me a better explanation than life."

He was right. He deserved more. I'd give that to him, of course.

"Clean off the couch, and I will."

He sat his coffee on the coffee table. He grabbed his pillow and blankets and moved them to the lazy boy chair.

We sat on the couch. I turned my body so I could see him. I cradled my coffee in my hands, trying to figure out how to explain it to him.

He cleared his throat. That was my cue to talk.

"Why has life made it hard for you to trust?"

I settled into the couch, kicking my foot underneath my butt. Not too many people were aware, but it was appropriate to tell him. After all, he did put his life on hold for me.

"My dad is actually my stepdad," I admitted.

He opened his mouth to speak but closed it. He tried to find the right thing to say to me.

"Forgive me for prying, but did your dad pass away?" he asked.

That would be the easiest thing to say. Then he'd just say I'm sorry for your loss and avoid the rest of the conversation like the black plague. But I wouldn't lie.

"No."

I look away from Zach. I stared at the painting on the wall. A beautiful goldfish glistened, its body highlighted in different hues.

"He abandoned us when I was young."

I looked over at him before I sipped my coffee. The coffee burned the tip of my tongue. I winced in pain.

"I'm sorry to hear that."

The perfect response. Zach had a way with his words.

"Did you ever find out why he left?"

I shook my head. The many thoughts that went through my head.

Once I was old enough, my mom informed me that my dad was my stepdad. I'd asked my mom why my birth father wouldn't want to be in my life, but my mom never gave me an answer. Either she knew and didn't want me to know, or she didn't know herself. All I knew, my birth father was the reason I didn't trust anyone.

My stepdad made it a bit easier for me to trust. He came into my life when I was young enough to assume he was my dad. I didn't learn he wasn't until I turned twelve. Trusting was something I had an issue with until this day. I hoped I'd learn to get over that issue one day.

"No, I never did."

Zach looked down and fiddled with his hands. He didn't know what to say, and that was okay. Zach didn't need to say anything. He just needed to understand.

"I can understand why you don't trust," he said.

He sat back and kicked his leg over his other leg.

"Do you have an issue with trusting?" I asked him.

Everyone was different. Everyone had different upbringings and experiences. While some might trust anyone they came in contact with, others wouldn't. Others couldn't.

He smirked. He shook his head before he grabbed his coffee.

"We don't have time to talk about that."

What kind of response was that? That type of response let me know he had trust issues. The real question was, where did his trust issues stem from?

I raised my eyebrows. "We had time to talk about my issues, but we can't talk about yours?" I asked.

I sat my coffee on the table and then folded my arms across my chest.

His eyes flickered to my chest. He looked me

in the eye before he said, "We would be here all day and night if we talked about my issues."

What issues could he possibly have? He seemed like the perfect guy. He was attractive, had an amazing job, and took care for himself.

"I have nowhere else to go."

He smiled before he stood.

"Well, I do."

My heart skipped a beat. "Where are you going?" I didn't want to be alone. Being alone was the last thing I needed right now.

"We're running low on food and essentials."

Why else would he leave me alone? He wouldn't do it unless he had to. We couldn't survive without water or food. Someone had to go do some shopping, and I was too scared to walk out the door. I looked at the front door. The two locks made me feel safe before, but now I didn't feel so safe. What would happen if the murderer came after me once Zach left? What if the murderer had the strength to break through the locks and end my life, once and for all? All the while Zach went to the store to pick up meat and veggies.

"I don't want to be left alone."

I just started to feel safe in his presence. I didn't know how to feel if I was left here alone.

"I can't risk you going outside. It's not safe out there for you."

I looked around the cabin. Did it seem smaller now than it did a second ago? Or was it just me being anxious?

"Don't worry." He placed his hand on my shoulder. "I'll make sure everything is secure."

"Thank you."

He stood. "I'll check the area after I get dressed."

He looked great in his sweatpants and T-shirt, but that wasn't acceptable for the brutal winter.

"Thank you."

I was grateful for his generosity, but that didn't stop the fear that pumped through my veins.

"You'll never stop thanking me, will you?"

I smiled.

"Nope. Never."

He chuckled before he walked into the room and closed the door.

I stared at the wall beside the TV. What had my life come to? I used to be a boring elementary school teacher. The most exciting thing I did was throw holiday parties for my students. Now, I was on the run to save my life. With the help of an overly attractive detective who seemed to get under my skin more and more as the days went on. I might be in serious trouble.

The bedroom door closing snatched my attention five minutes later. Turning around, I looked at him. He wore a pair of dark blue jeans that were snug on his hips and a thick blue jacket.

"I'll be right back."

He produced a gun from its holster. He held the black steel tight in his hands, his stance strong. He walked to the front door and peeked out the peephole.

I checked him out. His butt looked nice in his jeans, his muscular frame prominent. His arms flexed in his jacket as he unlocked the door. Considering the situation, I shouldn't admire it, but damn. It was hard not to.

He walked out into the bright morning and closed the door. A gust of cold air traveled in, and I shivered. There were two great things about being stuck in this cabin. I avoided the cold outside and could stare at a nice piece of eye candy all day. Well, that eye candy was about to leave me for the first time since we arrived to get a few things.

What would I do without him here? I guess I could aimlessly watch some TV. I couldn't watch the series we had started together when he was out. Even though I had seen the entire series several times, and I'm sure he did as well, it felt wrong. I had to watch it with him. I had to find something else to watch on TV while he was gone.

The door opened and closed. "Everything is clear."

He was out there for a while. I knew he had done a thorough sweep of the area.

"Thank you."

I couldn't thank him enough for everything he had. Everything he had sacrificed to be here with me, protecting me.

"Turn your phone on and turn it off airplane

mood. I want you to be able to contact me if you need to reach me."

I looked at the end table. My phone sat in the same place where I had left it when we arrived. Picking it up, I powered it on.

"Thank you."

"Would you like me to make you some eggs before I leave?" he asked.

The coffee was all I needed for the time being. My appetite hadn't come back. I doubt it would.

"No, I'm fine. I'm not hungry."

He gave me a pointed look.

"You know you have to eat."

He wanted me to eat. I didn't want to eat. He needed me to eat. He cared about me.

"How about I make an early lunch when I get back from the store?"

Sacrifices. If we couldn't agree on the same thing, we'd meet in the middle.

"Okay."

He walked over to me, holding his hand out to me. I took his hand, and it was cold. "I'll be back." He dipped his head and kissed the back of my hand. My heart pounded rapidly. His lips lingered, the hair from his mustache tickling my hand. "Okay?"

I nodded, too stunned to speak.

With those parting words, he grabbed his keys and he walked out the door. Seconds later, the lock sounded.

What just happened? What prompted that

action? Did I like it? Hell yes. Why did I like it? I didn't know, but I needed to find out.

Grabbing the remote, I turned the TV on. I mindlessly flipped through the TV channels. I settled on a talk show for a while, watching as two women discussed makeup products and tried them on. After switching that channel off, I turned to the cooking channel. Four contestants competed in a game show to win the top prize. I switched off that channel once my stomach growled loudly. Finally, I settled on the crime channel for a few moments. Once I saw the episode talked about solving a young girl's murder, I quickly clicked it off.

Candace. No matter how hard I tried to keep her out of my mind, she kept creeping back into it.

Candace and I were dining at an Italian restaurant.

Candace phone chimed.

The air smelled of garlic and tomato sauce. Italian music serenaded my ears.

She grabbed it from her purse and opened it. She giggled after looking at the screen for a few seconds.

"What's so funny?" I asked her.

I looked up from my food.

She shook her head. Her thumbs flew across the screen. "Nothing." She tucked the phone back into her purse.

"It can't be nothing," I drawled.

I sipped my Pepsi.

111

She looked at me and flashed the brightest smile.

"My friend from work sent me a funny picture."

Candace was a fanatic over funny images.

"Yeah." I agreed. "It had to be funny to make you laugh like that."

At the time, I believed Candace told the truth about her coworker sending a funny picture. It wasn't rare, as she had shown me funny images in the past. Thinking about it now, I realized Candace didn't share the picture with me. I now knew she had lied to me about what she had received.

Why would she lie to me? She had no reason to. We shared everything with each other. Or so I thought.

Maybe she chatted with someone and didn't want me to know about them.

Why, though? I had never judged Candace for the actions she took. I supported her with everything. I supported her with her dreams, and that wouldn't have changed.

Who was she in contact with? Time would tell. A person could lie all they wanted, but phone records told the hard, naked truth.

***

The door opened and closed. I pulled my eyes away from the wall. Zach walked into the cabin carrying a handful of bags.

Stuffing my phone into my pocket, I jumped up from the couch.

"May I help unpack?"

"Of course, you can."

He smiled as he walked past me and into the kitchen, warming my heart.

I followed him into the kitchen, where he placed the bags on the dining table.

"I hope you're hungry," he said.

He unpacked the bags.

"I could eat," I responded.

"Great. I'm going to make a hearty lunch."

I took groceries out of the bag, pleased with the quality of the food he selected.

Once I went into another bag, my mouth dropped open.

"Zach."

I turned around. He stared at me with a smile so big.

"Yes?"

I picked up the sketchbook, number two pencils, and colored pencils.

"You bought these for me?"

He nodded. "Yes, I did." He paused as he grabbed some vegetables out of the bag and sat them on the counter. "Since you're away from everyone you love, I figured I'd bring you one thing you love doing."

He remembered my love for drawing. He went out of his way to bring me something that might bring me a small amount of joy in this hard time. His generosity meant everything to me.

"Thank you."

I threw myself into his arms. His scent, all too

familiar to me, evaded my nose. I loved his scent. It brought me comfort every time I placed my head against his chest. His heartbeat quickened by the second. He wrapped his arms around me and held me tight. His arms settled around my waist, just above my hips.

Tears escaped my eyes and touched my cheeks. In such a horrible situation, he managed to make me smile. He managed to make me feel special.

His hand grazed my butt.

Did his hands linger on my butt for a second extra? Or did I imagine it?

I looked into his eyes. They sparkled with something special, something similar to love.

"You're welcome."

"Why don't you draw something while I prepare lunch?"

Zach and his thoughtfulness.

"Are you sure you don't want me to help you with lunch?"

He shook his head. "No, I want you to relax and draw."

Surprising myself, I kissed him on the cheek before walking into the living room with my supplies. I didn't know what I wanted to create yet, but I knew I wanted it to be colorful.

Once comfortable sitting on the couch, I opened my drawing pad. I drew from the emotions that dwelled within me. Right then, I could breathe freely. Zach was back.

My phone vibrated in my pocket. One

vibration indicated a text. When it vibrated for the second time, I knew I had a call coming through. Who could be calling me? I hadn't contacted anyone since I turned my phone on. The thing I did most on my phone was check the weather.

Grabbing my phone out of my pocket, my heartbeat quickened. A lump lodged in my throat when I looked at the person calling. My mouth went dry.

Candace.

My heart dropped.

The room that seemed so big a minute ago was now the size of a shoebox. That shoebox suffocated me.

Candace's phone called me. Glancing at the dining room door, it didn't swing open.

Without thought, I swiped my finger around the screen and placed my phone to my ear.

Breathing. The breathing was constant. Rhythmic. Measured.

Pulling the phone away from my face, I checked the name once more. Candace wasn't calling me from the dead. Her phone wasn't found at the scene.

It had to be Candace's murderer calling.

My heart pounded. The sound echoed in my ears.

"H-he-hello," I stuttered.

More breathing.

As I opened my mouth to say something, the phone was pulled out of my grasp.

Zach's eyes widened when he saw the caller

ID.

"Listen here, you son of a bitch…"

That's all I heard before all the sounds around me ceased. Zach's mouth moved, but I didn't hear anything. Locating a beautiful picture of a fish on the wall, I stared at it. I admired the intricate details the person noticed when they took the photo.

I didn't hear anything until he grabbed my face and forced me to look at him.

"Did you call Candace's phone?"

I shook my head. I couldn't find my words.

"Did you contact anyone when I left from here?"

"No."

My voice. I found it, but I didn't sound too confident.

"Who was that on the phone?"

"I-I don't know," I admitted.

I didn't know anything. Gosh, how didn't I know anything?

"Did they say anything to you?"

"The only thing I heard was breathing," I admitted.

"Did the breathing sound like a man or a woman?"

What kind of question was that? I didn't know sex recognition could be heard in breathing.

"I don't know."

The questions continued. Yet, I had no answers. I had no answers to satisfy either of us.

"Oh my gosh. Candace's murderer just called

me," I yelled.

Standing, I looked around. It no longer felt safe to be in this cabin. I had to get away from here. Now.

"I can't be here," I called out.

Storming towards the bedroom door, I was mere feet from entering when Zach wrapped his arms around my waist. His strong arms stopped me in my tracks. He spun me around and placed my head on his shoulder.

"You can't go anywhere."

"I have to."

Tears stung my eyes. No matter how hard I tried, I couldn't swallow the lump lodged in my throat.

"They're coming after me."

I knew it. I couldn't shake the feeling. They were close. Closer than I thought. I could feel it.

He backed me up against the bedroom door. Caressing my face, he made me look into his eyes. They mesmerized me.

"They might be coming after you, but guess what?"

"What?"

"I won't let them touch a hair on your little head."

Gasping, my eyes flickering to his lips. They were juicy and kissable.

"I'll rip them to shreds before they ever get the chance to touch you."

Silence.

So many words crowded my head, yet I

couldn't form one sentence. One word.

"You have to believe me. I'll always protect you."

More silence.

"I'll protect you with my life. I'll die for you."

Chapter Ten

Destiny

The sun peeked through the blinds, ripping me out of my deep sleep. Turning over, I snuggled closer to Zach's side of the bed. I peeked an eye open. His side of the bed was empty. Where was he?

Zach came to bed with me a few nights ago, per my request. I couldn't fathom going to sleep alone, especially since I received that call from Candace's phone. I was spooked. No matter how hard I tried, a dark figure haunted me whenever I closed my eyes. The same dark figure that claimed my best friend's life was after me. Anyone in this situation would have an uneasy feeling.

Especially after receiving that call. Whoever had Candace's phone didn't mean to call my phone... or Zach spooked them once he got on the phone because they hung up shortly after. All I knew was that I wanted to fly across the country to anywhere but here until Zach calmed me down. He talked me off the ledge that I was ready to jump off. I doubt anybody else could do that for me. I couldn't thank him enough for that.

Zach's scent calmed me. His heartbeat was music to my ears. His ambiance managed to calm me enough at night to allow me to sleep.

I surprised the hell out of myself when I invited him to sleep with me a few nights ago.

We hung out in the living room after eating a hearty bowl of vegetable soup he made for lunch. I helped cut up the veggies he used for the soup, so I offered my assistance and gratitude by helping. The soup warmed my insides while providing me with the nutrition I needed.

With my legs curled underneath me, I worked on an image of a horizon over a field of flowers. I couldn't wait to shade it in with my colored pencils. He didn't just get me the basic pack of twelve. He bought me a pack of one hundred, and I couldn't wait to use all the colors to make a colorful picture.

"Can you teach me how to draw?"

My hand came to a stop mid-sketch. I looked at Zach. He sat on the other side of the couch, only a few feet between us. His eyes were trained on me.

Was he serious? Was he kidding? The look in his eyes said the former. But I needed to be sure.

"Really?" I asked.

He laughed. He rubbed the stubble on his chin.

"Yes, really. I'd love for you to teach me how to draw."

I shrugged. "I don't know." I tossed a wink his way. "I'm not sure if I can do that."

He hummed. He smoothed his hand over his long, flawless ponytail.

"Why is that?"

"If you can't draw a stick figure, I can't teach you anything."

We laughed. Our laughs went together so beautifully. The sound was a beautiful harmony to my ears. I hadn't laughed since... I didn't want to think about it.

I motioned for him to sit closer. He scooched over to the middle cushion. His tan skin tone contrasted my melanin skin tone perfectly.

"That's beautiful," he complimented.

Looking at the strokes on the paper, I admired them. My abilities were pretty good. It was almost done. It just needed the finishing touches.

"Thank you."

"If you could teach me how to draw like this, I'm going to feel like a professional."

I smiled.

"If I could do that in a few minutes, then I'd be the professional."

He leaned closer to me. His hand brushed against my pant leg. My heart skipped a beat.

He looked at me, puzzled.

"What do you mean?"

I pointed at the drawing.

"It took me years to draw like this."

"Practice makes perfect is a true saying, isn't it?" he asked.

"Yes, it is. I can show you a few of the ropes."

He smiled.

"I'd love that."

Nobody had ever expressed their interest in learning how to draw to me. It was nice to have someone who wanted to learn things from me besides my children at school.

My heart. What were my children doing without me? I missed their sweet faces and gestures. It was nothing more special than being a first-grade teacher. It was the perfect age when they were still friendly and willing to offer a helping hand around the classroom. I hoped they received the same love and care from whoever took over my class.

Gosh, I hoped the murderer would be found soon so I could go back to work. I couldn't wait to return home and sleep in my full-size bed again in our apartment.

Oh. I couldn't afford our apartment anymore. I only afforded it with Candace's help. Since she was no longer here, I'd have no choice but to move in with my parents. They wouldn't mind. They've wanted me to move for some time now. This decision wouldn't be my choice, though. I didn't want to leave California, but there was nothing else that could be done. I had come to a dead end on this journey.

"Are you okay?"

Zach pulled me out of my thoughts.

"Yes."

My voice came out shaky, lacking every bit of confidence.

"Destiny."

Zach slipped his hand into mine. His hand was warm and inviting. Our hands fit perfectly together.

"Yes?" I answered.

"You're not okay."

He already knew me like the back of his hand. It had only been three days.

"How did you know?"

"May I?" he asked, motioning to my sketch pad and pencils.

I nodded.

Letting go of my hand, he gathered them into a pile before he placed them on the coffee table. He slipped his hand back into mine.

"I know when something's bothering you."

I stayed silent, deep in my own thoughts.

How could Zach read me so well? Was he trained in reading people from his years as a detective? Or had he learned my quirks in just a handful of days?

"Can you be honest with me?" he asked.

Honesty? It was such a strong, powerful word. My vulnerability was already on full display.

"Can you sleep with me tonight?"

His eyes grew wide as saucers. For me to be a teacher, those words didn't come out in the right text.

"I mean, can you come to bed with me tonight?"

I fumbled over my words.

He opened his mouth to say something, but I interrupted him.

"I mean..." I began.

"I know what you mean," he finished for me. He squeezed my hand. "Of course, I'll come to bed with you, gorgeous. I'll do anything that will make you feel better."

He just called me gorgeous. It sounded amazing, rolling off his tongue. An overwhelming sense of gratitude came over me. Leaning forward, I wrapped my arms around him.

"Thank you."

"What did I tell you about thanking me?" he asked.

He held me in his arms.

"I know, but I can't help it."

He smiled.

"We'll work on it. Now, can you teach me how

to draw?"

Teaching him how to draw for the next few hours entertained me, to say the least. I hadn't laughed that much in a long time. I laughed so hard I couldn't catch my breath, and my stomach ached.

Something about Zach made me want to forget about my trust issues. He made me want to trust him. Did it have something to do with him protecting me? Maybe. Did it have something to do with me starting to experience feelings for him? Maybe. I hoped I wasn't stupid for falling for the man who protected me. Maybe he treated me like this from the goodness of his heart, and I mistook his kindness for flirting.

I opened my other eye and groaned. I wanted to stay in bed all day. I didn't want to get up. If Zach allowed it, I would lay here all day with the covers pulled up over my head. He wouldn't allow me to wallow in my misery, though.

January first.

A new year.

I dived into a new year without my best friend. New Year's Eve was spent out on the town as a tradition. We'd hit up different bars to see what the scene had to offer before we settled at the last bar of the night and brought the new year in on a shot of tequila.

My new year came in with tears streaming down my face this year. Zach held me tight, cradling me in his arms as the time changed from 11:59 to 12:00.

"Wake up, gorgeous."

Groaning, I placed the pillow over my head. I loved it when he called me gorgeous. I knew he was being nice, but it was wonderful to hear.

"Wake up, sleepyhead."

He removed the pillow from my head.

Squeezing my eyes closed, the sun evaded my sleep.

"No. I'm not getting up today."

I didn't plan on getting up tomorrow. Or the next day. Or the following day. I just wanted to lay in this spacious, comfortable bed.

A warm hand cupped my face. My eyes fluttered open, and Zach's handsome face swam into view. His brown hair was pulled up into a messy bun, and his smile was bright.

"It's a new year. I know you're sad, but let's try to start the year on a positive note."

Positive? I was anything but positive this morning. My eyes ached from all the crying . My head pounded as if I was hit in the head with a baseball bat. I was a mess.

"Can I just stay in bed all day?"

He gave me a pointed look. "No, you can't. I need your company today. We have plans."

I perked up. Plans? What kind of plans? What did he have in mind? Would I like those plans? Would I approve? Would I be up for it?

"What plans?"

He shook his head. "Not so fast. You can't find out the plans until you get up and get ready."

His psychology to get me out of bed worked.

I had to know what he planned for us to do to start the new year.

"Okay. I'm getting up."

Zach yelled out a whoop as I pushed the covers off me. I smiled, his enthusiasm rubbing off on me. I stretched my arms above my head.

Through my yawning and scrunched eyes, Zach's eyes danced across my breasts, hidden underneath the thin fabric of my shirt. Clearing my throat, he tugged his eyes away from my chest.

He ran his fingers through his messy bun, and he looked away.

"I'll be ready in fifteen."

He smiled.

"I'm glad to hear. I'll see you soon."

After I handled my hygiene, I pulled on a pair of light blue jeans and a thick gray sweater. I pulled my hair into a high ponytail and walked into the dining room.

Two cups of coffee sat on the table. Zach hovered over a pot on the stove.

"Are you fine with oatmeal for breakfast?" he asked.

He didn't turn around to look at me. Did he sense my presence?

I folded my arms across my chest.

"Of course. You make the best oatmeal."

He looked over his shoulder, an adorable smile peeking through.

"I hope you aren't just saying that."

Walking over to the counter, I leaned my hip on it. As the oatmeal cooked, a bubble would pop occasionally from the heat.

"No. I mean it. You make it better than I do."

"Do you think I could compete with a top-notch chef?"

Laughing, I covered my smile with my hand.

"I wouldn't go as far as saying that."

He stirred the oatmeal before he turned the stove off.

"Can you do me a favor?"

His tone went from playful to serious.

Did I do something wrong? Had I said something out of line?

"What is that?"

"Never hide your beautiful smile. I'm glad I made it come to the surface."

Wow. My heart. Did he just say that? Or did I imagine a conversation like this would happen between us these past few days?

"Thank you." I gasped.

I grabbed bowls out of the cupboard for us. Zach filled the bowls and added in extra sweetness before we ate at the table.

I sipped my coffee. Closing my eyes, I moaned.

"Was that a good moan or a bad moan?"

I opened my eyes and looked at him. He had a quizzical look in his eyes.

"A great moan."

"Great? Have I mastered the art of creating your perfect coffee?"

I couldn't help but be honest.

"Yes, you have."

Over the next few hours, we enjoyed each other's company while we sat around and watched more TV. I swore I watched more TV this past week than I had in the last six months.

When you're stuck inside with limited things to do, you have no choice but to do things you usually didn't do.

"How did I do with this drawing?" he asked.

He showed me a picture of a fish. His lines had come together perfectly, creating an almost realistic-looking fish.

"You did amazing," I commented.

"But..." he began.

He looked at me, his eyes wide with intent.

"There's no but," I answered.

"Are you serious?" he asked.

I folded my arms across my chest.

"Would I lie to you?"

He smiled. He pointed at the fish. "It does look awesome."

"I must say, your drawing has gotten much better."

He pointed at me.

"I have you to thank for that."

"Are you saying I'm a great teacher?"

"The best."

"So, are you finally going to tell me what plans we have?"

It had been on my mind ever since I got out of bed this morning.

"I thought it would be great if we went outside."

My heart dropped. Deep in my heart, I knew it involved us going outside.

"I don't think that's a great idea."

I knew it wasn't a great idea, but I didn't want to be negative. I was frightened out of my mind. Someone had already called me from Candace's phone. That one call had me ready to jump on the next flight out of town, but I couldn't do that. Zach had done so much for me already. The last thing I wanted was for him to think I wasn't grateful.

"Why not?"

My eyes darted around the cabin. I settled on an image of a big fish. I could look anywhere else but at him. His eyes alone could make me say yes. They were something fierce.

"What if the murderer has tracked us down? They're coming after me."

"Please." He grabbed my hand, and I looked at him. His eyes pleaded with me. "We are in a small part of town. Not a lot of people come up here besides the locals. You'll be safe with me. I won't let anything happen to you."

"Okay," I heard myself say. Did I truly mean it? No, but I had to trust Zach.

"You'll be fine. I promise."

After piling our art supplies on the coffee table, we walked to the front door. A pair of bright pink tennis shoes sat beside his shoes.

I checked them out as I picked them up. They were adorable. They were the type of shoes I would buy myself if I were to exercise.

"Your mom loves bright colors?" I asked.

I slipped one foot into the shoe. My shoe fit perfectly like it was made for my foot.

"No. Those are your shoes." He slipped his shoes on. "I bought them for you."

Slipping the second shoe on, I looked at him.

"You don't have to spend all this money on me."

He shrugged as he picked up a black coat. I turned around, and he helped me into it, his hand brushing against my side. "You didn't have any other shoes, and I won't allow you to walk outside barefoot." He paused. "They look amazing on you."

Lifting my book, I analyzed them. They fit the personality I used to have, bright and bubbly. I couldn't wait for that personality to come back. It might not ever come back. It might be permanently gone, right along with Candace.

"Thank you."

He held his hand out for me.

"Are you ready?"

My mouth went dry. No, I wasn't ready. With my sketch pad, pencils, Zach, and the TV, I was content in this cabin 24/7. I wanted to say no, but I said yes. I had to get over my fear of going outside. I couldn't live in these four walls forever. I'd have to go outside one day, and today was that day.

Placing my hand in his, my heartbeat so loud I could hear it in my ears.

"Are you sure it's safe?"

He squeezed my hand. "Yes, it is, gorgeous."

He pulled me close, and I breathed in his scent. His scent reminded me of home. "I won't let anything happen to you."

Looking at him, his eyes glinted.

"It'll be fun. Let's go."

Zach opened the door. A gush of cold air rushed in as my heart warmed. Was I the only one who felt the connection? Did I imagine it all?

Following Zach out of the cabin, I looked around. When Zach first brought me to the cabin it was the middle of the night and I couldn't see anything, but now as dusk descended I saw it in all its beauty. The cabin was painted a beautiful mahogany shade with black trimmings. It was surrounded by gray pines and a massive yard. I imagined myself sitting on a lounge chair in the dead of spring, drawing a magnificent landscape.

"We are in the mountains." He pointed.

The mountains across the way were massive and stunning. They were inviting yet intimidating all at the same time.

I gasped. "This place is beautiful."

I couldn't believe I allowed my fear to prevent me from looking out the window to see such beautiful scenery.

Zach let my hand go, my hand immediately missing his warmth. He locked the cabin, and to my gratitude, he grabbed my hand again. Safety. That's what resonated within me when he touched me.

We walked on the road. A gust of wind traveled through, chilling me through my coat. I shivered, another reminder why California's winters weren't for me. The sound of our feet against the paved road rang out, our feet in perfect unison.

He looked at me, a smile peeking through.

"I come here when I need an escape from reality."

The cabins had plenty of land between them, giving them ample space to have the desired privacy.

As we approached the next cabin, I said, "I'd think that would be often."

"Why do you say that?"

"Your field of work can't be peaches and cream."

He squeezed my hand.

"You got that right."

I exhaled, my breath visible in front of me. This was the perfect explanation of how it was too cold.

"Is it hard being a detective?" I asked.

I hadn't dived too much into asking him about his career choice since I arrived. I'd been mentally unavailable. It hadn't even been a full week since I ran into the police station and met Zach, but I felt like I'd been living this nightmare for eternity.

"It's hard, but the great outweighs the bad," he answered.

As we passed another cabin, I looked at him. All the cabins were small and intimate, everything I always imagined a cabin would be.

"Almost always, I have to report bad news," he continued.

"How does the great outweigh the bad, then?"

I needed to understand his philosophy. It was always great to understand someone else's point of view, even if it differed from mine.

"Even though I report the bad news, the victim's family getting closure is the great result of my hard work."

Looking over my shoulder, I searched for someone spying. Nothing but trees and cabins could be seen. Zach's cabin was in the distance now. I couldn't wait until we received news of who did this to Candace. Once they were locked away in a jail cell for the rest of their lives, I'd be able to sleep peacefully. Well, I hoped I'd be able to. Zach still woke up in the middle of the night, breaking me out of my disastrous nightmares. I'd be lucky if I got through two nights without them coming to me.

"What motivated you to become a detective?" I stepped over a small tree branch in my path.

"I've always wanted to help people." I looked at him, and he was focused on our path. "I wasn't smart enough to become a doctor or nurse…"

"I know you didn't just say that," I interrupted him.

He came to a stop. I turned and looked at him.

"I mean, I thought the best career path for me would be in law enforcement."

I smiled. "That sounds better. I never want to hear you say you aren't smart enough again."

We continued to walk and talk. The amount of laughing I had done on our journey around the area caused my stomach to hurt. Zach was genuine, and I had to face it, I liked him.

We came to a stop in front of his cabin. The darkness had arrived   , and the temperature had dropped at least another five degrees.

He stepped closer to me, and my heart sunk into my chest. I looked at him, and he licked his lips. Was he going to kiss me?

Closing my eyes, I prepared myself for the fireworks to shoot off within me when a rustling sound nearby forced my eyes open.

"Go inside," Zach said.

Chapter Eleven

Zach

I didn't know what had happened, but it interrupted a kiss I had anticipated from the second I laid eyes on her. Whatever was going on, I needed to get Destiny to safety. Now.

"What's going on?"

Her eyes darted around, wide as saucers.

I grabbed her hand.

"I just need to get you inside." Pulling her up the stairs, I led her to the front door. Looking over my shoulder, I dug the keys out of my pocket. It had gotten darker since we left for our walk. The sun had already set. My body shivered uncontrollably from the frigid air. After what seemed like forever, I unlocked the door and pushed it open.

"Get inside."

She walked through the door and turned to look at me. Her face revealed every fear imaginable running through her mind.

"Where are you going?"

Did I need to be honest with her and freak her out? Or did I need to lie so she wouldn't freak out once I went to investigate?

"I think there's something out there."

Her mouth dropped open. I drew my gun from its holster.

"Lock the door. I'll be right back."

She nodded before I closed the door. The lock sounded, and I turned around, ready for action. I looked around the darkened area. Where did the noise come from?

I walked down the steps of the cabin. After surveying the front of the yard, I walked to the east. The cabins were spread out. Any noise that loud had to be close.

"This is Detective Miller. Come out with your hands up."

I walked stealthily, the gun firm in my hold. I saw no movement and heard nothing.

Walking further beside the cabin, my eyes were trained on the surroundings ahead of me.

Whoever was out there made it difficult for me to hear or see them. Maybe they took off once I placed Destiny inside.

Walking into the woods, the darkness was still. Scrunching my eyes, I waited for them to adjust to the darkness.

Rustling sounded to my right. I pointed my gun in the direction, my index finger on the trigger.

A baby raccoon darted across my path. Sighing in relief, I lifted my finger off the trigger. The raccoon was probably lost and searching for its mother. They didn't visit quite often during the winter, but he appeared to have made a special trip.

It was nothing but a baby raccoon. I was sure Destiny was spooked, but she should be fine once I told her it was an animal.

I walked to the front of the cabin. Once I walked up the steps, I knocked on the door.

"Destiny, I'm back," I called out.

Silence. The wind swirled around me.

I knocked once more. Destiny had the keys. I tried to turn the knob, but it didn't budge.

Where had Destiny gone? Was she okay? Was she still inside?

I entered the passcode into the door and opened it. I had the security system installed when I first bought the cabin, having issues with keys sometimes. I had to ensure that if I came to visit and left the cabin keys at home, I'd still be able to get in and out whenever necessary.

"Destiny," I called out.

Looking around the living room, I couldn't see her. I opened the bedroom door, and she wasn't sitting on the bed.

Where had she gone?

As I was about to head into the dining room, I heard a muffled cry.

Destiny. I turned towards the closed bathroom door. I tried to turn the knob, but it wouldn't budge.

"Destiny?" The muffled cry ceased. Silence resonated. "Sweetheart? Can you open the door?"

Moments passed before I heard the faint sound of the door unlocking.

I opened the door. Destiny leaned against the edge of the bathtub, her face in her hands.

"Where did they go?" Her voice cracked with pain. "Did you see where they went?"

I walked over to her and sat in front of her. Grabbing her hands, she looked at me with tear-filled eyes.

"It was just a raccoon."

Her mouth wobbled. Her eyes darted around the bathroom.

"Are you sure?" she asked.

I squeezed her hands.

"Yes, I'm sure."

She gave off a nervous laugh.

"The raccoon scared me half to death."

I nodded, enjoying her beautiful smile. She allowed it to come out more and more over the past few days. Whenever she smiled, it warmed my heart.

"Same here," I said.

I couldn't believe I had admitted that to her.

I didn't know what I would confront, but I'd rather confront the threat headfirst than have it come for Destiny. I cared about Destiny. No matter the costs, I had to protect her.

"You didn't let your fear stop you from going after the threat," she said in a small voice.

I rubbed the back of her hands with the pad of my thumb. She was right. The only thing I cared about was removing the threat.

I had feelings for her. It was foreign to me. I hadn't felt like this in years. I hadn't felt like this since... God, I didn't want to think about her. She was long gone in the past, which is why I had my trust issues. All I knew, I was scared.

"I made a promise to you the night at the police station."

Her eyes scrunched. I knew it was hard for her, and she probably tried her hardest to forget that day. She looked like she was deep in thought.

"What promise?" She paused. I could see the hurt that danced across her face. "That day is a blur."

My heart hurt for her. I hated that I had her remembering that day, but I needed her to understand.

"I promised you that I'd never let anyone hurt you."

She pressed her lips together. She analyzed me, waiting for me to continue.

"I've had promises broken in my past." I took a deep breath. I didn't usually express my feelings or talk about my past, but she deserved to know why I was the person she saw today. "I've sworn to never break another promise in my life. That is one promise I won't break."

Her eyes softened. She looked at her hands and puffed her lips out before she looked at me.

"Who broke a promise to you?"

Her question caught me off guard. I expected her to ask me one day, but I never thought it would be today. In the bathroom. While I comforted her. Somehow, the conversation switched to me.

The answer lingered on the tip of my tongue. Could I tell her? Others usually confided in me, not the other way around. Did I need to tell her about my past?

At the last second, I replied, "No one."

Defeat danced across her face. It hurt to see her like that, but I wasn't ready to open up about my past yet.

"I know you aren't telling the truth," she pointed out.

Was it written all over my face?

"You can tell me when you're ready."

She was understanding. I appreciated that.

"Thank you."

"Why do you care so much about me?"

Her question caught me off guard. When it

came to cases, I had sympathy for the victim and the victim's family and friends. I always grew a connection with them, so they knew I cared.

With Destiny, the connection was instant and special. The connection was different than I had ever experienced.

"From the moment I laid eyes on you, I was smitten."

Her mouth formed a small O. I couldn't read her expression. Did I do a horrible thing by telling her that? Should I have kept my feelings to myself? I didn't want to ruin the professional persona I'd built with her. That was the last thing I needed to do, but honesty was best in this situation.

"Zach..." she began.

"Wait," I interrupted. Placing my hand up, I stopped her. I didn't want to hear her rejection. At least, not yet. I needed to finish what I was brave enough to say. "Please, don't hate me for saying this. I promise if you don't feel the same way..."

Destiny placed her finger against my lips, silencing me. She leaned forward. Her eyes fluttered closed, and she kissed me.

Every thought I had escaped my mind. I traveled on a merry journey of heaven on earth as my heart exploded with adoration. A tingling sensation traveled through me. My penis grew hard. Thankfully, I wore a pair of jeans, and my bulge was hidden.

I grabbed the back of Destiny's head. Tilting her head slightly, I captured her lips. Her lips were soft and luscious, just as I had imagined. Our mouths moved in sync.

Had we shared the same feelings this entire time and didn't know?

Destiny's lips separated from mine. I groaned, missing the physical contact. After trying to hide her smile, she rubbed her thumb across her bottom lip. She looked at me before she looked at the floor.

"Wow."

That's all I could say. I had so much to say before Destiny kissed me. Her irresistible lips took my thoughts away. How did she do that? Did she have magical powers I wasn't aware of?

I touched my lips, afraid the kiss was a figment of my wild imagination. What a vivid imagination I had. If only I'd have another one.

"Was that okay?" she asked in a soft voice.

Maybe it wasn't my imagination. I grabbed her hands and kissed the back of them several times. "Yes." I paused, thinking of a better response. "Hell, yes."

She smiled and winked. "Good, I had to stop your babbling somehow."

We laughed before I helped her to stand. My hands settled on her hips. I pulled her close to me, inhaling the scent of her shampoo, enjoying the closeness. It hadn't been long since I had a woman pressed against me. It was just last week that a woman was in my bed. I just hadn't felt this way towards a woman in years.

She placed her head against my chest.

"Thank you for protecting me."

Cradling her in my arms, I tucked a strand of her hair behind her ear. I didn't want to let her go.

"What did I tell you before?"

She was silent for a second too long. She looked away.

"I can't help it. Especially for everything that you've done for me. You've gone above and beyond for me. I could never thank you enough for that."

I kissed her forehead. She deserved to be taken care of. She deserved to be protected.

"I'd do anything for you."

Her eyes met mine. "I knew that when you brought me here." She motioned her hands around. "Now that I'm not scared of my mind, I think it's time to get dinner started."

She walked around me and out of the bathroom. I turned and watched her walk away. The sway in her hips and long legs didn't help my boner. I adjusted myself before I cleared my throat and ran my fingers through my hair.

It was hard for me to think that I might feel something so intense. I hadn't felt the L-word since… I couldn't even say her name. She was the last thing I ever wanted to think about. She hurt me. She ruined me. She was the reason I became the person who couldn't trust anyone.

I didn't know what was going on between us, but I couldn't wait to figure it out.

Chapter Twelve

Zach

My heart. It beat like crazy. It wasn't doing it just sporadically throughout the day. Try around the clock. Maybe it had to do with Destiny's presence. Something about her energy had me addicted. I couldn't get enough, and I kept going back for more.

Was I in love?

All I knew, I wanted to keep Destiny happy. So, I contacted Destiny's apartment complex and paid for her apartment for the next six months. Her worries of being unable to pay for her apartment could be placed on the back burner until this situation was over. Then, she could decide her next moves, but I didn't want her to worry about it now.

Bustling around the kitchen with her last night while we prepared minestrone soup was nothing short of what you'd see in the movies. She waltzed around as if she was the woman of the cabin. I waltzed around as if she were my partner in crime as we prepared vegetables, meat, and noodles to simmer on the stove into a flavorful soup.

We talked and laughed as if we'd known each other for years. Was our connection that strong? Or was I just blinded by a beautiful woman under my watch?

I didn't want to lie to myself. We had a connection. I just didn't know how to deal with it.

"Are you deep in thought over there?"

She poured chicken stock into a pot.

Clearing my throat, I smiled. I stuffed my hands into my pants pocket.

"No," I answered.

She gave me a pointed look. "You can tell me the truth, you know." She winked at me. "I think we are past that part of our relationship."

Relationship? Is that what we should call this?

"Well, you know what I mean," she added, her eyes dancing across my face.

Relationship. That word has been etched into my brain since she said it last night. I hadn't been in a relationship since Charlotte hurt me. She ripped my heart out of my chest and shattered it into a million pieces. It's crazy how one person could change my outlook on the world.

Destiny might've done the hard work of changing my outlook again. She did it without even trying. Maybe not every woman was out to break hearts.

I rubbed Destiny's arm. We lounged on the couch in the living room. I stared at the TV show that played. It was a comedy, and it kept my mind occupied.

"Have you heard any updates on Candace?"

My hand stopped mid-rub on her arm. Destiny's question startled me. Yes, I knew this wasn't some special vacation with a stranger turned possible love interest. Yes, I knew we were in my cabin for business. For a split second, I could forget the hardships that caused Destiny and me to come together. That hardship was brought up, and I wished I had an answer for her. An answer that would make all her worries and sorrows disappear. Sadly, I didn't have that answer. There was only one thing that I could tell her.

"I haven't heard anything yet."

The look in her eyes once I finished my statement made my heart sink into my stomach.

The last time I had an update, Trevor informed us that Destiny's wallet was missing.

That was a big pill for Destiny to swallow. She knew that she was in danger. Whoever killed Candace now knew where they lived if they didn't already have that information.

She opened her mouth to speak, but I placed my finger to her lips.

"I will call Trevor and see if there are any updates."

She nodded. Her eyes were full of sadness. How could I take someone else's pain away so they didn't have to endure it on their own? I wish I knew how to because I would do that for her. In a heartbeat.

"I'll be right back."

Grabbing my phone off the coffee table, I walked outside. The air chilled me to my bones. I only wore a pair of sweatpants and a long-sleeved shirt. I'd do anything for Destiny, even shivering in the freezing cold, to make a call.

I dialed Trevor's phone. Tapping my foot on the ground, the phone rang several times. I hung the phone up once it went to voicemail.

He must've been busy. Or, he didn't want to answer and had no news to share. Hopefully, he'll reach out to me soon. I had yet to tell him about the phone call Destiny received from Candace's phone the other night. It was pertinent information. The suspect was getting sloppy with their movements, or they did it to ruffle feathers. I hoped for the former and not the latter.

On one hand, I didn't want to step away from the case. Frank was a great detective, no doubt.

I wouldn't have chosen anyone else over him, but I was more thorough, and my pace was on point. Frank had me by about fifteen years, give or take. He was slower with finding out information. I just knew if I worked the case, I'd have some type of information by now.

I made a sacrifice when I decided to protect Destiny. I sacrificed the speed of the investigation. I'd do it all over again if it meant protecting her. Her safety meant more to me than the speed of the investigation. The only thing that mattered was if we got thorough information. Frank provided just that with all the cases he worked on.

I hated walking back into the cabin without new information, but I had nothing.

She looked over at me, her brown eyes full of determination.

"Did you find anything out?"

I didn't want to tell her the truth, but I had no choice.

I bit my lip, contemplating my response.

"You can be honest," she continued, reassuring me. "I want you to be honest."

Walking to the couch, I sat beside her and placed my hand on her thigh.

"Trevor didn't answer..."

What was going on with Trevor? Trevor always answered. I hoped he was okay.

"Is there anyone else you can call?"

I had to tread lightly with the information I received. Frank was my partner, but I was supposed to be on FMLA. What I had done was considered unethical, requesting time off to watch a victim. We had people in place to do this type of job, but I couldn't bear not having Destiny under my watch. I put my job in jeopardy for her safety. I'd do it all over again if I had the opportunity.

The only person I trusted enough with this information was Trevor. We weren't the best of friends. Hell, I considered him more of a coworker than a friend, but he was the officer on duty when all of this unfolded. I had to trust, regardless of whether I wanted to or not.

I shook my head. "No."

The look of sadness settled on her face. I had to do something to cheer her up. I wanted to see her smile, not sulk.

"I have to run a quick errand."

Walking into the bedroom, I pulled out a pair of jeans and a jacket.

"How long will you be?" she asked.

I checked the time on my phone.

"I shouldn't be more than an hour," I called out.

"Can you promise me you'll be safe?" she asked.

After I pulled on my jeans, I walked into the living room.

"Of course. As long as you promise me you won't answer any phone calls that come through on your phone."

I walked over to the couch.

"I promise."

She stood, and I wrapped my arms around her waist. I held her tight before I kissed her forehead.

"I'll be back."

After locking the cabin, I checked the premises for anything out of sorts. This area wasn't frequented by too many people besides the locals. It was a nice area tucked away from many.

After starting my truck, I headed out on my journey to improve Destiny's mood.

***

A few minutes short of an hour, I parked outside the cabin.

Grabbing the bags from the back seat, I walked into the cabin.

"I'm back, Destiny," I called out.

She walked into the living room from the bedroom. She placed her hands on her hips, a hint of a smile showing.

"You weren't kidding when you said you'll be back in less than an hour."

At least she was in a better mood now than when I had left. Let's just hope what I bought her would brighten her mood even more. "Were you keeping count?" I asked, smirking.

"Maybe," she responded as she shrugged. "What did you get?"

"Come in here and find out for yourself."

She followed me into the kitchen. I sat the bags on the counter and moved out of her way.

She rummaged through the first bag. Once she combed through the second bag, she stopped. She didn't move for a moment. She looked over at me, her eyes brimming with tears. Her bottom lip wobbled before she threw her hand over her mouth and ran out of the kitchen.

What just happened?

"Destiny, wait."

I followed behind her. She ran into the bedroom and closed the door.

Placing my head against the door, her soft cries were painful to hear. Her mood went from cheerful to sad in a matter of seconds.

The only things I bought were a few candles and some sushi, which I thought she'd love. Or so I thought.

"Destiny, can you tell me what's wrong?"

Silence resonated. What could I do? I didn't think it was proper to give her space right now. She only had me. I had no choice but to be her rock. I grew to love being her rock.

Turning the doorknob, I walked inside. Destiny sat on the bed with her head in her lap.

"Destiny, can we talk?" I walked slowly, with grace. I didn't know her mindset. I didn't want to startle her.

I took her silence as a yes. I sat on the bed and rubbed her back. Her soft cries vibrated through her body.

"Can you tell me what's wrong?"

More silence. Should I continue talking to make her warmup to me? Should I be silent until she decided she was ready to confide in me?

"I thought sushi was your favorite."

More silence.

"That's why I bought it. To cheer you up."

Wrapping my arms around her, I held her against my chest.

We sat in silence for what seemed like an eternity.

"I'm sorry."

I closed my eyes, dreading whatever I had done to spoil the night.

"It's not your fault." Her voice was faint, soft. "You didn't know." She sat up and looked at me. Tears streaked her face. She leaned her head against my shoulder. "Sushi was Candace and my favorite meal to eat together. She loved the California rolls, and I loved the Shrimp Tempura. Plus, it was the last meal we ate together before..."

She didn't have to finish her sentence. It all made sense. I vaguely remember that they were out at the sushi restaurant when everything went wrong. I didn't realize how significant it was to Destiny. I didn't realize sushi was so involved in their friendship. My attempt to create a relaxing night for Destiny wasn't successful.

I failed.

Miserably.

"If I would've remembered, I wouldn't have brought it here," I admitted.

I wouldn't hurt her on purpose. That's the last thing I wanted.

"Let me get rid of it."

I didn't expect either of us to eat the sushi, no matter the hoops I went through, to get a decent package. Finding sushi in this area that wouldn't restrict you to the bathroom for days was difficult.

Destiny grabbed my hand.

"No, you don't have to..." she began.

Squeezing her hand, I interrupted her.

"Yes, I do. It's only right."

She held onto my hand.

"Please. Don't leave me."

Her eyes pleaded for my presence. She blinked, a tear escaping her eye.

What else could I say?

"Okay. I won't."

She curled into a ball in the middle of the bed, her butt poked out. I followed suit. Our bodies fit like the perfect puzzle piece.

I breathe in her delicate scent. "I'm here for you." I leaned forward and kissed her neck. It was perfect, just like the rest of her. "I won't leave you." I paused. "I won't ever leave you."

The feelings I denied for the longest came to the surface. I couldn't deny them anymore. No matter how hard it was for me to admit it, I just couldn't. I refused to.

I loved Destiny. I hadn't known her for more than two weeks but spent almost every second of the day with her. She was my ray of sunshine on a cloudy day. I never thought, after my years of having multiple one-night stands to get the urge off, that it would result in me falling for a woman that I hadn't even had sex with. I fell in love with her soul, not her body. What a wonderful woman I fell in love with.

Her soft snores filled the room minutes later. Caressing her face, I kissed her tears and her forehead. My lips lingered for seconds longer. I couldn't tell her my feelings. It would crush me if she didn't feel the same way, but I knew I had to tell her. I had to tell her soon if I had any respect for myself.

Chapter Thirteen

Destiny

Leaning my hip on the counter, I sipped my coffee. I winced. The hot liquid reminded me that I had poured a hot cup of coffee not even two minutes ago.

I was on edge. Zach hadn't heard any updates on Candace's case from Trevor in days. Trevor was our only lifeline to the case. I feared the case might go cold, and we'd never find out who caused such a disruption in my life. In so many people's lives.

I couldn't wrap my mind around the fact that Candace passed away. I had survived ten days without my best friend in this life with me. How could I survive eleven? How could I survive twelve?

Some might say I put one foot in front of the other. Some might say take it one second at a time. One minute at a time. One hour at a time. It was easier said than done.

The call from Candace's phone didn't help my sanity. It nearly brought me back to when she was alive and would call me just to hear my voice. This call was far from an innocent call to see what dinner I'd prepare for the night. The call had a meaning that I didn't understand. I doubt I'd ever understand.

Last night, I fell asleep with tears in my eyes. Sushi. Sushi caused the cascade of tears to fall. Sushi was our favorite meal. Zach's intentions were pure and thoughtful but had the opposite effect. He thought it would make me happy. It would've made me ecstatic under different circumstances, but in this situation, it just depressed me.

Anything that reminded me of Candace had this effect. I struggled to sit back and think of the great moments we shared when I grieved her death. She was too young to die. She had her whole life ahead of her. What sick monster did this?

Three ideas came to mind. It could've been

someone Candace interacted with while she worked. She bartended at one of the most popular bars in town. She worked there for years. Destiny was their best bartender. She encountered plenty of people. There were too many people to count. Too many people to track. Did one of those people hurt her? The time frame could be limited, though. From what Zach said, they'd look at who she had contact with the month leading up to her death.

It could've been Candace's ex-boyfriend. He didn't want the relationship to end. He begged her to take some time to think about what she gave up, but Candace had her mind made up.

It also could've been someone in Candace's life. Someone she hadn't made me aware of. Candace wasn't dating or seeing someone, to my knowledge, but someone killed her. Why would they care about her phone if it was random? Why would they care about my wallet? Either this person had something to hide, or they were intentionally diverting the attention away.

Hopefully, Zach would receive some news. He'd been outside for some time now. I knew we wouldn't have all the answers today, but I needed something. Anything. I just hate that I needed to be in protective custody. Zach and his partner could handle this case if I didn't need protection. Two heads together were better than one, I'm sure. What could have been missed in the investigation by one set of eyes would have easily been picked up if two sets of eyes had been on it.

Zach knew in his heart that he could provide better protection than those hired to do that job in the department. I supported Zach's thoughts.

This past week and a half had been confusing for me. I'd had some of the worst days of my life while having some of the best moments as well.

Something about Zach had me falling hard. Harder than I had ever fallen for any man.

Relationships had never been my thing from my experience over the years. I'd meet someone, whether while I'm out and about or when I decided to be spontaneous and take a chance on an online dating app. They might have kept my interest for one or two dates. By the third date, I wanted to explore something or someone that would hold my interest for a little longer.

Zach might've changed it all for me. He might've changed it for the better, but I wasn't searching. It's crazy that what I needed this entire time fell into my life when disaster occurred. He was my savior when I needed help the most.

I didn't know what Zach thought of me, though. How could such a handsome and thoughtful man be single? Men like him were hard to come around. Most of them were already in a committed relationship. What was up with him? Did he want to date? Did he want to settle down? He could get any woman he wanted. He was handsome, smart, had an amazing personality, and had a great job. I hoped he felt the same way about me.

I was tired of the occasional one-night stands. An occasional one-night stand would get my sexual urges to leave me alone for a while. Not to say I expected us to touch each other anytime soon, but I knew this felt different from anything else I'd experienced.

Adding a spoonful of sugar to my coffee, I stirred it before I took a sip. I moaned in satisfaction. My coffee had the right amount of boldness and sweetness I desired. Zach knew how to make the perfect coffee.

The door opened and closed. Cradling my coffee cup, I walked into the living room. Zach bent over and removed his shoes. His butt looked amazing in his dark blue jeans, smug on his hips.

He turned around. I tugged my eyes away from his butt to meet his eyes. He chuckled, revealing his beautiful smile. Oops, he caught me staring.

"Great news?"

I was hopeful.

"Good news."

Good excited me more than no news or bad news.

He motioned for us to sit. Once we sat on the couch, I put my coffee on the table.

"Candace's phone records are being tracked."

"Wow. That's amazing."

I smiled. That was better news than I expected. Especially since Candace's phone was removed from the scene. Especially since I received a call from her phone, possibly baiting me.

"How long should it take for us to get an update on the records?"

He squeezed my knee.

"I'm hoping it'll take a few days, but it could take a few weeks."

"Why a few weeks?"

That seemed long and a bit excessive.

"If we could locate the phone, we wouldn't have to wait for the records. We would just pull the records directly from the phone."

The killer must've thought having the phone would stop phone records from being pulled. The only thing it did was slow the process. They weren't as smart as they thought they were.

What Zach said made sense. The killer only slowed the process. They didn't prevent the process from occurring, though. Whoever committed the crime either committed previous crimes or watched a bunch of crime shows and knew the ins and outs of the processes. This killer was calculated. Calculated scared me. It scared me to my core.

"We will get the answers we want."

Grabbing my coffee, I took a sip. I surely hoped so. I wasn't sure if I wanted the answers or needed them. I've had my fair share of watching crime shows when boredom struck. I'd click on a random channel and stare at the TV, but crime shows always piqued my interest.

Ninety-five percent of the time, the killers

were caught quickly. The other four percent took quite some time for them to be caught. There was a loophole in the case that the investigators just couldn't figure out for a while, but once they combed over the evidence with a fine-tooth comb and a fresh pair of eyes, they found the prized information. The one per cent is what I feared most. The one percent where the case went cold, the family never received justice, and the killer wasn't found.

I had to get up and move. I couldn't sit anymore. Standing, I walked over to the window that overlooked the front of the cabin. My breath escaped me.

"It'll just take some time."

The hair on my arms stood up.

"Destiny."

A streak passed by the window and disappeared around the corner. My mouth went dry. The room grew smaller.

"Destiny."

Sticking out a shaky finger, I pointed out the window.

"Someone's outside," I trembled.

"What?"

Zach moved me to the side so he could see out the window.

"What way did they go?"

I pointed towards the left side of the cabin.

"Stay here. I'll be back."

I opened my mouth to object, but Zach had already left the cabin, gun in hand.

Was Candace's killer here to finish me off? Were they here to kill me, once and for all? Was the call from Candace's phone a warning that I'd see them soon? Were they here to kill me, once and for all? No matter how much I wanted to run and hide in the bedroom, I couldn't bring myself to move my feet. Frozen in front of the window, I watched Zach go around the corner searching for the threat.

"Destiny."

Turning around, Zach looked at me. A tear rolled down my cheek.

"Where did they go?"

He grabbed my hands. He rubbed the back of them with the pad of his thumbs.

"There's no one outside."

I pointed out the window.

"They were just out there. I saw them."

Was I losing my mind? Was I going crazy? What the hell was wrong with me? It couldn't have been a figment of my imagination.

"Destiny."

What would happen if Candace's killer wasn't caught? What if…

"Destiny."

What would happen if she never received the justice she so desperately deserved? What would happen if they successfully harmed me this time? They had already failed at doing it one time. Would they fail during their second try? All because I knew nothing at all and too much at the same time?

Zach squeezed my hands.

"Destiny."

I looked at him.

"Yes."

He rubbed his thumb across my cheek, wiping my tears away.

"Everything is going to be okay. You are okay."

I wanted a heavy weight to lift off my chest with his statement, but I felt dreadful. Nothing was okay, especially with my imagination running wild on me. Was it truly my imagination? Or was it someone outside, and they just disappeared before Zach could locate them?

"I'll never let anything happen to you. Do you believe me?" he asked when silence resonated.

Did I lie and say yes? Or should I be honest and say no?

I searched his eyes for sincerity before deciding which answer to give.

"To be honest, I don't believe too many things."

I could be honest with him. I didn't have to sugarcoat anything with him.

"Or too many people, for that matter."

My experiences from a young age had everything to do with that.

"Well, I think it's time for you to start."

How can I start something I have never considered? As a teacher, I'd thought that would be easy for me to do. Starting something new. Learning something new. It might be one of the hardest things I'd ever have to do in this situation.

"How do I do that?"

It was a genuine question. I didn't have the slightest idea of where to start, but I knew Zach would help. He helped me in more ways than I could count.

"Well, first things first."

He paused as he squeezed my hands.

"You have to forgive."

How could I do that? How could I forgive the person that forced my mother to be a single parent? How could I forgive the person who walked away, leaving me with no father figure?

Thank goodness for Robert. He stepped in when Mom needed him the most. When I needed him the most. It's nothing like having a father figure growing up.

It bothered me when children in my class didn't have a father figure. Or a mother figure. Having two parents in the home sets the child up for the best opportunities possible.

"It's easier said than done," I answered.

"How so?"

Analyzing him, I puffed out my cheek.

"Seriously?"

This conversation would get deep. Deep is what we need to understand each other better. Meaningful conversations meant everything to me.

"Are you going to allow your father to have that control over you for the rest of your life?"

Letting go of Zach's hands, I sat back.

Crossing my leg over my knee, I carefully choose my response.

"It's just like you to call the kettle black."

He scrunched his eyebrows. His lips formed a thin line.

"What do you mean?"

I crossed my arms over my chest.

"I know you don't trust either."

Zach scoffed.

"How do you figure that?"

I sipped my coffee before I answered.

"Your actions."

He smirked. "You know me better than I thought."

I smiled.

"We haven't been stuck together for the past week and a half for nothing."

His silence answered my question.

"If you want me to learn to trust, you must do the same."

His eyes narrowed in on me. He considered my words. Would he open up to me?

"You're right," he said after what felt like an eternity. "It is easier said than done."

"The first step in healing is admitting what has caused our distrust."

His eyes darted away from mine. This was a hard subject for him to discuss.

"How do you know that?"

I pinched my lips together. Here I go, talking more about myself. About my life. Sharing more personal information.

"My mom might've told me that a time or two before," I admitted.

Speaking of my mom, I missed her dearly. I missed her and my stepdad. Er, rather my dad. I didn't see him as anything besides my dad.

"We'll arrange for you to talk to your parents soon, don't worry."

Could he read my mind? Or were my emotions all over my face? I missed them so much. This was the longest I'd gone without talking to them. I felt empty inside.

"Why didn't you listen to your mom?"

Clearing my throat, I carefully chose my words. I loved my mom with all my heart. I had the utmost respect for her. She was easier to forgive than I was. She forgave my dad right when he left. I didn't have it in myself to do that.

"Stubbornness, mostly."

Zach hummed his response.

"What?" I asked.

He shrugged.

"I didn't take you for the stubborn type."

"There's still a lot you don't know about me," I pointed out.

He smiled.

"I'm ready to learn everything there is to know about you."

There he goes again. Flirting without overdoing it. He didn't force the flirtation. It just came naturally. I loved how it came naturally.

"Well, I can say the same thing about you."

We stared at each other. Time passed, and

nothing was said.

"Are you going to tell me who betrayed your trust?"

My question struck a nerve. Zach opened his mouth and closed it.

"It's kind of embarrassing."

What could have caused him not to trust and have embarrassing aspects? Did someone pull his gym pants down in middle school in front of the popular girls? Did he slip on a puddle of spilled water and fall on his butt in front of the entire cafeteria?

"I doubt that." I crossed my legs. "Who betrayed your trust?"

"My ex-girlfriend, Charlotte."

He paused before he continued.

"She was my first girlfriend, and we were serious. We dated a little longer than two years."

I beamed. "She sounds like an amazing woman."

What could possibly be embarrassing about that?

"It started out that way."

He cleared his throat before he continued.

"It's a lot to tell, though. Long story short, she cheated on me."

Gasping, I threw my hand over my mouth. I hadn't been cheated on before. I never stuck around long enough for that or settled down in a relationship, but I could imagine the type of trust issues that could cause. Especially when branching out in the dating field.

"I'm sorry to hear that."

My heart broke for him. I searched his eyes, and I could see the pain. I could see that the experience still hurt him. He carried it on his shoulders to this day.

"It's all good."

"No."

I grabbed his hand.

"It's not all good..."

"It's embarrassing," he interrupted me.

I squeezed his hand.

"That's not embarrassing. You put your trust in the wrong woman. That's all. That's no reason to be embarrassed."

His honesty poured out.

"It has prevented me from pursuing relationships."

That's the reason Zach didn't date. I knew it was a reason for him being single. I assumed it was for a different reason. I seriously had no idea.

"You can't let a foolish girl prevent you from trusting." I paused. "Especially an amazing woman."

He raised his eyebrows. I regretted the last four words that seeped out of my mouth.

"Just like you can't let your birth father prevent you from trusting."

I let his words sink in.

"You have to trust me, whether you'd like to or not."

He had no idea how much I wanted to trust him. I had a difficult time doing it. I had to trust my safety in someone I had met less than two weeks ago. I had to trust Candace's case in someone's hands that I had never met. A lot of trust needed to be done. I had to find it within me to summon up that trust and I needed to find it pronto. Just like that, the fear that tingled in my bones disappeared for the time being.

Chapter Fourteen

Destiny

"What are you thinking about?"

Zach's question pulled me from my thoughts.

Turning around, I tore my eyes away from the window. The night was still. The coolness seeping in from the window showed how cold it was outside. The sun had set, and the night came in beautifully.

"How do you know I'm thinking?"

I leaned my weight on one leg.

Dangers in Love

He smirked, stuffing his hands into his front pockets.

"You've been doing a lot of that lately."

All I could do was think. I thought about Candace and her family. I knew when her parents learned of the devastating news, they didn't take it well. Who would take that type of news well? No parent should ever have to lose a child, especially in such a horrific manner. She had her whole life ahead of her, and someone had just ended it. Ended it as if her life meant nothing.

I shrugged.

"I can't help it."

He was right. So many things were on my mind.

Like how my students were doing, I missed them so much. Hopefully, whoever covered my class taught my children just as wonderfully as I did.

Or how I'd continue to pay for the apartment, which I couldn't afford. Teachers were important in teaching the children what they needed to know for the working world but weren't compensated as such. Being the wonderful man that Zach is, he paid my apartment up six months. If he had informed me in advance of his plans, I would've asked him not to do it. He had done more than enough thus far, and I could never thank him for that. Time wasn't stopping for anyone, no matter how my life came to a screeching halt. I only had a few weeks to pay the rent and wasn't even working.

Or how my parents were handling the situation. Granted, I was thankful Zach allowed me to call them yesterday, but my heart ached once the phone call ended. Candace's parents had called mine and informed them of the news. I fell into a deeper depression when my parents offered their condolences. I didn't think that was possible, but I surprised myself. When I curled into bed last night, the only thing that helped to dry the tears was Zach. He held me in his arms, and he kissed my tears away. Nobody had ever done that for me before. He was one of a kind.

He stepped closer. Only mere inches from me, he said, "I'd love to get your mind on something positive."

Positivity came less than usual these past two weeks, but Zach tried his damnest with me. Every day. I couldn't thank him enough for everything he's done for me. Everything he continues to do for me.

"How do you plan to do that?"

He placed his hands on my hips. My heartbeat quickened, his touch inviting.

"A nice, relaxing night."

I smiled. That sounded exciting. We were more than just a victim and protector hanging out. From the vibe I received, it would be personal. More relaxed. I craved that.

"What do you have in mind?"

He took my hands in his. He kissed the back of them before he stared into my eyes.

"It's a surprise."

Surprise? I didn't know how I felt about surprises. Since being around Zach, I did feel more open to being spontaneous.

"When do I learn of this surprise?"

Zach hummed.

"All you need to do is wash up and relax."

Wash up? Relax? I couldn't argue with that.

"Okay."

"Okay?" He raised an eyebrow. "Why did that seem so easy?"

I folded my arms across my chest.

"You think I'm easy?"

His eyes widened. He raised his hands and shook his head.

"No. I didn't say that."

The look on his face caused an eruption of laughter to vibrate within me. He looked like a deer caught in headlights.

"I'm only kidding."

A smile appeared before he laughed with me.

"You had me scared for a second." He paused, narrowing his eyes on me. "I'd never disrespect you."

Those four words. A man had never spoken those to me, and it felt amazing. He had the utmost respect for me. I appreciated that.

I smiled.

"That's great to know."

"Get washed up."

Zach wrapped his arms around my waist. He kissed my forehead, his lips lingering longer than necessary.

"Everything will be ready when you're out of the shower."

With a parting smile, I walked around him. I threw another glance over my shoulder before I walked into the bathroom. His eyes were trained on me.

After I closed the door, I looked at myself in the mirror. On one hand, this woman was a stranger, thrown into an environment who she didn't know. She was to come out of her shell and learn to trust a stranger who didn't seem much like a stranger anymore. On the other hand, this was the new me. The woman who was forced to learn a new life, whether she liked it or not .

Turning the shower on, I stripped out of my clothes and stepped into the hot stream of water.

A lot of learning had to be done between us.

Learning of Zach's distrust made me understand him even more. We both had issues with distrust, but for completely different reasons. His distrust came from a girl breaking his heart into a million pieces by cheating on him. That is the reason he was single. He feared being hurt again.

I didn't blame him, though. Relationships weren't for everyone. I hadn't had a traumatic experience as such to cause me not to date. I would go on a date every now and again just to see what was out there.

I experienced a handful of one-night stands just to satisfy my sexual urges. I'd be fine for another six months to a year. I just never found the right person I could connect with on a romantic level... until, possibly, now.

Zach was a nice man. He had a good head on his shoulders. Would I go on a date with him? Heck yes, if I wasn't hiding in his cabin for my safety. I would've already gone on a date had the situation been different. I knew we wouldn't have met if this situation hadn't occurred. I hated saying things happen for a reason, but I believed that to be so.

After the bathroom filled with steamy cinnamon, I stepped out and dried off. Hot showers were so refreshing. They allowed me to wash away the day's events as I could be in deep thought with no interruptions.

After I dressed in a matching pajama set, I walked into the living room. The smell of steak swirled in the air, causing my stomach to growl. I hadn't eaten since the sandwich I had for lunch. Zach sat on the couch in his pajamas. He patted the seat beside him.

"I'm glad I dressed for the occasion."

"Casual and comfy is what I aimed for."

I sat beside him, taking in his scent. He smelled delightful. He looked even more amazing, his brown hair flowing freely down his back.

"What's the special occasion?"

Zach smiled, my heart skipping a beat.

"What do you mean?"

I ran my fingers through his hair. His strands were smooth and luscious, free of split ends.

"Your hair is down." I paused. "What's the reason?"

He opened his mouth to respond when a beep from the kitchen interrupted him. He stood and rubbed his hands together.

"Dinner's ready."

Why the complete change of conversation? He wouldn't get away from this conversation that easily.

"Can I help?"

"No." He turned and looked at me. He winked before he said, "All you need to do is relax."

He disappeared into the kitchen.

The sound of pots and pans ranged out. Crossing my legs, I patiently waited. What did Zach have up his sleeve?

Not even two minutes later, Zach called for me to come into the kitchen.

I walked in to see the dining room table transformed. A dark red tablecloth adorned the table. Four taper candles sat in the middle of the table, burning bright. Two plates of steak and a medley of veggies displayed beautifully beside a glass of water.

"Dinner is served."

"Oh, my goodness." I placed my hands over my mouth. "This is so thoughtful of you."

Zach smiled.

"Anything I can do to bring some light to your day."

He did great, I had to admit. He pulled my chair out for me, and I sat. Once he sat across from me, I beamed.

"Thank you."

I wasn't thanking him for the meal he had prepared or the attention he gave. I thanked him for dealing with my mood swings and emotions.

He picked up his knife and fork.

"What did I tell you about thanking me?"

"I doubt I'll be able to stop." I followed suit with my utensils. "You've been nothing but amazing to me."

Zach shrugged. "That's my job." He pointed at my plate. "Try your food before it gets cold."

Silence settled upon us as we cut into our food. After I ate some vegetables and a piece of steak, I gave him a thumbs up.

"This is the best steak I've ever had."

Zach laughed. "You don't have to lie to make me feel good."

"Oh, no." I wiped my mouth with my napkin before I pointed at him. "I'm serious. The steakhouses have nothing on you."

Zach winked and smirked.

"Well, thank you. That's one of the best compliments I've received about my cooking."

"I'm only being honest." Grabbing my water, I took a sip. "I feel it's only fair for me to correct you when necessary."

"Is there anything else you'd like to be honest about?"

"Yes. Your job is to help find justice for Candace. You've been nothing but amazing to me..."

Zach gave me a quizzical look.

"What do you mean?"

I considered my words carefully. "Everything you've done for me. Protecting me. Caring for me." I paused. "That's not in your job description."

He nodded. "You're right about that." He cleared his throat. "I've never done this for anyone else."

Did that make me special? What was special about me that wasn't special about his other victims?

I clasped my hands on the table. "How come?"

He smiled before he cut into his steak and ate a piece.

"I've never felt this way about anyone before. I've experienced feelings I never thought were possible to feel."

Oh. My. Goodness. These feelings I had weren't one-sided. They were reciprocated.

"I hope I didn't make you uncomfortable." Zach's face turned a bright red. "That wasn't my intention."

This was the first time I'd seen him embarrassed.

My silence must've given him the wrong impression. That's the last thing I wanted.

"No, I'm not uncomfortable." I ate some more of my food before I continued. "I'm just shocked."

"Well, don't be."

Placing my fork on the table, I folded my hands under my chin, and I looked at him. He looked irresistible with his hair down. It fanned his face perfectly. He could go for a supermodel. His lips looked kissable and soft. I bit the side of my lip, anticipating what would happen next.

"Is your hair down for a reason?"

His answer would determine how this night would go.

"Whatever reason you want it to be."

My desire for Zach replaced my hunger for dinner. I had only known him for two weeks, but our connection made it seem as if I'd known him for years.

We stood, the chairs screeching across the floor. I walked into Zach's strong arms, his scent inviting and familiar. Zach grabbed my face. He rubbed the pads of his thumbs on my cheeks. His lips crashed against mine. Experiencing our second kiss was just as amazing as the first one.

Our lips moved in sync. My heart exploded with adoration. I hadn't felt this way in... never. I had never felt this way for anybody.

Grabbing a fistful of his shirt, I pulled it over his head. His chiseled chest came into view, and I ogled the beautiful man before me. I kissed him all over his chest.

Zach tilted my face up. Staring into his eyes, they screamed so many unspoken words. He grabbed my shirt and pulled it over my head before his lips captured mine.

Chest against chest, we studied each other's mouths. His mouth tasted both sweet and salty. I loved every bit of it.

He pulled his mouth away from mine. My eyes fluttered open. I didn't want this to end. Not now, not ever.

His mouth traveled from my lips to the side of my face. He peppered kisses into my neck. I shivered involuntarily, the movement alone inviting.

"Do you want..." he began.

"Yes." I didn't even have to wait for him to finish his sentence. "Now." I gasped.

I pulled his pajama pants and boxers down, and his erection sprang to life. He pulled my pants and panties down before I grabbed his hand and tugged him to the bathroom. The bathroom still smelled heavily of cinnamon from my shower earlier.

"Another shower?" he asked as I turned the shower on.

"It's hot and steamy." I winked. "Why not?"

Zach winked before he pulled us into the hot shower. The water danced down our bodies, blanketing us in a hot waterfall.

"No more questions," he growled into my ear.

Stern. I liked that. Maybe a bit too much.

"Your wish is my command."

His sweet tongue entered my mouth. My eyes fluttered close, enjoying the bliss of the moment. I'd never felt these feelings before. I couldn't wait to show my love and affection.

He pressed me against the shower wall, pressing his body against me. His erection pressed against my stomach. I couldn't move. I didn't want to move. He towered over me. He stared down at me, rubbing the side of my face. His eyes were filled with love. Desire.

He bit his lip before cupping my face, then traced my lips before dipping his tongue back into my mouth.

Desire stirred in my stomach. I responded to his kisses with affection of my own.

"Now," I moaned.

I couldn't handle the foreplay anymore.

"What?"

His lips hovered over mine. They were so close, yet so far. When I leaned forward, he pulled back.

"Now," I repeated.

"I can't hear you," he whispered devilishly.

"Now," I yelled.

Zach smirked before he lifted me into his arms. He eased me onto his erection, and I released a breath. Holy shit, he was huge. He eased in and out of me as he stared deep into my eyes. Deep into my soul. Completely exposed, I served everything up to him on a silver platter.

A moan escaped my lips. My eyes rolled to the back of my head as he peppered kisses on my neck.

"Do you like that?" His voice came out raspy.

"Yes," I moaned out as I held onto his arms with all my might.

He knew what he did to me. He rocked my body with a rhythm I'd never experienced before. His lips found my neck. My neck was my tender spot. My pleasure zone. The passageway to unlocking the sexual desire I had pushed away for way too long.

"Zach, I'm..." I left off as euphoria came over me.

I lost all control.

He grunted and stilled his rhythm. He kissed my forehead before he placed me on my feet. My legs still weak from climax, I leaned against the wall. Staring at his naked body, I placed my hand over my heart.

"Damn, that was amazing."

"Yes, it was."

Chapter Fifteen

Destiny

Kisses touched my forehead, nose, and cheeks, pulling me out of my sleep. The smell of sausage swirled in the air. I bunched up the covers around me, snuggling closer to the source. The source of my warmth, comfort, and happiness.

"Good morning, sleepyhead."

I moaned my response. It couldn't be morning already.

I was beat, tired, and I needed more sleep.

"Breakfast is almost ready."

Breakfast? Morning had arrived. Ugh.

"I'll be up in a few," I mumbled.

Zach kissed me once more before leaving the room and closing the door.

How did Zach have so much energy? Last night, we made love in the shower, the living room on the couch, the dining room on the kitchen table and the bedroom. He ran off adrenaline.

Pushing the covers off me, I stretched my arms above my head. How did I go to sleep naked?

What happened last night? Why did it happen? I couldn't lie, I enjoyed myself. I just hoped it didn't change anything. I didn't want to ruin our relationship.

Could we go back to the way we were?

I doubted it.

Grabbing my discarded panties from the night before, I slipped them on. I went into the drawer and grabbed a pair of sweatpants and a shirt.

Walking into the bathroom, I stared at myself. Aside from my messy bun, I didn't look different, but I felt different. I felt like a new woman. After I handled my hygiene, I searched for Zach.

My nose guided me to the dining room. Zach stood with his back turned towards me. Two plates of sausage, eggs, and fruit sat on the table.

I clasped my hands together.

"Hello."

Zach turned around. Dragging my eyes down

his chiseled torso, I remembered how I touched him as he sent me to pleasure-town over and over again.

Clearing my throat, embarrassment took over. How would I face him today?

"Hey."

He sat glasses of orange juice on the table and smiled at me.

There was something about this irresistible man, something I couldn't get enough of.

He wrapped his arms around my waist and hugged me. His scent relaxed me and warmed my insides.

"How did you sleep?" he asked after he kissed my forehead.

He wasn't being distant or different. It didn't seem like last night... and this morning changed anything.

"I slept great." I sat at my place at the table. "How did you sleep?"

"I slept amazing." Picking up his glass of orange juice, he took a sip. "Last night was magical."

Magical? Damn. That was the best way anyone could describe our night together.

Picking up my fork, I stabbed into a piece of sausage.

"Are you okay?"

"Yes." I nodded. "I'm okay."

"Are you sure?" He stared at me. "You're acting kind of different..."

I opened my mouth to respond when he

continued.

"Shy, perhaps."

I pinched my lips together. "I just don't want anything to change between us."

He pursed his lips together. He shook his head.

"Nothing has changed."

"But..." I began.

I should just be quiet and eat.

I ate a piece of sausage.

"But what?"

Did I want things to change? I wanted to explore what could blossom between us. If nothing blossomed, I didn't want our friendship to dwindle.

"Nothing."

Time will tell what would happen between us. If we depended on fate, everything would work out.

"Are you sure?"

I loved his need for reassurance from me. It made me feel important, like I had a voice.

"Yes. I'm sure."

"Good."

We ate in silence. Every now and again, I'd sneak a look at him. He'd shoot me a smile or a wink, which sent flutters through my stomach.

"Are there any updates on Candace?"

Zach stopped mid-chew and looked at me. His eyes were full of sorrow.

My heart dropped. Zach had received some news, and it probably wasn't positive.

Or we were headed in the right direction with information, but we still didn't have a solid lead. Grabbing my orange juice, I took a sip.

"Yes."

I folded my arms, a bit perturbed.

"When were you going to tell me the news?"

Zach exhaled before he rubbed the stubble on his chin. "After breakfast." He paused. "After you actually ate something. Dessert cut our dinner short last night."

I smiled at his attempt to lighten the mood. We had fun last night. All night. Now, it was time for business.

"What new information do we have?"

He sat back in his chair.

"We are still waiting for the phone updates. They haven't come in yet." He paused. "Seems like there's a backup in that department."

Ugh. I wasn't happy to find that out. Candace's case was serious. Her situation should've been a top priority since we were dealing with a murder, but what did I know?

"Do you know when we should have some results?"

I worried too much time would pass by, and the murderer would have more time to escape their sentence. The longer it took to solve a murder, the less likely it would be to locate the suspect. I couldn't live with knowing Candace's killer wasn't behind bars for the crime they committed.

"Hopefully, in the next few days."

Hopefully? Hopefully didn't rub me the right way. Hopefully, it made it seem as if this situation wasn't a top priority.

"Is there anything else?"

Zach twisted his lips side to side before he rubbed his jaw. He stalled. When he stalled, it wasn't good.

"Zach." My voice was stern. "Tell me. Please."

After an eternity, he spoke.

"I'm not supposed to tell you this. I shouldn't tell you this, but I don't want to keep anything from you. The autopsy report came back."

The autopsy report? Why would we need to know the results of that? We knew Candace died from a gunshot wound. Did it say something beyond the gunshot wound? Was there something more that I didn't know?

"The gunshot hit a major artery."

I threw my hand over my mouth as tears threatened to fall. Did this mean what I thought it meant?

"If the bullet had moved over just an inch, she would've survived."

Oh. My. Gosh. I sniffled. Tears escaped my eyes and cascaded down my cheeks. I never thought my heart would break anymore, but I was wrong. Candace didn't have a chance to survive. She had no chance of surviving the second the bullet left the gun.

"I'm so sorry," Zach called out.

Sadness washed over his face.

I stood, and Zach followed suit. He took a step towards me. I shook my head and held my hands out in front of me, stopping him in his tracks.

"I'd like to be alone right now."

Zach looked defeated, but he nodded.

I walked out of the dining room and headed straight for the bedroom.

As I closed the bedroom door, I dropped to the floor in a heap. I sobbed my soul out, my heart in pain.

Candace had no chance of surviving her injury. Whoever did this wanted blood. Candace's blood .

It felt like our last night together was decades ago. I missed our conversations. I missed having only a few minutes together on the days we both worked. We'd sit down for those few minutes and catch up with each other on what was new or what we were running low on in the apartment.

I picked myself up off the floor. I needed a distraction. Drawing would distract me.

I walked into the living room. Thankfully, Zach hadn't made it in there yet. Grabbing my drawing pad and colored pencils, I went to work. I used my passion and ability to craft my pain.

Why didn't I hug her? Why didn't I hug her the last time I saw her? We were always affectionate towards each other. We were those best friends that said I love you all the time.

We didn't hug that night because we didn't know that would be the last time we'd see each other. The only person who knew that besides me was Candace's murderer.

Would Candace still be alive if we hadn't gone to that restaurant? Would Candace still be alive if we hadn't gone out at all that night? Was this a random act? Or was this planned and calculated? I had so many questions, and they have yet to be answered. Would they ever be answered?

"Destiny."

My thoughts ceased. Tearing my eyes away from my drawing, I looked at Zach.

"Yes."

My voice was a murmur, barely above a whisper.

Cupping my face, he kissed me softly before he whispered, "I'm so sorry."

Tears left my eyes. I looked away from him. I didn't want him to see me this emotional over the news he just shared. Yes, Candace died two weeks ago, but it didn't hurt any less learning this new information.

"I didn't want to tell you because I knew how the information would impact you."

Zach's face swam back into my vision.

"I promise you, Frank is doing everything in his power to get as much information as quickly as possible."

I knew he told the truth. That didn't help how I felt, though. Even if I knew the truth. Even if I knew who killed Candace and why, would I feel better? I highly doubted it. I might've felt worse after I knew.

"Thank you."

Zach kissed me once more, sending a rocket off in my chest. How did he have these effects on me? In such little time? It felt unreal.

"You're drawing is..."

I looked at my artwork. Somehow, in a few minutes, I had completed my picture. I had drawn an eye, outlined with the most beautiful makeup work. A single tear fell from it. The strokes of the pencil were fierce and bold. The colors on the page were sorrowful, lacking every bit of happiness.

"Meaningful and beautiful," Zach finished.

The picture was me.

Chapter Sixteen

Zach

Destiny made me want to be a better man. Not that I didn't consider myself a great man already. She just made me feel different inside. Since she'd been in my protection, I didn't remember the last time I thought about responding to one of my flings. Hell, this was the first time, and it wasn't because I needed to pleasure Mr. Happy. Destiny did just fine in the sexual department. Not that I planned for us to do anything together. Or anytime soon. It shocked me that she felt the same way. When you spend 24/7 with someone locked inside a small one-bedroom cabin, you tend to grow feelings for them.

My feelings for Destiny were real. Having feelings felt foreign, though. I never thought the day would come when I'd consider what my life would be like having a significant other around. Now, I thought about it often. Multiple times throughout the day. Destiny's aura was addicting, and I just needed more of it.

What did Destiny mean yesterday when she said she didn't want things to change between us? Did she mean she didn't want to explore what could possibly be? Did she regret our night together?

Either way, I didn't know what to think. All I knew, I loved her. I hadn't told her that yet, though. I didn't want to scare her away with my feelings. How could someone be so broken from a previous relationship years ago, love someone so amazing now? After they had sworn off love for eternity?

It was difficult for me to wrap my head around the fact, but it was possible. I was the living testament.

I rubbed Destiny's shoulder. She looked over at me and smiled. We hung out in the living room, and the movie we watched had just ended. I saw the movie several times before, but it was Destiny's first time watching it.

"How did you like it?"

"It was amazing." She paused, placing her hand on mine. "I can't believe I've never watched it before."

Her affection breathed life into me.

"There's a second one if you'd like to watch it next."

She beamed.

"Of course I want to watch it."

My phone vibrated in my pocket. When I saw Trevor returning my call, I kissed Destiny's head before I stood.

"We'll start it when I come back inside."

"Okay."

I answered the phone as I closed the front door. The weather called for a jacket, but this phone call trumped my warmth.

"Hello."

"Hey. I'm sorry I missed your call."

I had called Trevor earlier in the day, but he hadn't answered. It took him some time to call me back, but people were busy.

"It's okay. I'm just glad you returned my call."

Rusling sounded on his end before he spoke.

"How is Destiny holding up?"

I walked down the porch steps. The farther I could get away from the cabin to have this conversation, the better.

"She's okay right now. The recent information you provided bummed her out yesterday. She was a mess."

"Man, I'm sorry." Trevor cleared his throat. "That was hard information, even to just relay.

How are you holding up?"

Considering the situation, it was common and perfectly normal to worry about the victim. What wasn't common and normal was to worry about the person protecting the victim. His asking about me was considerate, to say the least.

Yes, the protector wasn't the person in immediate danger, but the protector carried the brunt of the victim's pain by offering as much comfort as possible. Well, in my case, I carried as much as I could for her. That's the least I could do.

"I'm doing good."

"Is she a lot to handle?"

I stopped in my tracks. Trevor's question didn't rub me the right way. Was he being an asshole, or was he genuinely concerned about me? I cared so much for her. I needed to protect her at every cost. Against everyone. I decided to consider the latter to decrease any type of tension that could be created between us. I didn't need to burn my bridges with the only lifeline that I had in this case.

"No, not at all." I looked down the road, no movement to be seen. "She's actually a joy to be around."

Immediately, I regretted my response. To someone with a mind like mine, it would seem innocent. To a man with a mind like his, he would make it into something dirty.

Trevor whistled. "Wait." He paused. "Is there something going on that I should know about,

Miller?"

I'd never disrespect Destiny and discuss our business. What we had going on would stay between us. No one needed to know what blossomed between a victim and their protector. What we shared was special. Nobody on the outside looking in would understand.

I chuckled, trying to loosen myself up.

"No, nothing at all."

Trevor hummed.

"Are you sure? She's kind of hot. Something would've happened the first day if I were her protector."

My blood boiled. I went from cold to hot. How dare Trevor say Destiny was hot. Granted, I thought the same thing when I first saw her. Anyone with great vision would think the same. How could he be so rude as to say something would've happened the first day? On her first day, she wasn't herself. She was a shell of herself, housing a traumatic event who saw something they shouldn't have seen. She was in no manner to accept anyone's advances.

"Yes, I'm sure," I boomed.

Silence. That's what I wanted from him. He had dug a big enough hole for himself already.

Enough with the small talk. We needed to get down to business. "Do you have any updates?"

"No. We still haven't received the phone records. Things are still backed up."

Vacations at the end of the year surely slowed things down. Yes, I understood the end of the year was when people needed to spend time with their family and friends, but it was a hindrance for our victims. Our victims were priority.

"I'll call you as soon as I know something."

Trevor might've said stupid things now and then, but he wasn't that bad of a guy. Considering all he'd done for me, I had no choice but to overlook his sly comments and remarks.

"Thank you."

Once I hung up, I turned and looked at my cabin. I had nothing positive to relay to Destiny. I had to do something to keep her in good spirits.

I walked into the cabin, the warmth inviting. I grabbed my coat and car keys.

"Are you going somewhere?" Destiny asked.

"I'm running to the store to get a few things for tonight."

Destiny perked up.

"Things? Do you want me to come?"

Did I want her to come? Hell yes. Was it safe for her to come? The suspect could be anyone. We had no leads in the case, and I'm sure Frank put in long hours to try to figure everything out.

"I want you to go but..."

"But..." Destiny drawled out, flashing me her smile.

Damn. Instant boner. Scratching at the stubble on my chin, I regretted my other head's reaction.

"I want you safe." I pointed towards the door. "It's not safe for you out there."

She stood and approached me. She grabbed my hands and squeezed them.

"Please, let me go with you. I don't want to be left alone right now."

It wasn't a good idea, but could I say no to her? She planted her beautiful eyes on me, and I was smitten. I turned into putty.

"You can only go if you stay in the car when we arrive."

"That's perfect."

She looped her arm around my neck. Her lips hovered inches from mine before I kissed her firmly. Her lips were warm, soft, and inviting. I didn't want our kiss to end.

After checking the surrounding areas of the cabin, I walked Destiny to my truck. I helped her inside before I walked to the driver's door. Thankfully, when I bought my truck, I had tint installed. No one would be able to see inside unless they walked up to the truck and cupped their hands to look inside.

It would be the first time Destiny came out since she came to the cabin.

When the truck roared to life, I looked over at Destiny. She looked out the passenger window.

"Are you ready?"

Her eyes were glossy when she looked at me. She'd cry at any second.

"Yes." She paused and looked around. "I'm ready."

Silence filled the cabin as we drove out of the neighborhood. I just knew she reminisced about her trip up there. It was right after we found out Candace didn't make it.

Once I pulled onto the main road, I grabbed her hand. She looked over at me and smiled. Her smile didn't quite reach her eyes.

If only I could make this trip back to the cabin a great one for her.

The beauty of the location of my cabin was that we were tucked in the middle of nowhere, but we were close enough to the local store to make purchases.

Tonight, I would give her the night of her life. Even though we couldn't go out and have a date, it didn't mean we couldn't have one at the cabin.

Pushing the middle console up, I patted the seat beside me. Destiny unbuckled her seatbelt before she slid over and snuggled against me.

I hadn't opened myself up to affection in years. Boy, I missed something amazing.

The grocery store came into view. Glancing in the rear-view mirror, I flicked on my blinker and completed my right turn.

The store was surprisingly empty for the time of the day. I parked as close to the front door as possible.

Grabbing her chin, I tilted her head up. "Please, lock the doors once I get out." I outlined her chin with my finger. "Don't get out of the truck. Under any circumstances."

"Okay."

Kissing her tenderly, I savored the taste of sweetness and the feel of her soft lips on mine.

As soon as I closed the door, I heard the truck lock. I walked into the store with one mission in mind. Cue romantic date mind.

After I grabbed a meat, some veggies, and a delectable dessert, I walked to the checkout.

"Are you shopping for a date night?" The cashier asked as she rang my items up.

I grabbed my wallet and pulled out my credit card.

"Yes."

She smiled.

"She must be really special."

"She really is."

After paying for my groceries, I grabbed my bags and walked to the truck.

She unlocked the doors, and I placed the bags in the back seat.

"What did you get?" she asked.

I slid into the driver's seat, put on my seatbelt, and placed the truck in reverse.

"It's a surprise."

"I'm starting to like surprises," she responded as she wrapped her hands around my arm and snuggled close to me.

I never thought I would miss love. I received love from my mother. She gave that to me daily. I didn't think I'd need love from anyone else, especially a companion. The things I had missed out on from holding onto the past.

The trip back to the cabin entailed running my fingers through Destiny's hair as I told her about my childhood. I didn't tell many people how my father left me and my mother to start another life with another woman and take care of her two children, but I told Destiny. It helped her understand me more, which was the most important thing for me.

"It was nice to get out of the cabin," Destiny said as we got out of the truck.

"Are you saying you don't like my cabin?" I joked.

We walked up the steps to the cabin.

"Of course not."

I opened the door, and she walked inside.

"It's just hard being in the same place all the time," she admitted.

I could agree with that. I only stepped out of the cabin to pick up the necessities we needed around the house. Frank needed to get this process to speed up. We needed this monster behind bars so Destiny and I could return to our everyday lives and go on dates like ordinary people. If only her life could go back to normal. Honestly, I didn't think my life could go back to normal after this. It wasn't normal to fall for the person in protection, and it had already happened.

"It is hard, but I'd do it all over again if it meant I could protect you."

I slipped my shoes off and made a beeline for the kitchen.

"Would you really?"

She leaned her hip against the counter.

Removing the items from the bags, I revealed

our dinner plans for the night.

"Yes. Obviously, the circumstances weren't ideal. I just feel we've connected on another level. I wouldn't have had the opportunity to open up to anyone else as much as I have opened up to you."

Destiny grabbed the vegetables. She opened the container and rinsed them off.

"Did we come into each other's lives for a purpose?"

We made eye contact. We both knew the answer to that question, but I needed to respond.

"Yes. Yes, we did."

Chapter Seventeen

Destiny

I couldn't believe how much he opened up, especially to me. When I learned of my situation, I never knew he'd need me to heal as much as I needed him.

"I'm guessing a delicious meal and dessert, grouped into a date, is my surprise?"

"Don't sound too excited," he said as he winked at me.

I bumped my hip against his. "I'm very

excited." I looked at the salmon, veggies, and petite fours. "This is the first date I'm actually looking forward to."

He grabbed a frying pan from the cabinet, placed it on the stove, and turned it on.

"Really?"

We were opening up to each other. I might as well be honest about everything.

"Yes."

"How come?"

He opened the salmon and rinsed it in the sink.

"We've taken the time to get to know each other before we decided to go on a date."

He placed the salmon in the frying pan. The cabin filled with a sizzling sound.

"Wait." Grabbing a cutting board, I placed the veggies on it. "You never asked me to go on a date."

He smirked. "You're right." He grabbed some seasonings out of the cupboard. "How rude of me."

I folded my arms across my chest. "I'm waiting," I playfully responded.

"Destiny."

I beamed. He would really ask me out.

"Yes, Zach."

"Would you like to go on a date with me?"

Grabbing a knife, I chopped the zucchini.

"No."

Zach looked at me, eyes wide with surprise. "Seriously?"

"You have to try a little harder," I teased.

Zach washed his hands in the sink. Once he dried his hands on a dish towel, he slipped his hands under my butt, picked me up with ease and placed me on the counter. He stood in between my legs. His closeness excited me yet sent nervous chills up my spine.

"Woah. I like this," I muttered.

Gripping the edge of the counter, I anticipated what would happen next.

His hand brushed against my inner thigh as he leaned close. He was inches from my face. All I had to do was lean in, and our lips would meet.

"Would you like to go on a date with me?"

I hummed.

"What will we do?"

His eyes flickered over to the salmon on the stove.

"Eat a delicious dinner while we get to know each other more. Finish off the night with some dessert."

"What kind of dessert?"

Zach winked. "We have options. You can either have petite fours or the freaky kind that ends with you falling apart in my arms."

I didn't think he'd go there, but he went there. Oh la la.

Cupping my face in his hands, he kissed me. His tongue darted out of his mouth, meeting mine. Fireworks were set off in my body, tingling all the way down to my toes.

"Do you want to eat, or can we just skip to

dessert?" Zach growled against my lips.

Dessert sounded amazing, but I knew we needed sustenance. Sustenance would get us through anything and everything we decided to do tonight.

"I want that date you promised me."

Zach tilted my head up. He kissed my neck before he whispered, "Your wish is my command."

He walked over to the stove and tended to the salmon. Hopefully, it hadn't burned.

Even though there was some distance between us, I still couldn't breathe. How did he have this effect on me?

He finished cutting the zucchini before he tossed them in a separate pan.

"You must really like my countertop."

Zach turned the salmon over, a loud sizzle rang out.

"Why do you ..." I still sat on the countertop.

"I mean, I favored this countertop as well." He shrugged. "That's why I chose it."

I pushed myself off the counter.

Bustling around as Zach cooked, I made the table ready for dinner. I grabbed the candles Zach had just bought, placed them on the table, and lit them.

I stood back and admired the set-up. Right now, we couldn't do too much outside of this cabin. For my safety, I had to hide. It was amazing how much effort Zach put into making this time for us extra special.

"Dinner is ready," Zach called out.

I looked at myself once more in the mirror. Even though I didn't have too much of anything there outside of the necessities, I could still make myself more presentable. I had pulled my hair into a formal bun, a change from the messy bun I usually wore.

I walked into the dining room. A lull of classical music played from his phone. The food and glasses of ice water sat in the middle of the table, in between the candles. The mood for tonight was set.

We sat across from each other at the table. We passed the food around family style.

"I didn't take you as the classical type."

Zach grabbed his glass of water and took a sip.

"Really? What kind of music did you think I'd listen to?"

I cut a piece of salmon.

"Country."

"That's my second favorite," he answered.

"How did you come to listen to classical?"

Forking salmon into my mouth, I was hit with an explosion of flavor.

He cut into his veggies before he smirked.

"Do you not like my classical music?"

"No, it's wonderful." I smiled. "It just surprised me."

"My mother. She listened to it when I was younger."

That explained a lot.

"Your mother is a big part of your life as well, isn't she?" I asked.

He nodded. "I'm family-oriented." He paused. "Even though I grew up without a father figure, nothing will change me of that."

It's crazy how we had that one thing in common. Our fathers didn't want anything to do with us. I was fortunate enough to have Robert come along and take over the father role. Robert didn't have kids of his own. Not that he didn't want to, he biologically couldn't have any. So, he came along and was the best father he could be to me.

"How old were you when your father left?" I asked.

This usually wasn't the topic for a first date, but Zach and I were on another level. We were different. I liked different.

"I was so young, I didn't remember him." He paused in deep thought. "My mother said I was in pre-k when he left."

My heart broke for Zach. To find out that your father left you as a young child to be with another woman and raise her two children as your own? I'm glad I didn't know too much about my birth father. I don't know how I'd feel if I had learned of something so horrible.

I remembered bits and pieces about my birth father, but it wasn't anything spectacular that stood out to me about him.

Cutting into my veggies, I took a bite. Officially, Zach was the best cook ever.

"How did you learn about his other family?"

Zach rubbed the stubble on his face.

"In seventh grade, my friends at school would always talk about their wonderful weekends with their fathers. I hate to admit it, but I was jealous. They had their fathers in their life. Why didn't I have mine?"

I sipped my water.

"I searched for him online one day after school, and I found him. Shockingly, the kids were around my age, maybe a little older."

Clasping my hands on the table, I leaned forward, completely invested.

"I showed my mom what I found, and she told me the truth. It hurt me, but I couldn't be too upset. My mom did everything in her power to raise me to be such a respectful man. Why should I look for the man who didn't want to be in my life?"

"What a respectful man you are," I commented.

He smiled.

"You're only saying that to make me feel special."

"I wouldn't do that." I continued eating. "I'm only being truthful."

After we finished dinner, we grabbed the dirty dishes and walked them to the sink.

"You don't have to help me with the dishes," he said as he rinsed off a plate.

"Yes, I do." I grabbed the plate and loaded it into the dishwasher. "Teamwork makes the dream work."

"So, I've come to realize something," Zach said.

He washed off the utensils and handed them to me.

"What have you realized?"

I placed them in the dishwasher.

"You waited for me to come along."

What? What did he mean? What did he imply?

"Um..."

I didn't know what to say.

"Do you trust me?"

He handed me another plate.

"Yes."

The trust I had in Zach grew over the past two weeks I'd been in his protection. At the start of this journey, I wasn't sure who I could trust. Zach showed me that my safety was in his best interest. He had done nothing but show me how important my safety was to him.

He handed me a pan.

"I think you've never settled down for two reasons."

I looked over at him. Two reasons? He didn't just think of one reason, but two reasons I hadn't dated. This had to be good.

"I'd love to hear what you've come up with."

He smiled.

"You want to give your students at school all your time and attention."

He had a great observation. My students deserved the world from me, and that was what they'd get. How did he know how I felt about my students at school?

"You also lack trust with the people you considered being in your life."

Could this man read my mind? How did he know so much about me?

I decided to become an elementary school teacher when I was a sophomore in high school. I wanted to teach kids at the most important grades in school. If they didn't have someone to confide in at home, I wanted them to confide in me. When I was younger, I always had my mother to confide in. When my stepdad came into my life, I had him as well. In school, I didn't have the luxury of confiding in my teachers when I wanted to talk. I gave my students and any other students roaming the halls the opportunity to talk if they needed to. I loved that they took advantage of the opportunity.

There's no way he learned that in the two weeks that we'd been together. Or had he? We mainly spent all our time together. There were many things I tended to learn when in close quarters with someone.

"How did you…"

"You think I'm an amazing man, and you obviously trust me. I think there's just one thing left to ask."

Was he going to ask me to be his girlfriend? Was I ready for that type of commitment? Was I ready to go to that next step with him? I'd already shared myself with him. Hell, I tended to do the occasional one-night stand to get the edge off when necessary, no strings attached. Was I ready to go to the next step with Zach?

"What is that?"

"Where have you been all my life?"

I released a sigh of relief. He didn't place me in a sticky position to answer a question I didn't know how to answer.

"I feel like I can talk to you about anything," he said.

"I feel the same way."

I placed the last of the dishes in the dishwasher. Besides Candace, I hadn't shared my trust issues with anyone. I never thought anyone would understand where I came from. Candace didn't even understand where I came from, but I still confided in her.

She had both her birth parents in her life, and they were happily married. Finally, I had found someone who understood me. That could relate to me on another level.

Zach grabbed my hands and squeezed them softly.

"Maybe we were placed in each other's lives for a reason."

"I'm almost positive that's the case."

Grabbing his face, I kissed him.

That was the case. Maybe I'd find it in my heart to give Zach a chance. Everything made him look like the perfect person for me.

Chapter Eighteen

Destiny

It was dark. Eerily dark. Too dark for my liking.

"Destiny."

Turning towards the voice, my heart sunk into my chest. Was that Candace? Where was she? Was she okay?

"Candace," I called out.

The hairs on the back of my neck stood up. I didn't want to walk or bump into anything. The darkness was thick and blinding.

An ear-piercing scream echoed.

"Candace," I yelled.

She needed my help. She needed me. I had to help. I ran blindly towards the scream. My feet slapped against the concrete, the air stilled around me. I couldn't see anything around me, but I had to help her.

"Candace," I yelled again.

I had to be closer to her.

"Candace, answer me," I screamed.

My voice cracked. Tears threatened to fall. If she could hear me, why wouldn't she respond to me?

Arms wrapped around me. The arms were too muscular. It wasn't Candace.

I screamed at the top of my lungs, fearful of the threat I encountered.

"Wake up, Destiny."

I pushed myself up to a sitting position. The blackness faded, and I looked around. I was in Zach's cabin. In bed. The room was bright, and he sat beside me. Sorrow and worry danced in his eyes.

"What happened?"

I wiped the sweat off my forehead.

"You were having a nightmare."

Oh dear. Not again. I thought the days of having nightmares were gone.

I dragged my fingers through my matted bun.

"I'm sorry."

"No." Zach caressed my face with his hands.

"I don't ever want to hear you apologizing to me. Ever."

He was so caring. Attentive. Selflessness.

"Were you dreaming of Candace?"

"Yes."

Closing my eyes, I was back in the nightmare, surrounded by darkness. I snapped my eyes back open.

"She called for me. I tried to find her, but I couldn't, no matter how hard I searched."

Zach dropped his eyes. He didn't know what to say to me.

"I miss her so much." I gasped.

Tears fell from my eyes.

"I know. I know." Zach rubbed my face. "I know you miss her."

"It feels like forever since I last had a conversation with her," I muttered between tears.

Zach released my face and wrapped his arms around me. His arms were warm, strong, and comforting.

"Why did this happen to her? Why didn't they shoot me instead?"

"No. Don't ever say that."

I looked at Zach through my tears. He had a serious, stern look in his eyes.

"I don't ever want to hear you say that again."

I stared into his eyes. He was serious.

"You matter. Your life matters just as much as everyone else's does."

"But..." I began.

He placed his finger on my lips. The move

was subtle and sweet. "No buts." He looked at his phone. "I want you to get some more sleep."

I hadn't slept well. No matter how hard I tried, my mind wouldn't rest. Candace crowded my mind. Maybe that's why I had the nightmare.

"Okay."

Zach kissed my forehead before I turned onto my side and closed my eyes. I gasped when Candace's face swam into my view.

"You're okay."

Zach wrapped his arms around me.

Closing my eyes, I drifted off to sleep.

***

The sweet smell of coffee pulled me from my sleep. My eyes fluttered open. The natural lighting from outside brightened the room.

Turning over in bed, I snuggled under the covers. What did I want more? Coffee or more sleep? The answer would be a lot harder if Zach's arms were still wrapped around me.

Pushing the cover off me, I decided on a delicious cup of coffee.

After I handled my hygiene, I walked into the dining room. Mid-sip with his coffee, he looked at me.

"Good morning, sleepyhead."

"Good morning."

Walking over to the cupboard, I grabbed a cup.

"Thank you for last night …"

I paused. Was it last night? Or early morning?

"Or this morning."

"You don't have to thank me, Destiny."

Grabbing the coffee pot, I poured coffee into my cup.

"I have to."

After I poured milk into my cup, I spooned sugar into my coffee.

Looking over my shoulder, I caught Zach staring at me. His eyes were full of something magical. It wasn't lust. Was it love?

"No, you don't."

Stirring my coffee, I took a careful sip. It was perfect. I sat across from Zach.

"How did you sleep?"

"Great actually." He winked. "My cuddle buddy is the best."

I beamed.

"She can't be that great if she's waking you up with screams."

Zach shrugged.

"I don't mind. I'm just glad I'm able to comfort her when necessary."

I honestly didn't know what I'd do if I didn't have his comfort.

"Have there been any updates yet?"

Zach sipped his coffee.

"I received some news from Trevor this morning."

My ears perked up.

"It's somewhat of a break in the case."

I placed my hand over my chest. Would I find out who murdered Candace? Was it someone we knew? Was it a stranger? Would I be able to handle this information?

"Did you find out who murdered Candace?"

Zach shook his head.

"We don't know that yet, but we received Candace's phone records."

Phone records? That would give us an insight into who she had been in communication with. Right?

"What did you find out?"

He told me this for a reason. He wouldn't have brought it up if we weren't closer to finding the identity of the monster that ruined so many lives.

Zach sipped his coffee. He cleared his throat.

"Were you aware of Candace communicating with anyone?"

I sat back, shocked. "No." I paused. "I told you that when you interrogated me."

"I know, I know." Zach held his hands out. "I'm not accusing you of withholding information."

Maybe this conversation should've been had after my first cup of coffee. Or third. I needed to bring up the case after caffeine fueled me.

"What are you saying?"

Sipping my coffee, I cradled my cup.

Zach rubbed the stubble on his chin.

"Candace was talking to someone before she was murdered."

"What do you mean talking?"

She had friends besides me. She communicated with her coworkers through text if someone couldn't make their shift or if they would be late.

He pressed his lips together.

"She was romantically involved with someone."

My desire for my coffee disappeared. I placed my cup on the table, then put my face in my hands, shell-shocked. Candace was romantically involved with someone? How long was this going on? How did she keep someone a secret from me? We told each other everything. Or so I thought.

"How long has this been going on?"

"At least six months."

Candace talked to someone for at least six months? How did I have no knowledge of this?

"Are you sure?"

I knew what he said was true. He had no reason to lie to me, but I needed his reassurance. I wanted him to be wrong.

"Yes. I'm sure."

Fumbling my hands in my lap, I looked at the fridge.

"How do we have text messages, but we don't have an identity?"

"This person has been communicating using a texting application that can be downloaded on your mobile device."

This person was smart. Or secretive. They communicated off a phone number that wasn't connected to them for a reason. What were they hiding?

We received such an overload of information but were missing the biggest part of the puzzle. Who was behind the texting app?

I opened my mouth to respond, but Zach continued to talk.

"We will contact the texting app once we have a warrant." Zach paused. He looked into my eyes. "We have to wait again, but the wait shouldn't be much longer."

"Do you think the person on the other end of that texting app is the same person that called me from Candace's phone?"

"Yes." He nodded. "I'm almost positive it'll be the same person."

Grabbing my cup of coffee, I walked it over to the sink.

"Is there something wrong with the coffee?"

"No." I looked over my shoulder at Zach. "I just don't want it anymore."

As I poured it into the sink, I watched the light brown liquid travel down the drain before I turned the water on.

"Destiny."

Zach exhaled.

"Yes?"

Turning around, I leaned against the kitchen sink.

He stood and approached me, towering so tall that I had to crane my neck to look at him.

"I have never seen you pour out your coffee. It's your favorite."

"I know," I answered.

He grabbed my hands and stepped closer, only a few inches between us. His cologne invaded my nose, relaxing me.

"This is why I don't usually bring up the case first thing in the morning."

I opened my mouth to respond but decided against it.

"Any time we discuss the case, you shut down," he observed.

"This whole case makes me sad."

Zach caressed my face. The pad of his thumb rubbed against my bottom lip.

"I know it does." He paused. His eyes flickered to my lips. "It makes me sad to see you sad. You don't understand what this situation does to me."

What did he mean by that?

"No. I don't understand."

Zach's hand left my face and caressed my neck. His touch sent shivers up my spine.

"I care so much for you. I placed my life on hold to make sure you were protected properly."

My heart exploded with adoration.

His hand traveled from my neck back to my face.

"Nobody, and I mean nobody, could protect you better than I can."

Did he say what I think he just said? Was he going to tell me something I had felt, but was too afraid to admit? Even too afraid to admit to myself?

"I haven't felt this way for anyone. Ever."

"What are you trying to say?" I asked.

I needed to hear him say it.

"I love you, Destiny. I love everything about you, and I don't ever want to see you sad. I hate seeing you go through these emotions every time there's an update. I just want this case to be solved to help you heal. I know it will take some time for you to heal, but I'm willing to put in the time and effort to help you do just that. You've made me want to become a better person. You've made me want to love again. I never thought the day would come when I would say that I love someone again, but I love you, Destiny. I love you so damn much."

Zach's lips crashed onto mine before I completely processed what he said. He said he loved me. I wasn't crazy to feel these feelings. I wasn't crazy to feel this way at all.

"I love you too," I said in between kisses.

Zach wrapped his arms around me. He held me tight.

"I promise, I'm doing everything in my power to protect you. I'm doing everything in my power to bring justice for Candace."

Tears fell from my eyes. They were a mix of happy and sad tears. They were happy since I had someone that loved me. They were sad since my best friend had to die for me to find it.

"Thank you."

Zach held me out at arm's length.

"If you thank me one more time," he said as he smirked.

He kissed my salty tears away.

"This might be informal to ask and at the worst time imaginable, but I can't wait any longer."

"What is it?"

He drew me closer to him. He rubbed his thumb across my lips again.

"Will you be my girlfriend?"

Butterflies fluttered in my stomach. I was on top of the world. I felt like I was in high school all over again. Giddy, about the young man that I wanted to come up to me and ask me on a date. I always imagined the first date would be at a movie theater or grabbing an ice cream cone.

In this situation, I fell in love with my protector after he moved me into his one-bedroom cabin. We shared a bed before we ever went on our first date. He held me in his arms while I had horrible nightmares and cried my eyes out. He was my savior. I couldn't expect any more from anyone else.

"I thought you'd never ask."

Chapter Nineteen

Destiny

"Mom."

Turning around, I looked over my shoulder at Zach. He stood on the porch of the cabin, watching me. He gave me some space to make a quick call to my parents.

"It's so wonderful to hear your voice."

"It's great to hear your voice, Destiny. How have you been doing? Where are you right now?"

There were some things I couldn't talk to my

mom about. I had discussed those things with Zach before I made the call. For both of our protections, I could only answer one of her questions.

"I've been okay. I just miss you so much."

It had been some time since I last called, but I had to do what was best for all of us to stay safe. Safety first, no matter how much it hurts not to be in constant communication.

"I miss you too." There was a pause. "Have you heard yet?"

"Heard what?"

I was out of the loop with the outside world.

"Candace's funeral will be held next week on Friday."

Funeral. Candace. I never thought those two words would go together in a sentence for at least another seventy or eighty years.

A lump formed in my throat. I tried to swallow it down before I spoke. Turning around, I looked at Zach.

"Where will the funeral be held?"

Zach's eyes widened. He placed his hand on his hip and looked off into the distance.

"California. Her parents are flying in from Argentina later this week."

"Are you and Dad going?" I asked.

On one hand, I wanted them to come and visit. I knew I could convince Zach to go to the funeral if my parents were there.

On the other hand, I didn't want my parents in harm's way. I didn't want to be in harm's way.

"Of course. We have to pay our respects to her parents."

I switched the phone from one ear to the other.

"Will you be there, honey?"

Zach motioned with his hand that I needed to end the call. My time talking to my mother needed to come to an end. My heart sank into my stomach. It couldn't have been more than two minutes that I talked to Mom.

"I'm not sure. I'll talk to Zach, but I have to go."

Mom exhaled.

"I love you, Destiny. Thank you for calling. I hope to see you soon."

The click of the call ending rang out in my ear. Closing my eyes, I willed my tears not to fall. I didn't want to cry. That's all I did now.

"Come here, sweetheart."

Zach's voice Soothed me. He wrapped his strong arms around me, holding me tight as the tears fell.

How could I go from talking to my parents multiple times a week, conversations over thirty minutes each time, to talking to them for two or three minutes, whenever it was fit for our safety?

It was impossible for me to be okay with it. All these changes that occurred in my life, all at once were hard for me to endure.

"I miss my parents," I said.

"I know you do."

He rubbed my back so tenderly, the touch

soft, yet demanding.

I hadn't seen them in person in over six months, but I always video-chatted with them. I felt stripped of everything. I wasn't in control of the situation. The murderer was.

"My parents will be in town this week."

Zach held me close but far enough that I could look up at him.

"For the funeral?"

"Yes."

Zach grabbed my hand, and we walked up the porch steps.

"I know what you are thinking..." Zach began.

"That I need to go to my best friend's funeral," I finished for him.

"Yes, but I don't think it's a great idea."

"Zach, I don't think I have a choice," I admitted. "She's my best friend. I cannot not go to her funeral."

Zach opened the door to the cabin, and we walked inside. The outside was a tiny bit cooler inside. It was finally warming up.

"It'll only put you in danger..."

"But…" I interrupted.

"There are no buts up for discussion."

Zach took my hands, and he kissed the backs of them. The kisses sent a message directly to my heart.

"I want you safe. If you go to that funeral, I can't guarantee your safety. That's the last thing I want for you. More often than not, the murderer usually attended their victim's funeral."

"There has to be something we can do."

My mind went through a million ideas. I didn't want to be tracked. There was a huge chance the murderer wouldn't show up at the funeral. There was also a chance that the murderer would show up, but we couldn't be sure of anything.

"There will be plenty of people at the funeral. We'll be safe while we are there."

"You'll be safe there. The thing I have to worry about is if you'll be safe once we leave. If this person is trying to hurt you down, they won't do it in a crowd of people." Zach squeezed my hand. "They hurt Candace when it was just the two of you outside. That's how they'll try to hurt you. When there are no witnesses around."

We walked over to the couch and sat. Zach wrapped his arm around my shoulder. Placing my hand on his knee, I gave it a squeeze. We had been official for two days, and I loved every second of it. How was he more affectionate now than before? I couldn't have asked for a better man to call my boyfriend.

"I have to admit, I'm frightened to go."

I looked around the cabin. It was perfect in its own way. It was my new home by default, but I had grown to love everything about it.

"I'm content with being in this cabin with you, but I have to pay respect to my best friend and her family. How can we go about doing this in the safest way possible?"

Zach stayed quiet for a few moments.

"I can call in a favor. Considering the manner

of the situation, I'm sure I can have the funeral crawling with police officers."

"If you could make that happen, I think it'll be safe for everyone present."

"I swear if I didn't love you…"

He kissed my forehead before he stood and walked out of the cabin to make a call.

***

"I don't know if I can do this."

I gripped the door handle. My heart beat out of control. Tears burned the back of my eyes.

"Destiny, you can do this," Zach encouraged me from my left.

We were in the church parking lot where Candace's funeral would be held. We were thirty minutes early. As arranged, the church parking lot crawled with armed police officers.

Could I really? I never thought the day would come when I'd have to bury my best friend. She was twenty-four years old, way too young not to be here with me. She was too young not to be living her life.

Now, we had to celebrate her life. The short time she was here on this earth, she made a difference in a lot of people's lives. I could tell with how packed the parking lot was.

"Are you ready to do this?"

I looked out the passenger window. People of all ages littered the parking lot, from babies who couldn't walk or talk to older people who needed a walker to get around. Some faces were familiar from middle and high school. Some faces

I had never seen before. Candace knew a lot of people through her job and the friendships she made in school.

"Let's do this."

Zach got out of the truck. He looked amazing in his black suit and black loafers. His hair was pulled back into a tight, low ponytail, and he wore black sunglasses. He walked around to my side of the truck and opened the door. He held his hand out and helped me step out of the truck.

I wore a floor-length, long-sleeved, loose-fitting black dress with a pair of black flats. I wore my hair in a ponytail and a black, wide-brim hat.

Zach locked the truck. I wrapped my arm around him before we walked towards the church's front door. I held my head low, fearful of being noticed by too many people .

We walked into the church. The smell of fresh flowers swirled in the air. An array of flowers surrounded the silver casket, enough to supply two florist shops. A beautiful picture of Candace sat in front of the casket. She smiled brightly into the camera with no care in the world.

Her smile. I came to a stop. Zach stopped a few feet in front of me. I lifted my head to look at him. Zach's eyes softened. I couldn't go farther. I couldn't bear it.

"You can do this."

Could I really do this? I didn't feel strong enough.

Zach reached his hand out to me. Placing one foot in front of the other, I grabbed his hand

and continued to walk.

"Is that Candace's parents up there?"

Zach pointed to the right side of the church at a small group of people. Immediately, I recognized her parents' small frames.

"Yes."

We made our way over to the group. Once the people in front of us walked away, I came face to face with Candace's parents. I hadn't seen them since the Christmas before last . Their faces were solemn and wet with tears. Their eyes were red-rimmed and laced with pain.

Hugging them, I tried my hardest not to allow the tears to flow. I needed to be strong for them. They were falling apart.

Zach offered his condolences before we walked over to a church pew and sat. This was all too much. I couldn't believe I had to say goodbye to my best friend. In the worse way possible.

Zach wrapped his arm around my shoulder.

"It's going to be okay."

"Will it, though?" I asked.

Not only had Candace's parents' lives had changed, but my life had changed. No longer did I have my best friend, the person I could tell everything to. No longer did I have my roommate. I was in California all by my lonesome now.

"Destiny."

I looked up. Mom and Dad stood a few feet from me.

"Mom, Dad." I gasped.

Standing, I walked around Zach and threw

myself in their arms.

"Honey, it's so wonderful to see you," Dad said, stroking my back.

"It's been too long," Mom said as she kissed my forehead.

The tears that I tried so hard to hold inside flowed down my cheeks, and the faucet turned on full force.

"I miss you two so much."

I held onto them tight. I didn't want to let them go for fear that they'd disappear. Our reunion was necessary.

Someone cleared their throat. Separating from my parents, I grabbed their hands and held onto them tight.

We turned and looked at Zach. For a second, I forgot where we were and the occasion.

"Hello. I'm Zach, Destiny's..." Zach drifted off.

What would he say? How would he introduce himself?

"Protector," he finished off as he looked from me to my parents.

Dad spoke first. Releasing my hand, I held it out to shake Zach's hand.

"I'm Robert, Destiny's father."

Mom introduced herself next.

"I'm Angela, Destiny's mother."

Zach smiled.

"It's wonderful to put a name to the face."

Small talk was exchanged as I slipped my hands back into my parent's hands. Them being there with me at the funeral was the closest thing to being at home. Their warmth and presence just made me feel safe.

Zach looked off into the distance.

"If you'll excuse me, I need to have a word with my colleague."

Zach excused himself and we sat on the pew.

"I'm so glad you're okay," Mom said as she kissed me on the cheek.

"I know all of this must be scary for you," Dad continued.

He gave my hand a comforting squeeze.

"It is scary, but I feel protected with Zach around."

"Are you sure you don't want to come home with us?" Mom asked.

I looked at Mom. Her eyes were soft and filled with worry.

"We can get you a plane ticket right now," Dad added.

I looked at Dad. He looked happy to see me, but I could see the concern in his eyes. I could only imagine what life had been like since I called them and told them I'd be going away for a while.

No matter how much I wanted to say yes, I couldn't. I had to be strong for all of us.

Crossing my legs, I exhaled. "I have to stay here." I pursed my lips. "It's only right. I don't want to endanger you two with me being here."

"Don't say that sweetie." Mom squeezed my hand. "We can protect you at all costs."

My parents had done enough to protect me over the years. They didn't need to do it anymore.

Turning, I spotted Zach. He talked with Trevor. I turned and looked at the back of the church. Two officers stood guard. The place crawled with several officers. I could breathe easier.

Right before the service began, Zach sat beside Mom.

The service went on for an hour. We sang songs, a few people shared their experiences with Candace, and we listened to the pastor talk about Candace's wonderful soul.

There wasn't a dry eye in the church, especially from my eyes. I kept my head tucked low and went through an entire tissue pack. I should've been talking about Candace and our special friendship at that podium. Sadly, it wasn't safe for me to do so.

We all walked outside. My heart ached. Zach and I wouldn't go to the burial ground. His place consisted of getting me back to the cabin as quickly as possible.

Looking at the sky, I willed myself not to cry any more tears. I wasn't sure how my eyes weren't dried out yet.

By the end of the day, my eyes would hurt so much. I already knew they were bloodshot.

I pulled my parents into a hug.

"I love you two so much."

"We love you too, honey," Dad said.

Mom kissed my cheek.

"Call us when you get a chance."

Zach said his goodbyes before he grabbed

my hand and walked me to his truck. I kept my head low. I couldn't turn around and take another look at my parents. I just couldn't. One foot in front of the other. That's all I needed to do. That's all that I could do.

"Are you okay?" Zach asked once we were in his truck.

I looked at my lap. Honesty flowed from my lips and my heart.

"No, but one day, I will be."

Chapter Twenty

Zach

Destiny had been out of it since we buried Candace three weeks ago. She said she was okay, but she didn't tell the truth. She was there in the present, but I knew her mind was elsewhere.

When we sat down to have dinner, she would become quiet, zoned out, and stare into space. I had to repeat her name several times before she'd come to, smile, and attempt to carry on a conversation as if nothing had happened.

I wasn't sure if she was out of it because she buried her best friend or because she wasn't sure if she'd ever see her parents again. As long as Frank found a suspect, and soon, she'd be able to reunite with her family.

I refused to allow her to put her family in danger. It would be unethical for me to allow her to do that. It might've appeared selfish on my end, though.

I loved being around her. Her presence did something positive to me, but if the suspect tried to hurt Destiny that night, I knew they were doing everything in their power to track her down. She needed to be under my protection. Nobody could protect her better than me.

Destiny's nightmares came back more often than I had expected. She had more nightmares than she had peaceful nights. Whenever she woke up in the middle of the night screaming, I provided comfort until she could fall back asleep. I'd run my fingers through her hair. I'd rub her arm and wrap my arms around her waist. I'd wipe her tears away.

I did everything I could to provide comfort, and show her the love she so desperately needed from me. I hated to admit it, but I believed attending Candace's funeral caused Destiny to have a setback.

We hadn't received any more updates on who Candace had been in communication with. Once we figured out who was behind that phone number, we'd make the connection to who killed Candace. I yearned for that update. I wanted Destiny to be content.

There were two ways Destiny could be content. Bring Candace back or get justice for Candace. I could only get justice for Candace.

Destiny sat in the dining room, drawing a banquet of flowers. The vase was completed with her flawless pencil strokes. The flowers were yet to be started.

I kissed her cheek.

"That drawing is beautiful," I commented.

Destiny jumped slightly before she looked at me.

"I'm not finished yet."

I had not seen a real smile from her in weeks. I didn't want it to go away.

I sat beside her.

"Well, what you have completed already is beautiful."

She gave me a warm smile.

"You want to help me finish it?"

"No. I'll only mess it up. I'm no great artist like you."

She pursed her lips. Her sweet lips looked amazing. I wish she'd press them against mine, but I hadn't pushed the boundaries too much with her. She received all the space and time she needed from me to grieve. I was there with open arms, ready to dive back into the relationship we agreed to pursue.

"I've taught you." She winked. "You can't be

that bad."

I tucked a strand of hair behind her ear. Today, she wore her hair down. It flowed down her back and fanned her face perfectly. She looked like a goddess in the flesh.

"Are you up to do something different today?" I asked.

She sat her pencil on the table.

"Like what?"

"I have a date planned for us."

She scrunched up her eyes and hummed.

"Really?"

Was that a good really or a bad really?

"Yes. Only if you are up to getting out of the cabin."

She clapped her hands.

"Of course. It'll be nice to get out for a while."

"Awesome." I stood. "Whenever you're ready to head out, I'll be waiting."

"Wait."

Stopping in my tracks, I turned to look at her.

"Aren't you going to ask me out?"

Destiny was too cute. Her desire to be asked out on a date just showed me how loveable she was. It showed me how seriously she took this relationship. Our relationship.

"Destiny, will you go on a date with me?"

She closed her sketch pad and sat her pencil on top.

"I thought you'd never ask."

She stood and placed her hands on her hips.

"Wait. Do you know something I don't know?

I thought I wasn't supposed to be out in public."

"Nothing has changed. I want to take you fishing and I know of this private location we can visit." I pointed at her sketch pad. "Bring your sketch pad and your pencils. You'll need them."

Her face brightened.

"I'll pack what we need for the day. Meet me outside whenever you're ready."

After I packed up a cooler with food items and grabbed blankets, I left the dining room and made a beeline for the front door. I put my tennis shoes on before grabbing my gun from its holster and walked outside. The air had a touch of warmness creeping in from the sun. The perfect weather for a fishing trip.

I checked the area around the cabin. There wasn't anything hiding or lurking behind the trees or bushes. An occasional chirp from a bird perched nearby rang out.

After I placed the cooler on the back of the truck, I walked up the porch steps and the door swung open. Destiny stepped out. She wore a pair of blue leggings that hugged her curves and a black sweater. She wore her hair in a high ponytail. She carried a bag.

"You look beautiful." Grabbing her hand, I walked her down the steps. "Why did you put your hair up?"

She played with the ends of her hair. "We are going to do an intense sport." She flexed her arms, which had a small amount of muscle tone. "I have to keep my hair out of my face."

I laughed. "It's not that intense, but you'll have fun doing it."

I helped her in the truck before I got in.

"Is the location far?"

The truck roared to life. "Not at all. Maybe a ten-minute drive."

Turning the radio up, country music came through the speakers. With a hand on her knee, we drove to our location. It felt great having my girlfriend on the passenger side of my truck. My woman. This was the first ride we had done together, excluding the trip to the funeral since we entered into a relationship. We needed to celebrate this. It was a one-in-a-million chance for me to enter into another relationship. This all felt oddly amazing.

"That was a quick drive," she commented once we parked on the side of the road.

We were on a one-lane road. Thick wood lined both sides. This place was severely secluded.

"I told you it was right up the road."

Turning the truck off, we got out.

She looked around.

"Are you sure it's safe?" she asked.

"Of course. I come here often."

Looking around, the scene became familiar to me. I had come here several times a year, and I knew the place like the back of my hand.

I grabbed the cooler, fishing poles, bait, and blankets from the bed of my truck.

"Are you ready for our trek?" I asked.

"Trek?" Her eyes widened in horror. "Is it like five miles?"

I laughed.

"No. It's only half a mile."

She smirked. "That's easy." She walked a few steps ahead of me before she turned and looked at me. "Do you need help to carry anything?"

"No. I can carry it all."

This area was so discreet nobody frequented it often. Only the locals knew of it, and of all the times I've come to visit, I've only come across one other person.

"Lead the way?"

Stopping in her tracks, she motioned for me to walk ahead.

"I'd rather you lead," I commented as I walked ahead of her.

"Why? I don't know where I'm going."

"I know, but I love the view."

Destiny laughed.

"Inappropriate much?"

I shrugged.

"You love it."

We walked the path I knew by heart. We avoided tree limbs that had recently fallen and wet ground that turned into mud.

Within minutes, we walked into the clearing. It was a diamond mine tucked into a diamond rough. Green pasture surrounded the pond. The pond was calm and expansive.

"This place is beautiful," Destiny observed.

I sat the cooler, blankets, and fishing pools down.

"That's why I come here when I'm in town."

Destiny walked closer to the pond. She stood in silence.

Grabbing the blanket, I opened it. I laid it on the ground, grateful for the bright and warm sunshine that dried the ground up.

"Admiring the beauty?"

"Yes." She looked around and motioned her hands. "I'm used to the city. It's not often I have the opportunity to visit the country."

I grabbed the fishing pools and the bait.

"It doesn't seem like you've visited the country before."

She walked over to the blanket and sat her sketch pad and pencils down.

"I have, but not as often as I'd like."

I showed Destiny how to set up the fishing pool line and where to hook the bait. She squealed when I opened the container of worms and stuck them on the hooks.

I went through the motions of showing her how to move the bait before she threw the line into the water.

"How come?"

She flickered her eyes over to me. She held onto the fishing pole tight.

"How come what?"

"How come you don't visit the country?"

I wanted to know everything about the woman I had fallen in love with. From her favorite candy to her most memorable childhood memory.

"I haven't had someone who wanted to do such visits with me," she admitted.

"Well, now you do."

I thrived in the outdoors. Any outdoor activity I loved to participate in. I loved fishing, hiking, kayaking and everything in between. The cold weather wasn't for me, so I stayed inside when the cold temperatures hit , but this was the warmest day we had since the new year. We had to take advantage of it with some outdoor fun.

She looked over at me and smiled.

"It's a wonderful environment to relax in and just be creative."

I couldn't help but agree.

"Perhaps a wonderful place to finish your drawing?"

She shrugged.

"Or start another one."

I felt a slight tug on my pole but knew it wasn't anything to bring in.

"You have to finish the banquet of flowers here. You have the perfect scenery."

"Yeah, I know."

She looked at her fishing pole. Setting mine aside, I stood behind her. My favorite scent on her, berries, surrounded me. Pressing myself against her, I worked with her to reel in her catch.

"Do you think we caught something?"

Her voice bubbled with excitement and giddy. She reminded me of the first time when Jake's father took us fishing. I felt excitement and energy when I caught my first fish.

"Possibly. Go ahead and reel the line in."

We worked together with the fishing pole. Within seconds, the hook appeared, and a bluegill dangled from it.

"Oh my gosh. We caught our first fish."

She let the pole go. She turned around and jumped up and down.

"No, you caught your first fish. You did it all on your own."

Her excitement and bubbly energy rubbed off on me. I was happy for her. For this to be her first time fishing, she did great.

"I can't believe I did it on my first try."

I grabbed the fish. He squirmed in my hand.

"You want to unhook him?" I asked.

She squinched up her face.

"Heck no."

I laughed. I unhooked the fish before I tossed it back into the water.

"Are you sure you haven't fished before?"

She smiled.

"Never before."

I winked.

"You could've fooled me."

"Why?"

She bumped her hip against mine. She wiggled her eyebrows.

"Is it because I fish better than you," she taunted.

I set the fishing pole down before grabbing her hands and pulling her closer. Her breasts rested against my chest. Eyeing her luscious lips, I stared into her beautiful eyes.

"You're great, but I wouldn't say you're better than me."

She pursed her lips. "Fair enough." She kissed me softly on the lips before she turned around and faced the pond. "I'm ready to catch more fish."

We fished for another thirty minutes. Destiny caught one more fish, and I caught two.

"I can't believe I never knew how amazing fishing was," she commented once we sat on the blanket.

We sat so we faced the pond. It went right back to being calm after we finished fishing.

I rubbed her back.

"You just needed someone to show you how amazing it is."

She leaned into my side and placed her head on my shoulder.

"I wonder what else you're going to show me."

"I can show you almost anything." I kissed her temple. "I need you to show me something, though?"

"What?"

She whispered her response as she turned to look at me.

"Your lips."

Cupping her face, I kissed her. I kissed her lips with so much passion. All the passion I held at bay since we returned from the funeral poured out of me like a faucet. I didn't want this faucet to shut off.

Destiny moaned before she slipped her tongue into my mouth.

Instant hard-on. The things I wanted to do to her.

Grabbing the back of Destiny's neck, I tilted her head back. I trailed kisses from her lips to her neck and to her ear.

"Zach." She gasped.

She shivered in my grasp as her eyes fluttered close.

"Yes."

My voice was raspy. I cleared my throat.

"I want you."

My penis was pressed firmly against my jeans. Hell, I wanted her too.

"Say please," I responded.

Taking control of her mouth, I savored every inch of her lips. Oh, how I loved her lips.

Destiny pulled away slightly. Her breathing intensified, but I didn't allow us to separate. I needed her close.

"What?" she asked in between kisses.

I groped her breasts. They were soft, yet firm. I wanted to bury my face in them.

"Say please," I repeated.

Her eyes widened. "Please." She panted. "Can we do it now?"

Nobody usually came to visit, especially on a day like this. It was one of the warmer days of February, but it was still chilly. Most would view it as too cold to fish.

"Hell yes," I growled.

Layers of clothing were discarded before I removed her ponytail holder. Laying Destiny on the blanket, I admired the exposed, beautiful woman before me. Her curly hair splayed across the blanket. Her breasts rose and fell with each breath she took. Her nipples were rock hard.

Leaning down, her breasts were inches from me. Making eye contact, I flicked one with my tongue before I lightly tugged on it with my teeth. She moaned, her eyes never leaving mine.

Growling, my penis grew uncomfortable and pressed against my jeans.

I repeated the same movement with her other nipple. She moaned as I ran my fingers through her hair.

"Are you okay?"

I knew the effect I had on her. I loved driving her crazy.

"I need you inside me now," she said, barely above a whisper.

"I didn't hear you," I whispered back.

"I need you inside me now."

Standing, I unbuttoned my jeans, and pulled my jeans and boxers down. My penis sprang up, happy to be free from its restraint.

Grabbing a condom out of my pocket, I tossed my jeans onto the pile of our discarded clothes.

"You planned to have sex with me?"

"No."

Settling in between her long legs, I rubbed my hands up and down her smooth legs.

"You brought protection," she pointed out.

"I only make love to my girlfriend."

My response shocked her. She opened her mouth to say something but decided against it.

Laying on top of her, I captured her mouth. Our tongues swirled together, small pants and moans flowed from her mouth as I tangled my fingers in her curls. She clawed at my back with her fingernails, sending shivers through my body.

Settling in between her thighs, I rolled on the condom. I stuck my middle finger into her wet folds.

She bit her lip and moaned. Testosterone took over, and I plunged into her wetness. Exhaling sharply, I moaned. She clawed at my back, no doubt leaving marks.

With a rhythm in my hips, I plunged in and out of her. Her wetness, mixed with her tightness, sent me into a frenzy.

"Zach, I'm..." Destiny's eyes rolled to the back of her head as her body shook with pleasure.

I continued my rhythm before I growled and exploded.

I could add making love to my girlfriend by a pond to my small list of memorial events.

Chapter Twenty-One

Destiny

"I have a few errands to run. Do you want to come along for the ride?"

Glancing up from the sketchbook, I brought my cup of coffee to my lips and took an attentive sip. Like always, Zach made the pot of coffee.

What did my boyfriend not know how to do? He made the best coffee. He cooked tasty and healthy meals. He had amazing love-making skills. He was perfect.

"No, I'm fine."

Zach raised an eyebrow. Grabbing a paper cup, he poured coffee into it.

"Are you sure?"

"Yes." I pointed at my unfinished drawing of the vase. "I want to finish this drawing since I didn't get a chance to finish it yesterday." I paused, thinking of the romantic time we shared yesterday. "Or the day before."

After we made love by the pond, Zach held me, and we talked. We talked for hours. We watched the sun be replaced by the moon. It was the most romantic date I'd ever had. Nothing could top it.

Zach smirked.

"We have been keeping busy."

Standing, I walked over to him. I placed my arms around his neck.

"Can you promise to come back as quick as possible?"

He kissed my forehead.

"I promise to make my trip as quick as possible. Turn your phone on in case you need me."

Grabbing my phone off the end table, I powered it on.

"Don't miss me too much, okay."

"I can't promise that. I love you, Zach."

He grabbed his cup of coffee.

"I love you too."

Once Zach left, I went back to the dining room. I had to finish the banquet of flowers so I could move on to another drawing.

Grabbing my pencil, I worked on a tulip.

What had my life come to? I was in a committed relationship with my protector. I stayed in his cabin, under his constant watch. If I were on the outside looking in, everything looked great. Nobody would expect I ran from danger. Running from my best friend's murderer who had a possible vendetta against me. Running from the person that would've killed me had their gun not jammed. It was a miracle I could run away from the scene and live another day. Even if it was in a cabin located in a rural area.

Sadly, Candace didn't have that opportunity. Candace didn't share one of the most important pieces of the puzzle that could've solved the entire case. Who she talked to for at least six months.

I couldn't believe it. We made a promise back in high school that we'd always share everything with each other.

"Girl."

I looked up from my fruit cup. Candace stood across the table, directly in front of me. She wore a blue dress that stopped mid-thigh and her famous black-heeled boots. Her hands were perched on her hips.

Looking around, I was in a crowded cafeteria, full of hungry students and chatter. I sat at a table with other ninth graders. It was only the second week of school, so the freshmen generally stuck together.

"Yes?"

"I've been looking all over for you."

She sat across from me.

"You've found me." Grabbing my water bottle, I took a sip. "What's up?"

"Oh, nothing." She grabbed a salad out of her backpack and opened it. "I just wanted to have lunch with you today."

"Your lunch isn't during this period today," I observed.

She shrugged.

"Well, it is today."

I laughed. Grabbing my ham sandwich, I took a bite.

"What class did you skip?"

She added dressing to her salad.

"Algebra."

I raised my eyebrow.

"Isn't that your favorite class?"

"Hell no." She forked salad into her mouth. "Try least favorite." She looked around the cafeteria. She stared in a direction for a second too long.

I looked in that direction. There was a table of junior and senior boys.

"What's going on?" I asked her.

She wound a piece of hair around her finger. "Uh, nothing."

I gave her a pointed look.

"Something's going on."

"How do you know?"

"You're glowing," I observed.

We hadn't known each other long, only for two weeks, and I already knew her like the back of my hand.

Her cheeks turned a rosy red before she busted at the seams.

"You're right. Something is going on."

"Well, spill the details."

She looked from her left and right before she leaned in closer. She cupped her hands over her mouth.

"I have a crush on someone."

My ears perked up. Candace had some juicy news. "Who?"

She flicked her eyes back over to the table.

"You see that hot brunette?"

I looked at the table. There were two attractive brunettes at the table. One wore a black shirt, and one wore a team's jersey.

"Which one?"

Candace smiled.

"The one in the jersey."

I squinted my eyes, analyzing him.

"Luke?"

She looked at me. She threw her hand over her heart.

"You know him?"

"Yeah." I ate more fruit. "We have journalism together."

Her eyes widened. "Journalism?"

"Yeah."

Journalism was one of my favorite classes. I could fully express myself in words with no judgment. Nothing in the world was better than that.

"Wow."

Her one-word response threw me for a loop.

"Why are you so surprised?"

She stabbed her fork into a tomato.

"I'd never imagine he would take that class. He doesn't seem like the type," she pointed out.

"You'd be surprised what you learn from someone. If you just take the time to talk and get to know someone."

"Yeah, you're right," she agreed. She opened her juice and took a sip. "I want to know everything about him."

I finished my fruit cup and set it aside. A group of girls walked by, talking animatedly.

"Well, how do you expect that to happen?"

She winked at me.

"Grab his attention and hope he makes the first move."

"Do you have a crush on anyone?" she asked.

I looked around the cafeteria. There was a sea of new faces. Obviously, there were a lot of attractive faces that I would do a double take on, but no one stood out to me that I wanted to get to know on a personal level.

"No."

Candace leaned closer.

"Come on, there has to be someone you have a crush on."

I shook my head.

"Not at all."

"Would you tell me if you did?"

"Of course." I thought for a second. "You want to make a vow?"

She raised her eyebrows. She folded her arms across her chest.

"What kind of vow?"

I sipped my water.

"We vow to always share everything with each other, no matter what."

She smiled.

"Hell, yes."

We locked hands.

"Best friends for life," we recited together.

I held up my end of the bargain. I told her literally everything you could think of from my one-night stands, both the horrible ones that left me sexually frustrated and the ones that made my toes curl. I told her how, up until the age of ten, I slept with a night light and my stuffed animal tiger.

Why hadn't she? Why did Candace feel the need to keep this relationship a secret? Did she think I would judge her? Did she think I wouldn't support her? There had to be something more to this relationship. Even though Candace didn't feel the need to include me in her personal life, I still loved her.

Candace's murderer had to have known her. No longer did I believe that this was a random act of violence. They had to have been the person she was in contact with or someone who had a close relationship with the person she had been in contact with.

It could've been anyone, though. A man she had a conversation with at work as she served his third drink for the night. A woman who might've seen Candace's sweet nature come off as flirtatious to her boyfriend or husband. Her ex-boyfriend who didn't like how things ended. It could've been a multitude of people.

Taking a sip of my coffee, it was cold.

I looked at the time on the stove. Forty-five minutes had passed since Zach had left. Had I daydreamed the entire time he was gone?

Wondering out the dining room and towards the front door of the cabin, I peeked outside. I couldn't see Zach's truck. He should be here any second, though.

A sense of bravery washed over me, and I stepped outside. The fresh air filled my lungs and I smiled. There was something special about stepping outside after being inside for an extended period of time. It was refreshing.

Walking down the steps, I came to a halt. My hands became clammy as a set of blue eyes danced over my face. A smile touched his lips.

A man in his early thirties stood in the front yard next door. He stood tall and was rather lanky. His eyes were planted on me.

Who was he?

He waved.

"Hello."

Where did he come from?

Did I speak? Did I ignore him? Everything in me told me to run back into the cabin, but my feet. They were heavy. They were planted. Why were they planted?

Is he the person I saw the other night pass by the window? Zach didn't inform me that we had neighbors next door. Did Zach know about this neighbor?

"Hello," I responded. I had no other choice but to speak.

Candace's perfect match stood in front of the cabin next door. From his tallness to his boyish smile. In Candace's mind, looks took priority, personality was last. He matched what she would go after. He pointed at me.

"Are you my new next-door neighbor?" he asked.

I nodded. No words came to mind.

He walked towards me.

"I'd like to formally introduce myself."

This didn't feel right. Taking a step back, I spun around as quickly as humanly possible. Taking the steps in long strides, I disappeared into the cabin. Slamming the door, I locked it and ran to the bedroom.

Sliding to the ground, tears blurred my vision.

Who was that? Was he a local? Or was he here with a vendetta? Perhaps, a vendetta against me.

I shouldn't have gone outside. It wasn't safe for me to do so. I should've known better. Gosh, what was wrong with me?

Zach. I needed Zach. Dialing Zach's phone number, I pressed the phone against my face. Silently counting to myself, I willed him to answer. I cursed under my breath when the call went to voicemail.

Where's Zach? I needed him. He said to call him if I needed him. Why didn't he answer?

I had to do something. I didn't need to wallow in my misery. I've done more than enough of that.

Art. That's what I needed.

Walking through the living room, I glanced once more at the front door before I made a beeline for the dining room. It was locked as tight as a drum. Good.

Looking down at my drawing, I had finished my tulip and had started on a rose. I should've been done with this drawing by now.

Placing my head in my hands, I exhaled. Candace had been on my mind lately. She nearly consumed my mind. There was nothing wrong with that. Was it?

The man outside didn't help my anxiety, though. Why was he freakishly similar to what Candace found attractive? Was he the man behind the call? Was he the streak I saw weeks ago?

Candace. I missed her. I grieved for her and her life, but I felt like I had no time to let my mind relax and rest.

I washed my coffee down the sink before I grabbed my sketch pad and pencils. I needed a change of scenery to finish this drawing and relax without feeling my head exploding.

I sat on the couch, sitting crisscross applesauce. Channeling my inner artist, my drawing went from incomplete to completely drawn.

I sat back and analyzed my work. It would be perfect once I shaded everything in.

Two buzzes drew my attention from picking out the perfect shade of blue to color my vase.

Looking at the edge of the coffee table, I noticed Zach's phone, face up. The screen was lit up.

That's why he didn't answer my call. He didn't have his phone. How did he leave his phone?

Scooting to the other side of the couch, I grabbed it.

Francesca: Hey, hot stuff.

The first message read. My heartbeat quickened.

Francesca: When can we do another round? I'm hot for you. Text me back soon, I need you.

Who was Francesca? Why did she text Zach? Did he lie about having a girlfriend? Was I that naïve to think a man of Zach's stature was single and available?

He was literally the perfect package. A respectful man of the community, and he had an amazing heart.

My stomach turned. My coffee threatened to make an appearance. Pushing myself back on the couch, I closed my eyes. I stuffed my face into my hands. Was this really happening to me?

There had to be some type of explanation for these messages.

Keys jingled in the door.

I'd get an explanation a lot quicker than I planned.

Zach walked in carrying a big paper bag full of groceries. He closed the door with his foot before he turned around.

"Hey, I'm back." He kicked his shoes off before he kissed my forehead. "Are you okay? You looked freaked."

Pointing towards the cabin next door with a shaky finger, I said "I met your neighbor."

Zach's face scrunched up. "What neighbor?"

I thought that was the end of his questions until he continued with more.

"Wait, did someone come over here? I told you not to open the door for anyone."

"I went outside."

Zach fumed.

"Why did you go outside? You have no reason to go outside. It's not safe, especially when I'm not here."

He disappeared into the dining room.

Why did I do it? I thought he would've been back by then, but I knew it wouldn't make a difference. I did something stupid.

He walked into the living room and made a beeline for the front door. His eyebrows were furrowed.

"I'll be back. Stay inside."

Zach wasn't outside for more than five

minutes before he walked into the cabin.

"Did you find him?"

"No. I went next door and knocked, but nobody answered."

Woah.

Who was he? Was he the streak that I saw a few weeks ago? Here one second, gone the next?

"Where did he go?

He shrugged.

"I don't know. I wasn't under the impression anybody lived next door."

What was going on?

"Are you sure he came from the cabin?"

At this point, I wasn't sure of anything.

"I-I don't know."

Staring into my eyes, he approached me. He caressed my face, nearly sending a calm feeling over me.

"Listen to me. I don't know who you saw, but they will not hurt you. Do you understand me?"

Everything in me wanted to say yes, but I couldn't bring myself to say anything. So, I didn't say anything.

"I'll keep an eye out for this neighbor. Nobody, and I mean nobody, is going to hurt you."

Zach kissed my forehead before he led me to the couch.

One burden lifted off my chest, but another one lingered.

"Did you miss me?"

"Well, that depends."

He squeezed my hands before we sat.

"Is there something wrong?"

I pointed at his phone on the end table.

Leaning forward, he grabbed it. "I knew I left my phone here." He laughed. "It's usually attached to my hip. Did Trevor call with an update?"

"No."

I was short and to the point.

Zach turned the screen on, and he scrunched his eyes.

"Did you..." he left the question hanging as he looked over at me.

"Yes."

"I can explain..." he began.

I held my hand out, stopping his speech. "There's no need to." I stood, willing myself to continue talking. "You didn't have to lie to me about having a girlfriend."

Zach stood. He reached to grab my hand, and I moved out of his grasp.

"You've got it all wrong, Destiny."

I folded my arms across my chest. What could I have misunderstood from those messages?

"How?"

Zach exhaled.

"It's kind of embarrassing to admit."

I tapped my foot on the floor.

"I don't judge."

Zach motioned with his hand for me to sit. After some thought, we sat together.

I stayed quiet. He had the floor.

"Francesca is one of my one-night stands." He paused. "Well, was." He reached for my hand. This time, I didn't pull away. I listened with an open heart and an open mind. "Other than sex, there's no relationship there."

"One of your one-night stands?"

How many one-night stands did he have?

"Yes. When Charlotte hurt me, I vowed to never date again. I have had quite a few one-night stands over the years. When I say quite a few, I can't even give you an exact amount because I've lost count."

This man was truly damaged. More damaged than I originally thought.

"I hit up some casual one-night stands when I have the urge. We do the deed, and we go on about our business, no strings attached."

I squeezed his hand comfortingly.

"Francesca was someone I had fun with." He exhaled, looking into my eyes. "Ever since I looked at you, you're the only woman I want." He paused. "Mentally, emotionally, sexually. I want all of you."

"I want you too."

Zach wrapped his arm around my waist, and he kissed me. He kissed my heart and my soul with his words. He kissed me like his life depended on it.

"I've had my fair share of one-night stands as well," I whispered against his lips. There was no reason not to share when he shared so much with me already. "I've done the same in my past. You have no reason to be embarrassed."

We pressed our foreheads together and stared into each other's eyes.

"If this is what being in love feels like, I don't want this feeling to ever go away."

Never in a million years did I think a man would ever voice those words to me. Never in a million years did I think I'd ever be in love. I never knew what being in love felt like. Nobody else but Zach made me fall head over heels. The feeling was so comforting, yet foreign at the same time.

"Me either."

I laid my head on his chest. His heartbeat was music to my ears, such a beautiful melody I could listen to on repeat for an eternity.

"I'm glad I found you," I said.

"We found each other," he responded back.

Chapter Twenty-Two

Zach

Was Destiny sent from Heaven above, specifically for me?

She understood me. She understood everything about me. She didn't judge. That's the most I could ever ask of her. No judgments, just love. I hated we were brought together under these terrible circumstances, but we had each other now. I had the opportunity to help Destiny heal, and that's what I intended to do. Even if it took every fiber of my being.

I ran my fingers through Destiny's hair before I kissed her forehead. Falling asleep with her in my arms every night was a dream. The dream I never imagined for myself but was forever grateful for.

A moan escaped from her lips as she turned over and pressed her butt against my groin. She was in a deep sleep. Thank goodness she slept through the night last night. It was the first night of many.

Slowly easing out of bed, I was careful not to wake her up. She deserved uninterrupted sleep.

Walking into the bathroom, I stared at myself in the mirror. I had a severe case of bedhead, my hair frizzy and messy from the night's events. I pulled my hair into a low ponytail and handled my hygiene before I went into the dining room and put on a pot of coffee.

The machine came to life and filled the dining room with the smell of coffee. What would I ever do without a fresh cup of coffee every morning?

After adding creamer to my coffee, I sat at the dining room table. I checked the time before I dialed Trevor's number. We hadn't heard any updates, and I would love to give Destiny some positive news when she woke up. Her receiving that call from Candace's phone and seeing streaks outside the window got the best of her. Fingers crossed, we'd know soon enough who Candace communicated with so an arrest could be made.

The phone rang four times before it went to voicemail. I hung up the phone and exhaled. Trevor would call me back when he had a chance. He had to busy. There was only a handful of us in our police department. Trevor helped all of us as much as he could. He strived to become a detective one day. With his hard work and dedication, I knew it would happen.

Destiny's and my relationship progressed well. We went from awkward roommates who second-guessed every word spoken to lovers.

I finally understood how Jake, my best friend, felt. He had a wife and two children to love and protect. I had a girlfriend that I loved, and I needed to protect her with all my being.

Jake contacted me last week. Over the past two months, I wasn't in contact as often as I should have been. Even though Destiny needed protection, I also needed to limit my contact with the outside world. As soon as this passed over and Candace's murder was behind bars, we would come out of hiding, and I'd show the entire world the amazing woman that I called mine. The amazing woman for whom I fell head over heels.

For now, our location and our relationship had to be kept a secret. On the outside looking in, nothing looked normal about a protector in love with the woman he protected. I saw no reason to further complicate things.

Should I call Frank? Would that throw him off? I shouldn't know anything about the case. I shouldn't even care about the case. Technically,

I lost all responsibilities to the case when I requested FMLA. I had requested an extension on my FMLA last week since this case took longer than I expected and I received another month. Hopefully, everything would be solved before my FMLA was up. I hated not knowing anything. Calling Frank would be the worst idea I could come up with. He'd wonder why I was curious, and we needed to avoid any type of questions.

Taking a sip of my coffee, I winced. My coffee was damn good, but it was hot. It needed to cool down.

Once Candace woke, I knew she'd ask for an update. I had nothing to give her, but I could give her something to look forward to. Perhaps we could hangout and do something fun together. No matter where we were, the time we spent together was important.

Being around Destiny these past two months, I'd learned two things. Life was too short not to take risks and go after what I wanted. So many things that were out of my control held me back for so long, such as my dad leaving and Charlotte cheating. Allowing that weight to lift off my shoulders allowed me to love myself better. Two, I finally knew what I wanted. I wanted someone to love me just as much as I loved them. I found that in Destiny. My sweet, sweet Destiny.

Finally, I knew what we would do today. I knew Destiny would love it. I just needed a bit of help from my mom.

I dialed my mom's phone as I sipped my

coffee. As always, she answered on the first ring.

"My wonderful son is calling me," Mom called into the phone.

Her excitement to talk to me always warmed my insides. She was always cheerful, no matter what. Her world could be falling apart, and she still had a smile on her face.

"Hello, Mom."

Sitting back, I crossed my legs.

"How are you doing?"

Shuffling sounded on her end.

"I'm great, and you?"

"Fantastic."

My words couldn't be truer.

More shuffling sounded.

"Mom, what are you doing?"

"I'm doing a quick walk on my treadmill."

My mom somewhat developed into a health nut in her older years. When it came to grocery shopping, she tended to stay in the meat and produce section. Very seldom did she stray and eat or drink something that was processed except for coffee. She couldn't go without a cup a day.

"Define quick."

"Forty-five minutes."

I laughed. Mom's definition of quick was the opposite of my definition.

"When you finish up your workout, can you help me out with something?"

Beeping sounded before she exhaled.

"I can help you now." She paused. "What can I do for you?"

After I explained what I needed from Mom, we got off the phone. In a few minutes, what I requested would come to my phone.

Once I finished my coffee, I placed my cup in the dishwasher and walked into the living room. At the same time, Destiny walked out of the bathroom. She wiped her eyes before she smiled.

"Good morning, sweetheart."

Her smile. That was the second thing I needed to complete my morning.

"Good morning."

Walking over to her, I wrapped my arms around her waist. I ran my fingers through her messy ponytail. I loved it when she was in my arms. I felt complete and at home.

"How long have you been up?" She looked around me for a moment before she looked at me. "I woke up to an empty bed, and I was disappointed."

Cupping her face, I admired her beauty. "I've been up an hour." Dipping my head, I kissed her. "I have something for us to do today."

She smiled against my lips.

"What is that?"

"It's a surprise."

She dragged her finger across my jawline.

"I'm starting to love surprises."

I loved her touch. "I'm glad you do."

"Did I tell you how amazing you look?"

Looking down at her pajamas, she laughed. "I'm only wearing pajamas."

"You look amazing in anything." I held her

outstretched in my arms. "You look amazing in nothing as well."

She swatted at my arm as a text message sounded on my phone.

"I'll be ready in thirty minutes."

I checked my messages.

"Perfect, that'll give me time to run to the store."

Before she walked into the bedroom, she turned and looked at me.

"Don't be too long. I'll miss you."

Why did statements as such turn me on? There was nothing sexual about what she said, yet something about her wanting me around did something to me.

"I won't be."

Withdrawing my gun from my holster, I walked out the door and walked around the perimeter of the cabin. Destiny was mine. I had to do everything in my power to protect her. Nobody would touch her. Nobody would lay a hand on her.

Driving to the closest drug store, I picked up all the ingredients we needed for our date. I waved goodbye to the store associate before I drove back to my cabin.

"Sweetheart, I'm back."

She walked out of the dining room with a cup of coffee. She pointed at her cup.

"If I haven't told you before, you make the best coffee."

I kissed her forehead.

"You've only told me a million times," I commented.

Walking into the dining room, I placed the groceries on the counter.

"I'm sure I'll tell you a million times more."

She placed her coffee on the counter and leaned her hip against the counter. She wore a pair of jeans and a long-sleeved shirt. She looked fantastic in those jeans. I swore they were made for her.

"Are you ready to bake?"

She raised an eyebrow.

"Bake? Bake what?"

I rubbed my hands together.

"Homemade chocolate chip cookies."

Her mouth dropped open. She covered her mouth, her eyes full of excitement.

"That's my favorite dessert."

I smiled, glad of my thoughtfulness.

"How did I guess that?"

I grabbed the ingredients out of the bags. Destiny finished off her coffee before she placed her cup in the dishwasher.

"You must have the ability to read people."

I shrugged.

"Or you might've told me before."

She had told me so many things, and I remembered every detail. Like how I slept with a night light and my stuffed animal tiger until the age of ten. She thought it was embarrassing, but I thought it was adorable. What could I say, I was obsessed.

"I'm glad you listened," she commented as she went into a cabinet and grabbed a bowl.

"I listen to everything you tell me. Everything you tell me is important."

She looked at me before she grabbed a mixing spoon out of the drawer.

No matter how big or small the detail, he cared. Nobody else in this world cared enough to listen to me, even when I babbled about nothing.

"Really?"

"Yes." Unlocking my phone, I pulled up the recipe. "Are you ready to bake?"

She smiled brightly.

"I was born ready."

As we measured out all the ingredients we needed to make the cookies, Destiny tossed a chocolate chip into my mouth after I drew two flour hearts on her cheeks.

"Is this your mom's cookie recipe?" she asked once we placed all the dry ingredients into a bowl.

"No, my grandmother's." I tossed a chocolate chip into my mouth. "It's a sacred recipe, no one besides my mother and I could have it."

She gasped.

"You must feel special."

"I do," I agreed. "I love my grandma with all of my heart."

She mixed the dry ingredients so they were combined.

"Is she still alive?"

"No. She passed away from a heart attack

when I was eleven years old. She's the reason I have this cabin. She left it for me."

Her death still bothered me to this day. My grandmother and I were so close. That's why my mother became a health nut. She feared she would have the same health conditions as my grandmother and wanted to get a jumpstart on turning her physical health around.

She placed a hand on my shoulder.

"I'm sorry to hear that she passed away, but she left you a wonderful cabin."

I smiled my appreciation.

She grabbed two eggs out of its carton.

"You said this is a sacred recipe?"

"Yes."

"How come you are sharing it with me then?"

I looked into her eyes.

"My grandmother always said, 'Share this recipe with the one you love and see yourself spending the rest of your life with'."

Her eyes softened. She opened her mouth to say something but closed it. I loved those reactions when she was so shocked about what I said that she wasn't sure what to say so she didn't say anything at all.

"My grandmother would've loved you had she had the opportunity to meet you."

Her face brightened and blossomed with love.

"Really?"

"Of course."

Any woman who can change my mind about

certain life choices would be loved by my grandmother.

"It's time to add in the wet ingredients."

We put all the ingredients together in one bowl, and we mixed it. The delicious smell of homemade cookie dough swirled in the air.

"It smells so wonderful in here," Destiny commented.

"It tastes even better."

Placing a dozen of cookies on a cookie sheet, we slipped it into the preheated oven.

"I don't think I can wait until after lunch to have a taste."

I placed my hands on her hips.

"You don't have to wait."

She chuckled, her teeth on full display.

"I referred to the cookies."

"You don't have to wait until after lunch to eat a cookie. I hope I don't have to wait much longer for a kiss."

She bit the corner of her lip as she wiggled her eyebrows.

"You don't."

She snaked her arms around my neck. Her soft lips touched mine, giving me an instant boner. She slipped her tongue into my mouth, sending me into a frenzy.

Slipping my hands under her butt, I lifted her with ease. I placed her on the countertop, and I stood between her legs.

Brushing my hand against her inner thigh, I cupped her face. She was too irresistible for words. I loved her dark skin, her melatonin speaking bold words. No other woman on this earth could compare to her beauty. No other woman on this planet was more perfect for me.

"Did you know making cookies would result in a make-out session?" I whispered against her lips. My forehead was pressed against hers as we stared into each other's eyes.

"No." She gave me a feather-soft kiss. "I'm glad it did, though."

Grabbing a fistful of her ponytail, our kiss deepened. Her lips. Her taste. Her soul. It was everything I desired. I was obsessed with her. Nothing could be done about it.

She moaned against my lips. It took everything in me not to rip her clothes off and bend her over the dining room table. The way I wanted to be inside her. She was too irresistible.

Her fingernails scratched at my back, giving me goosebumps all over.

"Do you want me?" she whispered into my ear.

Her tongue touched my earlobe, seeding tingles down my spine.

Pulling away, I looked at her. Her eyes were hooded with lust and hunger.

"Hell yes," I grunted.

She smiled before she touched my nose.

"Well, you can't have me."

Wait. What? What did she say? Did I hear her correctly?

"What?"

She smiled devilishly.

"You can't have me until I get a cookie."

I looked at the time on the cookies. There were five minutes left of baking time. They still had to cool for a few minutes.

"That's so far away," I groaned.

She shrugged.

"That's only ten minutes," she pointed out.

Only ten minutes? Did she not know what she did to me? Mentally? Emotionally? Sexually? One minute compared to a lifetime when it came to Destiny. Could you imagine what ten minutes would do to me?

Peppering kisses along her neck, her scent pulled me in. I dove back in for her mouth, her neck not satisfying my needs. Exploring her mouth with my tongue, I tasted every inch of her. Why did she taste so amazing?

The oven beeped.

Destiny pushed me away and jumped from the counter.

"Don't forget oven mitts."

She looked over her shoulder before she grabbed the fall-themed mitts.

"I was so excited, I almost forgot."

She placed the cookies on the stove. The smell was delightful.

Once the cookies cooled and formed slightly, we moved them onto a cooling sheet.

"I can't wait any longer," she called out before she grabbed a cookie and took a bite.

Her eyes rolled to the back of her head, and

she let out of a moan.
"How does it taste?"
She gave me a thumbs up.
"It's the best cookie I've ever had."
I smiled.
"I knew you'd say that."

Chapter Twenty-Three

Destiny

It was finally time. I was ready. The image I had in my memory over the years would suffice for the picture I'd sketch. Or I could use the obituary tucked away in the corner drawer beside my side of the bed in the bedroom.

Candace looked beautiful and radiant, a twinkle in her eyes. I missed that twinkle. I missed the smart remarks she used to give when she felt sassy and I missed that smile that could melt away any anger that could be felt within a second.

I had to start with her eyes. Everyone took notice to her eyes. They were bold and full of life. Well, they used to be. I still had to create the eyes that drew everyone in.

"What are you staring at?"

I looked around. We sat in the school's library, working on a research paper for English class. Five open books were spread out on our desk. Our research paper was due in two weeks and our teacher was kind enough to give us the period to get a jump start on our paper.

"It's nothing," I answered.

I looked at the book that sat in front of me. Boy, this research paper was going to be hell to complete. I had no issues doing my work, but I hated essays. They sucked.

"It's not nothing." She poked my hand with the eraser of her pencil. "Tell me."

I gasped. She wouldn't let up.

"Your eyes."

Candace widened her eyes. She tucked a strand of hair behind her ears.

"Um, Destiny, I'm not sure what..." Candace began as she held her hands up.

I laughed, interrupting her thread of words.

"I'm not flirting with you," I laughed. Candace joked a lot, to say the least. "You're my best friend, for goodness sake. You just have beautiful eyes."

She smirked. "Thank you." She fluttered her eyes. "My eyes have always been one of my favorite features." She tapped her pencil against her lip before she winked at me. "I have my parents to thank for that."

"Thank you for the update, Trevor."

Zach's voice pulled me out of my thoughts. I looked at my drawing, surprised I had completed Candace's eyes and her nose.

"I'll talk to you soon." Zach ended the call before he looked over at me.

I sat my pencil down, and I crossed my fingers.

"Please tell me that we received wonderful news."

Zach sipped his phone into his pocket before he sat beside me. "We're still waiting."

I dragged my hands through my hair. "What is up with the wait?" I asked.

The waiting game killed me. I couldn't fathom how people went months, even years, without discovering what happened to their loved ones. It had been about two months since the time bomb started. I was ready for that bomb to explode so Candace could finally rest. Candace couldn't rest while that evil villain was still on the loose.

Zach shrugged his shoulders.

"Things get backed up. It's not uncommon for something to take this long."

"Is it common, though?" I asked.

He looked at me. He stayed quiet as he analyzed his thoughts.

"Honestly, if I were Frank, I'd press that department hard to get the information we need.

We have a woman who was murdered outside of a restaurant. In my opinion, it's top priority."

"What do you think the holdup is?"

I searched his face for answers only his mouth could reveal.

"There could be an issue contacting the phone company. A problem on their end is prolonging the process. It could be many things."

"What you're saying is that we need to be patient?"

Zach scrunched up his face.

"I'd say understanding."

I blew air out of my cheeks. This whole situation was difficult to handle. Losing a loved one wasn't for the weak. The waiting game was the hardest part of it all.

"I have something that'll get your mind off the case."

I perked up. Maybe all hope wasn't gone. Maybe there could be a few hours I could get lost in time and just relax my mind.

"What is that?"

"Let's go into town."

Going into town. That sounded amazing. What a nice change of scenery that would be.

"That sounds like a wonderful idea, but I'm not supposed to go out."

Zach smiled as he looked off into the distance. "I'm going to call a friend of mine. I'll be right back." Zach kissed my forehead. "By the way, that drawing is beautiful."

I looked at my drawing. It wasn't close to

being completed, but what I had done looked amazing.

"Thank you."

He squeezed my hand before he walked out the front door.

Her lips. Candace had a peculiar set of lips. It would be a bit harder to draw them, but it wasn't impossible. My pencil flew across my sketch pad as tears escaped my eyes. This drawing came together so perfectly. It looked exactly like Candace. I brought her back to life in a sketch. Or the closest I could bring her to life.

Zach walked into the cabin. He walked around the couch, squeezed and rubbed my shoulders, giving me a massage I didn't think I needed.

Closing my eyes, I allowed the stress to leave my body.

"What did I deserve to receive such an amazing massage?"

"Hmm, let's see." Zach leaned down and kissed my cheek. "You're amazing. You're my girlfriend." He nuzzled my neck, tickling me. I giggled, feeling all giddy inside. "Did I mention you're amazing?"

"Yes. Yes, you did." I turned and looked at him. "All the time, actually."

"Are you okay?"

Zach wiped the tears on my cheeks.

"Yes, I'm okay." I motioned to my sketch. "It's just hard drawing Candace."

"Why don't you take your time with this

drawing? I know you want to draw your best friend, but it's okay to start something and put it on hold for a while."

What a great suggestion.

"Okay."

I closed my sketch pad, and I looked at him.

"How did your call go?"

"It went well." Zach kissed me once more before he sat beside me. "Can you be ready in twenty minutes?"

"I can." I grabbed his hand. "Are you asking me out on a date?"

"Yes, I am."

I smiled. The feelings I should've experienced as a teen, such as getting excited for a date, were what I felt now.

"Should I dress up for the occasion?"

Zach shrugged. "We are going somewhere casual. Wear whatever you like...or nothing at all."

I rubbed my nose against his.

"You'd like nothing at all, wouldn't you?"

"Hell, yes."

Kissing him softly, my lips lingered for an extra second. I snaked my tongue out and licked his lips.

"I'll be back."

I stood. Zach slapped my butt and whistled before I walked into the bedroom.

I didn't have much of a wardrobe there, but there was nothing a nice pair of jeans and a sweater couldn't conquer. I decided to wear my curls down for the rest of the day, something that happened on occasion.

"We had the same idea in mind," I said as I walked into the living room.

Zach turned around. He looked handsome, almost magical, with his hair flowing down his back. His smile pierced me. It warmed my heart.

"Yes, we did." He walked over to me, wrapped his arm around my waist, and tucked a strand of hair behind my ear. "You look beautiful."

"Thank you." I ran my fingers through his hair. "You should wear your hair down more often."

"I will. Only if you promise me something?"

I took a step back. What could Zach want me to promise him?

"Promise you what?"

Zach took a step forward.

"I'll wear my hair down if you promise to run your fingers through my hair just like this."

"That's a promise I can keep."

Zach laughed before he dipped his head and captured my lips. His lips. His touch. His everything. I swore I'd melt into a puddle if he wasn't holding me up.

"Are you ready to go out?" Zach asked once his lips left mine.

My eyes fluttered open. The things he made me feel.

"I'm as ready as I'll ever be."

Zach performed his routine check around the cabin before he walked me to his truck.

If I didn't have a class of first graders

depending on me to teach them all that their little minds could muster when I went back, I wouldn't mind moving to an area as such.

The drive to our location relaxed me. Country music played through the speakers. I stared out the passenger window, enjoying the scenery.

When we parked in front of a mom-and-pop burger joint twenty minutes later, my eyes brightened with joy.

"Are we going to pig out on cheeseburgers today?"

Zach turned the truck off. He looked over at me. "With a side of the best curly fries ever."

I smirked.

"Oh, I'll be the judge of that. I love curly fries."

We got out of the truck and walked into the restaurant. The restaurant was decorated like a 1950s burger joint with high-top tables and red stools. License plates and images taken around the world decorated the walls. 1950s music played through the speakers. This was a true hole-in-the-wall restaurant. As expected, the restaurant was empty.

"Zach, my main man," the guy at the counter called out.

We approached the counter, and they shook hands.

"How are you doing, Mike?"

"Amazing as ever, my friend." He turned his attention to me and stuck his hand out. "Who's your friend?"

He looked at me and smiled.

"This is my girlfriend, Destiny."

Never in a million years did I expect him to introduce me as his girlfriend. With everything going on, I expected to be introduced as a friend. Boy, was I wrong. Wrong in a great way.

I shook his hand.

"I'm Destiny."

"You're beautiful," he said before he kissed the back of my hand.

"Paws off," Zach called out, his voice stern.

Mike held his hands up defensively. "I won't step on your toes." He walked to the cash register. "What can I get for the beautiful couple?"

Zach and I contemplated the menu on the wall as he held me in his arms. We pointed at different items on the menu before we decided on our order. Zach ordered a double cheeseburger, and I ordered a cheeseburger. We ordered a curly fry and a strawberry shake to share.

"I'll bring your order to your table when it's ready."

We turned around to find a table when I stopped in my tracks.

"Is everything okay?"

Genuine concern was all over his face.

"Yes."

I took a deep breath. Zach went out of his way to protect me every day. He did everything in his power to make me feel comfortable. He even went through the trouble of requesting a restaurant be empty so we could have a date at a restaurant.

"Thank you for everything you've done for me."

Zach grabbed my hand and smiled. "You're welcome," he finally responded.

Zach walked me to a table, and we sat across from each other.

We sat beside a window. Staring outside, I could see that everything looked calm and relaxing. A red car passed by, followed by a white truck.

"Are you okay over there?"

Pulling my eyes away from the window, I looked at Zach and nodded.

"I'm fine."

Zach reached across the table and gave my hand a squeeze.

"Are you sure?"

"It just feels weird being out in public." I shrugged. "I guess I've gotten used to the four walls I now call home."

Zach looked out the window. "I never thought of my cabin as being just my home. It's my home away from home." He smiled. "I'm glad you're comfortable there, considering the situation."

Looking around, I lowered my voice.

"Do you think they are even close to finding Candace's killer?"

Zach's expression was unreadable. He looked around before he folded his hands on the table.

"I think they are. Whoever is on the other end of that texting app is the key to this whole mystery. We should know something any day now."

Any day now. I couldn't wait for Trevor to call and tell us they had tracked the murderer down. Candace would have justice, and I would finally feel safe again. I'd finally be able to return to the outside world without fear or need to look over my shoulder. I could do normal things again, such as go to the grocery store and look for the apple with the fewest imperfections. I'd be able to go back to work and teach my children. I missed them so much. It was nothing like going to work and being surrounded by children who loved to learn and thought the world of me.

"Are you ready for the world's best burger?" Zach asked, pulling me from my thoughts.

I looked up. Mike sat a tray of food in front of us. My eyes widened. My stomach growled on cue. The burgers looked delicious, and the fries looked crispy. The strawberry shake was served in a special cup with two straws.

"Enjoy," Mike said and patted Zach on his back.

"Where do we begin?" I asked.

There was so much food that I didn't even know where to start.

"The fries, of course."

We stuck our hands into the fry basket. Our hands brushed against each other before we grabbed a fry.

"Can I feed you?"

Zach was the cutest thing ever.

"As long as I can feed you."

Zach smirked.

"Of course you can."

We looped our arms around each other before we ate the fry. The crunch filled my mouth, and my eyes rolled to the back of my head.

"Is it the best curly fry you've ever had?"

I dove back into the basket for another fry.

"Hell, yes."

"I told you," he said.

"How did you find out about this place?" I asked.

Grabbing my burger, I unwrapped it.

"When I came here to buy my cabin, I stopped here for lunch. Mike and I became friends, and the food keeps me returning for more."

I bit into my burger, and I moaned my appreciation. The burger flowed with juices and flavor.

"I can see why you keep coming back."

I wiped my mouth on a napkin, impressed with my lunch.

"You can't say that until you try the shake."

Placing the shake in between us, we grabbed the straw. Taking a sip, the sweet strawberry goodness reminded me of summers in Florida. What a nostalgic feeling.

"I'm sold," I called out.

The shake reminded me of my hometown. The fries and the burgers topped any other burger place I'd try in years. I doubt I could find anything better anywhere else.

"Will you be a repeat visitor?" Mike asked from afar.

I gave a thumbs up, my mouth full of strawberry goodness.

Chapter Twenty-Four

Zach

If someone had told me years ago that today would consist of eating cheeseburgers and fries with my girlfriend while slurping down a creamy milkshake, I'd call them a damn liar. To their face. Yet, we dined in a 50s burger joint while music from another generation played through the speakers while we ate some of the best food in California.

If someone had told me a year ago that I'd

fall in love with the most amazing woman in existence, I'd say they were wrong. Yet, I held onto her hand as we walked through the woods surrounding my cabin.

"Are you listening to me?"

Snapping out of my thoughts, I addressed Destiny. Her smile halted slightly as her eyes darted across my face.

"What did you say?"

She exhaled.

"I want to know when I can meet your mom."

"Hopefully soon." I squeezed her hand. "I've told her so much about you, but I don't want to harm her."

She nodded. "I understand." She turned and gave my bicep a squeeze. "I'm just so excited to meet her. Do you think she'll like me?"

This woman and her thoughts. She was too adorable for words.

"Um, no. I don't think she'll like you."

Stopping in her tracks, I dropped my hand. Her smile disappeared, and her mouth dropped open.

"I'm positive that she'll love you."

She slapped my arm. "You just scared me half to death."

I laughed. "I didn't mean to."

"I think you did," she said as we continued walking.

A breeze whipped through the air, causing the trees around us to rustle in the wind. The temperature gradually warmed up.

"She's going to fall in love with you. Just like I did."

She smiled before she looked at her feet. The rhythmic sound of our feet sounded on the pavement.

"You think so?"

"I know so," I answered with confidence. "Jake and his family will love you as well."

"I can't wait to meet your best friend."

Jake learned of Destiny three days ago. We talked for about thirty minutes on the phone, and he could sense something was different about me. It had to be our best friend's telepathy because he sensed something right.

"You lucky bastard," he called into the phone that night.

A laugh escaped me. We didn't have a filter when it came to talking to each other. We were truly brothers from another mother and mister.

"How do you fall for the woman you're protecting?"

"She's magical. I swear, she's something else."

"Hmm." Jake was silent. "Is she magical or a certain body part?"

He got down to the nitty-gritty. "She's magical. Everything about her is magical." Looking towards the cabin, I stuck my hand into my jeans pocket. "She's different."

"I'm glad you've found someone worthy of your time. If only you had listened to me about Charlotte..." Jake continued with his rant.

If only I had. Jake warned me that Charlotte wasn't right for me, but I was so smitten I didn't care to hear him out. Obviously, he knew more than I did because I visited Heartbreak Motel for years. I didn't regret any decisions I made, though. If I hadn't held onto my heartbreak for so long, this situation wouldn't have happened as it did. I wouldn't be compelled to take Destiny into the comfort of my wing and protect her.

"Everything happens for a reason," I said once Jake stopped his spew of words.

"Once this is over, we can get together with them." Destiny pulled me back to the present.

"I look forward to that." I smiled. "I can see a lake day in the near future."

Destiny looked over at me. Her eyes were full of hope.

"Did you receive some news you haven't told me yet?"

"Not yet." I looked at the road and kicked a small pebble in my path. "We're getting closer to the truth, though. I can feel it."

"Are you sure? I feel like we are stagnant."

I shrugged. "I'm not sure. It's just a gut feeling." I squeezed Destiny's hand. "I promise we will get to the bottom of this situation soon."

"So, you never told me something."

"What's up?" Destiny asked.

We walked past an overgrown tree that needed a trim months ago.

"What do your parents think of me?"

Obviously, I knew she hadn't told them we

were involved. That type of conversation couldn't happen at her best friend's funeral over an open grave. She talked to them briefly when they arrived back in Florida, but the phone call was short and sweet.

"They think you're amazing for all you've done for me."

"Really? What do they know I've done?"

She wrapped her hand around my bicep and gave it a squeeze.

"They know that you've gone out of your way to protect me. You provided such a nice place for me to stay. You make sure I'm fed, even on the days I don't have an appetite. You make sure I'm okay."

That was music to my ears. If only her parents knew what type of relationship we had developed.

"I'll always make sure you are okay." My cabin came into view. "I'll make sure you are more than okay. That's my goal now."

As we walked up the steps, branches snapped in the distance. We stopped mid-step. I looked to my left, towards the noise. I didn't see anything noticeable.

"Zach," Destiny whispered.

Her voice wavered with terror.

Goosebumps raised on my arms.

I handed her the keys to the cabin.

"Go inside. Don't open it for anyone but me."

I pulled my gun from its holster. Destiny opened the cabin, and she disappeared inside.

Now, it was time for business. The gun pressed against my chest, I scurried down the front steps. My heart beat so loud, I heard it in my ears. Did Candace's killer finally locate Destiny to finish her off? So, there were no witnesses to testify against the crime they had committed?

Not on my watch. Nobody would hurt my Destiny. Nobody would lay a finger on her head. She was mine.

Aiming the gun, I rounded the corner. I was ready to fire and defeat the threat that lurked in the shadows.

No one was there.

Walking down the side of the cabin, I pressed against the wall. Maybe they were at the back of the cabin now?

Taking a deep breath, I rounded the corner. Nothing could be seen but an array of trees and greenery.

Rustling sounded to my right.

Jackpot.

Whoever lurked in the shadows would come to light now.

I went around the corner, ready to fire, when I saw a raccoon trampling away. Exhaling, I wiped my forehead. Animals were common. I just didn't think one would be out and about right now. The day turned to night, but they usually waited until the night arrived. The little fella scared us, but thank goodness for a false scare.

I walked to the front door and knocked.

"I'm back, Destiny. Let me in."

Moments passed by before she responded. "What's out there?"

Turning, I looked over my shoulder. She was freaked. The damn raccoon placed her in a bad mind space.

"It was just a raccoon."

The lock sounded, and she opened the door. Tears wet her face. Her eyes were red.

My heart dropped. It hurt me to see her in pain. To see her hurt. To see her scared of the unknown. If I could, I'd take this pain away from her and harbor it myself.

"Destiny," I said.

Closing the door behind me, I drew her into my arms and rubbed her back. She sobbed into my neck.

"I'm so scared," she admitted.

"Everything is going to be okay. It was just a raccoon," I reassured her.

Her eyes darted everywhere but never met mine. "Don't you see?" She paused. "Everything is not okay. I fear that everything will be the opposite of okay any day now. Someone is going to come through that door and hurt me."

Her worries were valid. Everything she felt was valid, but my priority was to make her feel safe.

"Destiny."

I tilted her head up. She still wouldn't look me in the eyes.

"Look at me."

Her sad eyes found mine, and I wanted to

crumple up inside. They yearned for happiness.

"I've been kidding myself this past week."

I didn't understand what she meant.

"What do you mean?"

She shook her head and looked past me again.

"I've been pretending that there isn't someone out there trying to hurt me."

She pointed towards the door.

I rubbed my thumb across her cheeks. They were so soft, I wanted to kiss them.

"I won't allow them to," I answered truthfully.

"But..." she began.

"Shh, no buts." I placed my index finger against her lips. "I promise I'm going to protect you. Nobody, and I mean nobody, is going to hurt you. I'll give my life before I allow someone to hurt you."

Her eyes searched mine.

"Do you understand me?"

After an eternity, she nodded.

"I understand."

"Stop crying, Destiny."

I wiped her salty tears away.

She chuckled as she shook her head. A small smile appeared briefly.

"What did I ever do to deserve you?"

"Everything." I kissed her firmly, then tucked a strand of hair behind her ear. "Absolutely everything."

She kissed me, giving me all her love and affection.

"How about you take a relaxing hot shower? I think it'll help calm you down," I offered.

Her eyes flickered to the left, on the side of the house where the bathroom and the room were located.

"That sounds amazing but..."

I raised an eyebrow. "But what?"

"I would love it if you joined me."

Was it sad to say I received an instant hard-on just from the mention of showering with her?

"I would love to join you."

She smiled before she grabbed my hand. "Well, come on."

She pulled me towards the bathroom.

I turned the water on.

We stripped out of our clothes, and Destiny's eyes zoomed in on my erection. She winked and smirked.

"Someone is a little happy," she commented.

"Someone is very happy," I corrected her.

Once the water was hot, we stepped into the shower.

The water danced down our bodies. Closing my eyes, the water saturated my hair, and I shivered, the feeling one of a kind and indescribable. Nothing beat hot water flowing through my hair in the shower.

Opening my eyes, I stood in awe. Destiny stood before me with love in her eyes. Her mass of curls curled more from the water. Her hair dripped water onto her breasts. She was a true goddess, created by God himself and placed in this world just for me.

"Are you okay?" she asked.

Pulling her into my arms, her breasts rested on my abs.

"I'm more than okay," I whispered into her hair. "Especially when you're in my arms."

***

Destiny turned over and snuggled closer to me, pulling me out of my sleep. Blinking a few times, I looked around the dark room. I had to pee, and it was nowhere close to daylight.

Kissing Destiny's forehead, I pushed the covers off me and left the bed.

I wasn't looking forward to brushing my hair in the morning. We dived into making love last night after we finished our shower, and we relaxed afterward.

I heard a noise as I finished in the bathroom and closed the door. Stopping in my tracks, I listened. There was another noise, yet quieter this time. I walked into the bedroom, and Destiny was still asleep. She didn't make any noises.

I walked to the bedroom window. Raising one of the blinds, I looked out. A figure in black crept along the side of my cabin. The walk, the mannerisms, they looked so familiar to me. The person turned around briefly before continuing their journey to the back of the house.

They had no business being there.

I knew who the person was.

Chapter Twenty-Five

Destiny

Pushing myself up, I placed my hand over my chest. My heart raced. Something jolted me out of my sleep. I wasn't sure what it was, but I didn't like it. I reached over to touch Zach, but he wasn't beside me in bed.

Where was he?

Pushing the covers off me, I stood. Stretching my arms above my head, I yawned. I wanted more sleep. I couldn't wait to find Zach so we could go back to bed and get more rest.

"Zach," I called out.

I walked into the dark living room. My eyes had adjusted to the dark, and he was nowhere to be found.

I walked towards the dining room.

"Zach, where are you?"

Flicking the lights on, I nearly blinded myself from the brightness. Scrunching up my eyes, I shielded my face before I turned the lights off.

Where was Zach? If he was headed somewhere in the middle of the night, I knew he'd let me know.

He had to be outside the front door. Maybe he couldn't sleep, and he needed fresh air. I walked towards the front door. Only a few feet from the door, it opened.

"There you are," I said.

Tucking my matted hair behind my ear, I gasped.

It wasn't Zach. A masked person in all black stood before me.

I opened my mouth to scream, but the person raised their index finger to their mouth and shushed me.

"Don't scream."

Their voice was stern. Too stern for my liking. I couldn't tell this person's gender.

Where was Zach? Had they done something to Zach before I woke up and got out of bed? My heart beat so fast, an anxiety attack threatened to appear.

My heart sank. This wasn't a random act. This place was unknown to most, but the locals found this gemstone relaxing a few times of the year or year-round.

This person was there for a reason. I was one-hundred percent positive they were there concerning Candance's death. I knew they weren't waiting for me to make a pot of coffee so we could sit and discuss how to reach a mutual agreement.

Looking towards the bathroom, I hoped Zach went in there and stood in the dark, waiting for the perfect moment to attack the intruder. After another few seconds, my hope dwindled.

"I don't know who you are…" I began as I held my hands up.

The dark figure who stood only a few feet from me scared me to death, but I had to do what was possible to live. To see another minute. To see another hour. To see another day.

"But I don't want any trouble," I finished.

"I have no choice."

It was a man's voice. He paused. I could sense the urgency in his voice.

"I must clean up her mess."

Her mess? What did he mean by that? Was there more than one person involved in Candace's death? I racked my brain back to the night of the shooting. It was hard to think of that night. I spent so many days trying to forget every event that occurred that day. I woke up screaming many nights because of the memories, but I had to go down memory lane. I had no other choice.

There was only one person there that night. After they shot Candace and their gun jammed trying to shoot me, I ran on foot. If anyone else was there that night, I wouldn't have had the opportunity to run. They would've laid in wait, waiting for me to come across their trap.

"Whose mess? Who are you talking about?" I asked.

"Just shut up," he yelled.

I stepped back, shocked. Why the change of mood? He was calm one second, going off the next. Anything could set this person off. I had to tread lightly. There was no telling what mind space he was in.

Where the hell was Zach?

"I'm trying to think," he called out.

He paced in front of the door, grabbing his head in his hands and growled.

"Turn on the light."

I looked at him. Seeing him in the dark scared the crap out of me. What would seeing him in light do to me? I'd finally know who was in this cabin with me, but I wasn't sure I was ready to see him. I wasn't sure I was ready to see the person who had an intent to cause harm to me.

"Don't make any sudden movements."

He produced a gun from his pocket, the silver glinting in the moonlight coming in from the window.

Holding my breath, I walked over to the light switch. Flicking the lights on, I turned around slowly, my eyes slowly adjusting to the light.

"I'm sorry I have to do this..."

He removed the hoodie from his head. I threw my hand over my mouth.

It was Trevor. The police officer who provided the information to us this entire time.

"Trevor."

I couldn't believe my eyes. They had to be playing tricks on me.

"I have to protect Melissa," he continued.

Melissa. Who was Melissa? What did she have to do with Trevor? What was their connection? Why was he there? What did she have to do with Candace? What did Trevor have to do with Candace?

"Who is Melissa?"

Confused, I needed clarification. I looked around the cabin, the coolness seeping in.

Where was Zach?

"My wife."

Why was he there concerning his wife? What did his wife have to do with Candace? None of this made sense. Would it ever make sense?

He opened his mouth to continue his rant when the front door swung open.

Zach walked in, his face balled into an angry scowl. Hot air steamed from his ears.

"You son of a bitch..." Zach fired off as he stormed into the cabin and slammed the door.

Trevor held the gun up and aimed it at Zach.

I screamed, clawing my face in horror. I had lost my best friend to gun violence. My boyfriend couldn't leave in the same manner.

"Come in here and take a seat on the couch. We need to talk."

"I'm not doing sh—" Zach began.

"No?" Trevor interrupted. "If you don't, I'll kill Destiny now." He paused for a moment. "Instead of later."

My legs wobbled. Trevor was there to murder me. Oh. My. Goodness.

"Join him on the couch, Destiny."

Trevor motioned his gun towards the couch. Zach and I plopped down at the same time. I looked at my hands in my lap. Everything in me told me to look the person who wanted to harm me in the eyes, but I couldn't bring myself to do it. I wasn't strong enough.

"What the hell are you doing, Davidson?" Zach asked.

"I'm here handling business. Whatever it takes to make sure Melissa doesn't go down for Candace's murder."

I looked over at Zach. His eyes were trained on Trevor.

"What does your wife have to do with this?"

Trevor scoffed.

"Miller, I respect you." He walked slowly in front of us. "That's why I'm going to tell you what happened before this whole thing comes to an end."

Grabbing every nerve in my body that I could muster, I looked at him. I knew he'd tell us why he was there.

Zach reached over and gave my knee an encouraging squeeze. He removed his hand just as quickly. I missed his touch. His touch told me everything would be okay. I needed his touch.

"Candace and I met one night at the bar where she works."

Candace knew Trevor? He never mentioned he knew her when I ran into the police station. Candace never mentioned an encounter with a police officer, either. If she had, that would've stuck in my head. Maybe she didn't know he was a police officer when they first met? She mentioned that two firemen came in after their shift at the fire department and were of great company. Not once had she mentioned a police officer.

He smiled as he looked off into the distance. "It was literally love at first sight." He chuckled. "Her eyes were the first thing I noticed about her. I swear her eyes could see every part of my soul. I loved every part of that."

Zach and I exchanged a look before we gave Trevor our full attention.

"We began an affair, and the moments I spent with her were the best days of my life. The best months of my life." He took a deep breath. "Melissa found out five months into the affair."

"What did Melissa do when she found out?" Zach asked.

Trevor and I both looked at Zach. I was surprised he asked questions instead of letting Trevor continue with his tirade of a story.

"She told me to end it, or she'd handle it."

I covered my mouth. I wasn't sure I could hear any more, but I didn't have a choice. Trevor wouldn't let me out of his sight for a second. Even if I wanted to get rid of my dinner from last night.

"I guess you didn't end it," Zach continued.

Trevor shot Zach a nasty look before he answered.

"I tried to end it, but I couldn't. I became so addicted to Candace. In more ways than you could even imagine."

"So, Melissa killed Candace?" I asked.

Trevor nodded, a sad look in his eyes.

"I didn't find out about it until hours after you came into the police station."

"Has Candace ever mentioned Destiny as her best friend? Her roommate?" Zach asked.

Looking over at Zach, I was grateful for his questions. The detective in him led him to ask the important questions. He asked the questions I had yet to even think about.

"She said she lived with her best friend, but I don't recall her ever mentioning your name."

Why did Candace keep me a secret? That didn't seem like something Candace would do.

Did I even believe him when he said he didn't know I was her best friend? I guess there was a small chance that he told the truth. What did I know? I knew nothing about Trevor. Candace didn't even tell me about him. Why didn't she tell me about him? Did she think I'd judge her? She was my best friend. I wouldn't judge her for the decisions she made in life. At this point, anything was possible. Absolutely anything.

"Did you ever go over to their apartment?" Zach asked.

Trevor shook his head.

"Never. Whenever we'd get together, we would get a hotel."

I sat back on the couch, shocked at what I heard. Never in a million years did I imagine Candace would be tangled up in a messy triangle. What did Candace get herself into?

"Melissa saw the relationship between Candace wasn't stopping, so she decided to take matters into her own hands."

I didn't want to hear any more about this madness.

Trevor looked at me. His eyes burned into mine.

"Melissa passed the sushi restaurant and saw Candace's car in the parking lot. She decided at that moment to make the problem go away." He exhaled. "She figured if she could make Candace go away, she could get my full attention again. The sad thing is Melissa and I had problems for months. Before Candace came along, but she decided Candace would be at fault for our marriage falling apart."

"Why are you involved in all of this?" Zach asked.

"My wife killed my mistress." Trevor shrugged. "I'm directly in the middle of this. My mistress is dead at the hands of my wife. If my mistress is dead, I need to protect my wife at all costs. That is why I am here."

He aimed the gun at me. My stomach gurgled.

Zach stood, and he aimed the gun at Zach.

"Zach, don't make this harder than it needs to be."

"I can't let you hurt Destiny. She has nothing to do with this."

Trevor scoffed.

"She has everything to do with this. She wasn't supposed to be at the sushi restaurant with Candace. The gun wasn't supposed to jam when Melissa tried to shoot her."

My mouth went dry. He knew everything that happened that night. Melissa told him everything. This wasn't just an odd, horrible coincidence of him showing up tonight. He planned this. He was calculated with his moves.

"That's why we stopped receiving updates," I said. "Frank found out it was Trevor's wife, and Trevor didn't want us to know."

"Ding ding ding." Trevor pointed at me. "Destiny is right. I've been looking for you two since Melissa told me everything. I put two and two together, figured out you were talking about my Candace in the police station that night, and I've been on the hunt ever since."

He disgusted me. How could he reference Candace as his when his wife killed Candace? His wife took my best friend away from me. He didn't have the right.

"Doesn't it hurt you that Melissa killed Candace?" I asked.

Trevor exhaled.

"It does hurt. Candace was something special, but she's dead. I have to take care of my wife now."

Zach took a step towards Trevor, and he cocked the gun.

"Don't come any closer."

Gulping, I tried to swallow the lump in my throat. The lump was lodged. It wouldn't go anywhere.

"I couldn't find you two. Trust me, I tried my damnest, but the only thing I could locate was your house." Trevor smirked. "I couldn't find this cabin. You're a hard man to track down."

"I am," Zach agreed. "So weird assholes like yourself can't track me down."

"Zach," I said in a stern voice.

The bear had a gun, and he was ready to fire bullets. There was no need to poke the bear. He was already agitated and on high alert.

Trevor laughed. "There's no reason to throw insults, Miller."

Insults wouldn't help us out of this situation. Honestly, I didn't think anything would help us.

"I was happy when I learned you two would be at the funeral. I knew I could follow you wherever you brought Destiny, but you two didn't go to the cemetery. Do you know that threw a wrench in my plans?"

Trevor was delusional. Absolutely delusional.

"I finally trailed your location once you two went to that burger joint. Boy, do they have some amazing burgers."

Was he really talking about burgers right now? While he held us hostage in Zach's cabin? In the middle of the night?

"Zach, it's time to say goodbye to your witness."

Trevor pointed the gun at me, and I closed my eyes. I saw Candace get shot, and it was embedded in my memory. I couldn't keep my eyes open when I got shot.

Tussling started. A slew of curse words flew through the air. Opening my eyes, I watched in horror as Zach and Trevor fought over the gun.

"Give up, Davidson," Zach yelled.

"Not in this lifetime, Miller," Trevor yelled back.

Dropping to the ground, I was scared the gun would go off at any second. Zach had this, didn't he? If I joined in the fight, I'd only make it worse. Right?

The sound of metal screeched across the floor. The gun flew across the room and slid under the couch. Jumping to my feet, I scrambled to locate the gun under the couch.

Sirens wailed in the distance as I grabbed the gun. Pointing the gun, I was ready to fire at my target.

"Freeze."

Zach and Trevor stopped tussling on the ground.

Trevor laughed as he spit a glob of blood out of his mouth and attempted to get up.

"You better be careful. You don't know how to shoot that."

A cocky laugh bubbled within me.

"Yes, I do. My boyfriend taught me."

Shock danced in his eyes as he looked back and forth between us. I handed the gun over to Zach.

"It's over, Davidson."

Trevor nodded as he held his hands up.

"Yes. In the biggest way possible."

Chapter Twenty-Six

Destiny

My life flashed before my eyes. Not once but twice. The first time, I saved myself. The second time, Zach saved me. I could never repay him for that.

The neighborhood flashed with red and blue lights. Neighbors littered the yard, watching everything unfold in their pajamas and robes.

I leaned on the hood of the police car. I had the blanket the police gave me wrapped tight around me. My eyes flickered around the yard. Eyes bore into my soul. I was one of the stars of a local scandal. The town that didn't have any action or excitement received it from my presence.

"Destiny."

Looking up, Zach walked towards me with open arms.

"Zach," I cried.

An ugly cry escaped my lips as I threw myself in his arms and held onto him tight.

"Don't ever let go of me."

"I won't, sweetheart. I promise I won't."

Our affection might've been looked down upon, considering the audience was the local police department and Zach's coworkers from his police department. We didn't care, though.

Grabbing his face in his hands, I kissed his lips.

"Thank you for saving me."

He kissed my forehead. "I'd do it again and again. In a heartbeat." He tucked my hair behind my ear. "I told you that I'd never let anyone hurt you. I meant that with all my heart."

I wrapped my arms tight around Zach. He was the only person I wanted to be with. The only person I wanted to be around at that very moment. He was my saving grace.

"Zach, Destiny," boomed a loud voice.

Turning, I looked at a tall, built man. He was bald, and he wore a pair of blue jeans and a black-collared shirt. He maintained a stern look.

Slipping my hand into Zach's, I wrapped my arm around his bicep.

"Frank."

Zach shook hands with him before he turned and looked at me.

"Destiny, this is Detective Lawson. The detective that's been handling Candace's case."

I reached my hand out to shake his hand.

"It's a pleasure."

"That indeed." He smiled. "I'm going to need you two to come down to the local police station. We need to ask you two a few questions."

I looked up at Zach. What was going on? Would he be in trouble for this?

"We'll meet you there," he said.

Zach led me to his truck.

"What's going on?" I whispered to him.

He opened the door and helped me inside.

"Hold on."

He strapped me into my seatbelt. As he walked to his side of the truck, I looked at the onlookers. Their eyes were trained on the truck. I hated being the center of attention, especially considering the situation.

"What's going on?" I repeated once Zach was in the truck.

The truck roared to life.

"We are going in to be questioned."

Questioned? I had already been questioned.

"Again?" This was unbelievable. "I thought I was done with the precinct."

Zach laughed.

"Sweetheart, you're far from done."

Once we got onto the main road, I asked the questions that flooded my mind.

"Where were you when I woke up?"

Zach tapped his fingers on the steering wheel.

"I woke up to use the bathroom and heard something outside."

The cold air blasting from the vents sent a shiver up my spine. Leaning forward, I closed the vents in front of me. I should've brought along the blanket the police gave me when they first arrived.

"I saw him creep around the back of the cabin. I put two and two together. We didn't receive any more updates from him because the updates led back to him being behind that texting app number and his wife being the suspect."

Everything Zach said made total sense, but I still couldn't fathom how Zach could figure everything out so quickly, especially under the pressure of the situation.

Zach was a detective for a reason. He had all the skills he needed and proved that to me tenfold tonight.

"Did you ever suspect anyone close to him could be responsible?"

It was a hard question to ask, but I needed to know what Zach thought. Never had I expected Trevor to be connected in any way to Candace. She never mentioned him once to me.

"Hell no."

He looked over at me briefly before he focused back on the road.

"If I had, I wouldn't have relied on him for information. I would've done my own investigating into him, but he never rubbed me as someone that would be involved in such a scandal that could lead to someone being murdered." He paused. "I considered him a friend."

I looked at Zach. His eyes were focused on the road and I couldn't see them, but I could sense this situation saddened him. I could hear it in his voice.

"I'm so sorry, Zach."

The only thing I could do was apologize. I had no other words to say. Nothing else felt right to say to him in this situation.

"I guess, no matter how much you might be around someone, you truly never know them."

Zach spewed some hard words. I thought Candace and I were inseparable. I thought we shared everything with each other, but that wasn't the case. She felt the need to keep this relationship a secret, and I had to face the facts.

"I wonder who called the police. They came rather quickly," I said.

"It was me."

I looked over at Zach. He looked at me for a few moments and smiled.

"You called?"

"Yes."

He placed his hand on my knee.

"I tried to intercept Trevor by meeting him on

the other side of the cabin, but he must've changed his direction after I last saw him outside the window. At that moment, I called for help and met you two inside after. I had to stall until help arrived. I refused to have anyone else get hurt in this situation. Especially my girlfriend."

Smiling, I basked in the amazing man that was in my presence.

"You made sure that happened."

We arrived at the police station. The parking lot was empty since every police in this area littered Zach's cabin. The building was dark, but it appeared big. It was bigger than the local police station where I met Zach.

"Where's Detective Lawson?"

Unbuckling my seatbelt, I turned around. There wasn't any sign of headlights.

"He'll be here soon."

Wait. Zach was supposed to be on family medical leave this entire time. Would he get in trouble for taking me into protective custody? I hoped he wouldn't get suspended or fired over this situation. It would literally kill me if he lost his job protecting me.

"Are you going to be in trouble?"

It took me some time to muster up my question. I didn't quite know how to ask.

"What do you mean?"

I fumbled my hands in my lap.

"You don't have to be nervous around me."

"How did you…"

"I've been around you long enough to know

that you do that with your hands when you're nervous."

Zach was observant. Too observant. I loved that about him.

"Speak what's on your mind, sweetheart."

We shared nearly everything with each other in more ways than one. I didn't know why I was nervous.

"Will you get in trouble for taking FMLA to protect me?"

Zach shrugged. "Honestly, I'm not sure what will happen. We will find out shortly, though."

My heart dropped. I didn't want him to get in trouble because of me. That wasn't fair for him.

"Zach. If you get in trouble for me..."

Zach held his hand up, and I stopped talking.

"I would die for you, Destiny. Getting in trouble won't hurt me."

Beaming, I pushed the armrest up, and I scooted over. Climbing on top of Zach's lap, I straddled him. I pressed my lips against Zach's. Running my fingers through his matted hair, he pulled me close. I needed him. I needed his touch. His care. His affection. His love.

He slipped his hands under my shirt and pressed his hands against my stomach. I sucked in my breath, his hands cool against my skin.

"You mean the world to me, and I will do absolutely anything for you."

"I love you so much," I responded before I found his lips again.

"I have to tell you something."

What else would be spilled today?

"What?"

"We do have a neighbor next door. He moved in last week, and when I ran next door to confront him, he said he wasn't home, but I could talk to him tonight. He checks out."

Oh, my goodness. Everything fell into place. I wasn't going crazy.

Five minutes later, headlights shone in the parking lot. Sliding off Zach's lap, I fixed my shirt.

The car stopped three spaces over from us. Detective Lawson stepped out. We joined him in the parking lot.

"Thank you for coming in for questioning."

They shook hands again.

"It's no problem, Frank."

We followed Detective Lawson up to the police station. He unlocked the door with a key, and we walked inside.

He turned the lights on, and the room lit up. A light in the far-right corner flickered once or twice before it stayed on. The air smelled faintly of burned popcorn.

"This is much bigger than our shoebox," Zach commented as he closed the door behind us.

Detective Lawson chuckled.

"Yeah, tell me about it. At least you can comfortably fit two chairs in your office."

He led the way through the room. Cups of coffee and half-eaten sandwiches sat on desks. The officers ran out of there in a hurry to get to the cabin. We walked down a hall, and he led us into an interrogation room. The temperature in the room dropped by several degrees. One bright light shone above the table. The chair on the opposite side of the table was a computer chair. The two chairs on the other side of the table were metal, old, and rickety.

"It's official. I feel like a suspect in a crime show," I commented as Zach pulled out a chair for me to sit on.

They laughed at my comment.

"You're not a suspect in anything," Detective Lawson reassured me as he sat in the computer chair.

"You're just a victim in a vicious crime," Zach continued.

"Zach's right."

"Where is Melissa? Is she in custody? Is she on the run?"

I needed to know what my life would look like once I stepped foot out of this police department. Would I go back to Zach's cabin? Or would I go back home to an empty apartment? An empty apartment that I'd have to clean out before I had to move back in with my parents.

"She's in custody."

He opened a notepad, and I looked at his cursive sprawled in black ink.

"Has she confessed to what she's done?" Zach asked.

"Yes. In detail."

He scrunched up his eyes as he looked at his notes.

"Melissa assumed Candace was out by herself and thought it was the perfect time to commit the murder."

"If Melissa confessed, why did Trevor hunt us down with the intent to harm Destiny?"

Zach and his million-dollar questions. I wouldn't have thought to ask that question, yet it was the most important question to ask. If Melissa had confessed to first-degree murder, Trevor hunting me down would do nothing positive for her. It would only hurt him in the process.

"He told us tonight that he thought if the only witness was dead, Melissa could plead mental insanity." He shrugged. "Instead of being sent to prison for twenty or more years, she'd go to a mental institution."

"Trevor's plan backfired, and they are both going to jail for a long time," I said.

"He won't go to jail as long as her, but his sentence won't be light either," Zach said. "Especially since he's an officer."

That made me feel somewhat good.

Detective Lawson looked between the two of us.

"So, did this relationship start when you took your FMLA and took her into protective custody?"

I let go of Zach's hand. I hadn't even realized I grabbed it.

Uh oh.

"I can explain," Zach began once he cleared his throat.

"There's no need," Detective Lawson said.

"Why not?"

Zach's voice was a mix of shock and determination.

"Do you know what you did for this young lady?"

He pointed at me.

I looked back and forth between the two of them. What did Zach do for me? Besides, pick me up when I couldn't see myself get out of bed? Make me eat when my body said no? Cared for my every need 24/7? Wake up in the middle of the night when I screamed at the top of my lungs, trying to claw out of a nightmare?

"No." Zach shook his head. "I don't."

"Zach, you saved her life by taking her into protective custody."

I knew Zach saved my life in more ways than one, but what did Detective Lawson's terminology mean?

"I would've had Trevor take her into protective custody that night if I were working."

My mouth dropped open. If Trevor had taken me into protective custody, I wouldn't be sitting in this police department right now. I'd probably be at the bottom of a river or in a field with a gunshot wound.

Zach smiled at me.

"You saved me," I said.

"I saved you."

His smile was priceless. I wasn't searching for an amazing man, yet he sat beside me . He came into my life when I least expected it. If

Candace could see me now, she'd give me a round of applause for the companion I found in Zach.

I couldn't fathom how Candace never told me about her relationship with Trevor. That was something I'd never know now. She was gone, and soon, her soul could rest in peace. That's all I wanted for her.

Chapter Twenty-Seven

Destiny

Leaving Zach's cabin was necessary. I had grown to love the atmosphere that the cabin carried. It was my home away from home for two months . It was my safe space until Trevor came along and took away that safe space.

I wouldn't say goodbye to the cabin forever, though. It would take some time for me to want to go back after what unfolded there.

Zach covered the rent on the apartment while I was in protective custody. I couldn't afford to cover the apartment on my own, and I refused to find a random roommate online, so I decided to let the apartment go. That was Candace and my shared space. If I couldn't share it with her, I wouldn't share it with anyone.

Zach invited me to move in with him. He lived in a two-bedroom house about twenty minutes away. At first, I was hesitant. I knew I couldn't afford anything in the area on my own, but I knew my parents would take me in until I figured out my living situation. Until I figured out what I would do with myself. Leaving California in the midst of everything going on wasn't ideal, but I'd be willing to do whatever was necessary to get my footing back in the world. I needed my world to go back to normal. It was anything but normal for the past few months.

Zach wouldn't take no for an answer when he invited me to live with him. I was hesitant to move in with him too fast, considering we were thrown into living with each other for the sake of the case. The last thing I wanted to do was move too fast in the relationship, but some might think that had already happened. All I knew, we were in love. I was so excited to see where the relationship would lead.

"Sweetheart, are you headed to the apartment yet?" Zach asked once I picked up the phone.

"Not yet."

I balanced the phone between my ear and shoulder. That day, I'd go to the apartment and pack up our things. Zach offered to go with me, but I thought it would be best for me to do it on my own. After I strapped on my sandals, I grabbed my purse.

"I'm about to walk out of the house now."

Once we met with Detective Lawson right after Trevor was arrested, we returned to the cabin, grabbed what we needed, and drove to Zach's house. Right after what happened, I couldn't imagine even taking a nap in the cabin. I was too frightened . So, we drove for two hours to get back to town and crashed after a nice hot shower.

"Make sure you stop and get yourself a cup of coffee. I can't have you running on no caffeine."

I laughed. Locking the front door, I walked to my car in the driveway.

"How does a coffee addict run out of coffee?"

"You'd be surprised how much coffee I used to drink," he commented. "Now, promise me you'll drive safe."

"I will. I promise."

I started my car up. Immediately, the phone connected to the Bluetooth.

"I love you." His voice sounded magical and vivid going through the speakers in my car.

He loved me. Those three words caused a flutter in my stomach, and a huge smile to appear.

"I love you, too."

Zach went back to work that day. It was

difficult to wake up to an empty bed that morning and an empty house. I was used to having company constantly, so it was a big change for me. Zach was ready to return to work, but he asked me several times if I was okay with being alone. Even if I wasn't okay being by myself, I would've still permitted him to return to work. He took time off from work to care for me. The least I could do was support him in going back to work.

Excitement tingled from within when Meg's Coffee Shop came into view. I parked in the crowded parking lot of the coffee shop. This shop had only been open for six months, and business flourished. I could see why. Their coffee was the best, and their pastries were to die for.

Walking inside, was immediately greeted with a "Welcome to Meg's Coffee Shop."

The dining area was nearly packed to capacity. The line leading to the order counter was long, but there was never a time when I'd go there and I'd have to wait more than fifteen minutes for my order.

After I ordered myself a caramel macchiato, I walked over to the pick-up counter. Pulling out my phone, I scrolled through the latest social media site.

"Excuse me, miss," came a deep voice.

"I'm sorry," I mumbled.

I moved over a few steps, engrossed in the video I watched.

"Excuse me, miss," repeated the deep voice.

Obviously, this person wasn't trying to get

around me. They were trying to get my attention. Maybe he needed help.

A Black man, in his early fifties stood in front of me. He had a small build, and he was bald.

"Can I help you with something?"

"Are you Destiny?"

My heart dropped. Who was this? How did he know me? Where did he know me from? How did he find me? Did he follow me? Was I in danger?

My eyes roamed the coffee shop. Light chatter mixed in with the occasional clink of glasses rang out.

"W-wh-who are you?"

"I'm Dennis..." he began.

There was only one Dennis that I knew. He left my mother and me high and dry when I was a child.

"Your father," he finished.

He took a step closer to me and opened his arms. Stepping back, I kept a safe distance between us.

Who was this stranger trying to hug me? Was he really my father?

"Um, I don't think I know you," I admitted.

He was silent for a moment. I could tell that he contemplated his next words to me.

"Yes, you do, Destiny. I'm your father."

He repeated father, but all that came to mind was Robert. The man who helped raise me. The man who stepped in when my father left me and didn't look back.

"Destiny," the barista called out as he sat my

drink on the counter.

Smiling my thanks, I picked up my drink. I turned my attention back to the stranger before me.

"How are you so sure I'm who you think I am?"

My mom had shown me a picture of my father so many years ago. It had to be at least fifteen years ago, but I vaguely remembered what he looked like. Was this man really my father? I couldn't fathom why a random man would come up to me and claim to be my father, but I didn't trust anything anymore. I had been through enough to question everything. Every. Little. Thing.

He pulled his wallet out of his pocket, opened it up and pulled out a tattered picture. Lo-and-behold, it was young me with the man I vaguely remembered as my father. We were at the beach, and I wore a red one-piece bathing suit, and he wore a pair of blue swim trunks.

I sipped my drink.

"It's really you," I gasped.

"Can I get a hug, lovebug?"

Lovebug.

That name brought up memories. Memories that I tried so hard to bury, but they came to the surface in full force. They came to the surface so hard it nearly took my breath away. My early years of childhood had been buried because I couldn't understand why my father didn't want to be in my life. Now, I had the opportunity to ask him. I had the opportunity to ask him everything.

"Yes."

After I sat my drink on the counter, we hugged. His scent surrounded me, an almost unfamiliar, yet warming nostalgia feeling settled over me.

"It's so great to see you." He held me outstretched in his arms. "You have turned into such a beautiful woman. You are truly your mom's twin."

Compliment after compliment flooded me as we hugged. I never imagined this day would come, and surprisingly, it came, and it slapped me in the face.

"Thank you." I picked up my drink. "Can I buy you a drink?" I offered.

"Dennis," the barista called out.

"There's no need for that, lovebug." He picked up his drink. "I have my own."

I looked outside and saw an empty bench right in front of the coffee shop. Perfect.

"Let's sit and talk?" I asked him.

He smiled.

"Sounds perfect to me."

He held the door open for me. I thanked him, and we walked over to the bench and sat down.

"What are you drinking?"

"Black decaf coffee," he said.

"Decaf?" I raised my eyebrow. "Why decaf?"

"With old age, comes some major changes." He shrugged. "Trust me, I miss all the goodness of caffeine."

We sipped our drinks, and I looked at everyone around me. An older, gray-haired couple walked by. A woman with a baby in a stroller walked into the coffee shop. I had been out of the cabin for a whole day and loved being around people. I loved observing everything that occurred around me. I never knew how much I missed daily interactions until I no longer had them.

"Where have you been for the past…fifteen, twenty years?"

He widened his eyes.

"You came in hard with that question."

I crossed my legs.

"I mean no harm with the question. I just want to know where you've been. What you've been up to."

He sipped his coffee before he set it down.

"I've been in Florida until recently," he answered.

What prompted his visit to come here? Was this a coincidence? Was this planned? What did he know that he wasn't telling me?

"I've been here about a week now."

"What prompted your trip here?"

It was time to get to business. No more tiptoeing around the subject. This wasn't a random visit where he randomly stumbled across the daughter he abandoned twenty years ago.

"I wanted to see you."

"How did you find me?"

He rubbed his bald head as a family of four

walked in front of us.

"Your mother."

My mother gave him my information? I had no idea my mother had contact with him. For all I knew, she thought he fell off the face of the earth. She had no knowledge about him once he walked out of our lives.

"I contacted her. I told her I wanted to reconnect with you."

"She just gave you my location?"

That didn't sound like Mom. The type of person Mom was, she'd contact me. Well, considering the fact that a week ago, I was still in protective custody, she couldn't.

"It took some convincing before she told me what state and city you were in."

"How did you get in contact with her?"

He smiled.

"Lovebug, the internet has changed our lives for the better. After doing some searching, I found her on social media."

Social media had changed the world for the better.

"You've always been on my mind. Even when I left, I never stopped thinking about you. I've always loved you."

I couldn't believe that someone who just up and abandoned me could love me. It was hard to think that I was always on his mind. If I meant something to him, there was no way he could stay gone for this long. Yet, I couldn't find it within me to be mad at him. There wasn't an upset bone in my body. Too much had happened in the past few months for me to be upset over this situation. I honestly had a different outlook on life now. Life was too short. Our days were numbered. I had to live my life to the fullest and with no regrets.

I tapped my fingers on my coffee cup. I had to ask a hard question. I just hoped he could answer it.

"Why did you leave?"

"I can only be honest with you," he began. He looked off into the distance. "I wasn't ready to be a father. I was young, and I wasn't ready to settle down."

The honesty flowed from his mouth. I had nothing but respect for him. I didn't expect him to be this honest with me.

"I've wasted too much time. I know it's been years, but I want to be in your life. I'll do anything to be in your life. Can we make this happen?"

I sipped my coffee. There was only one thing to say.

"It won't be easy. A lot of time has passed by."

He looked down. Defeat washed over his features.

"But I'm willing to work on our relationship. It will take me some time for me, but I'm open to a relationship with you."

The biggest smile appeared.

"Thank you, lovebug."

We stood, and we hugged. We hugged for an eternity. Never had I imagined the things that had happened these past few months would happen, but things happened for a reason. I lost my best friend at the end of the year, but my father came into my life at the beginning of spring. I was ready for what was to come. I was ready with open arms.

Chapter Twenty-Eight

Unknown

Melissa. Melissa was gone. She was taken away from me. She was thrown into prison. She'd probably spend the rest of her life in there if I didn't find her the best lawyer that money could buy. That was not the outcome I expected, considering the circumstances.

I couldn't deal with her being behind bars. That was not a part of the plan. If only Melissa had planned her execution better, I doubt she would've been in this position. I doubt she would've been caught. Without a witness, Melissa could've gone to a cozy mental institution for five years, ten years tops. She would've been free to enjoy the rest of her life. She was behind metal bars, and her backyard was decorated with electrical wire.

I shouldn't have trusted Trevor to make things better for Melissa. He made them worse, and he'd have to deal with my wrath. Now, I had to take care of the situation myself.

Destiny. She was the cause of all of this. She wouldn't get away with this. She wouldn't get away with Melissa going to jail. I'd get my revenge on her. Melissa would get her revenge. If it was the last thing that I did.

Stay tuned for Book Two of Dangers in Love Series. It is currently in the writing/editing process and will be available for purchase in 2025. I cannot wait for you to read it!

OTHER TITLES BY ANA DENISE

His Crazy Obsession Series

His Crazy Obsession

His Unstable Obsession

SIGN UP FOR MY AUTHOR NEWSLETTER

Be the first to learn about Ana Denise's new releases and receive exclusive content!

www.authoranadenise.com

Thank you for reading!

*Please add a review on Amazon
and let me know what you
thought!*

Amazon reviews are extremely helpful for authors, thank you for taking the time to support me and my work. Don't forget to share your review on social media and with hashtag #DangersinLove and encourage others to read the story too!

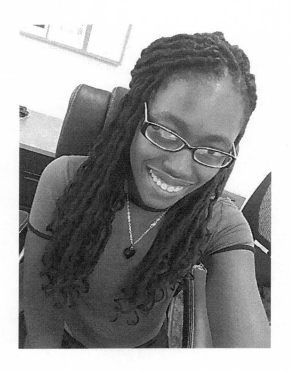

Ana Denise was born and raised on the Treasure Coast of Florida in 1999. She considers her family and friends to be most significant in her life. Growing up, she has always been fascinated with reading and writing short stories. Following her passion, she has decided to become a romance author after obtaining a Bachelor's Degree in Business Administration.